"Stella!" Mary Jean found hers[elf] ... time, after all her angst, Stella might walk away without even acknowledging her.

Did she not recognize Mary Jean, even now that it was just the two of them, face-to-face? Mary Jean, after all, had had the advantage of watching Stella through the years in photographs and in movies, whereas Stella hadn't seen her at all.

"Stella," she said, taking one step closer. "It's me. Mary Jean."

For the first time, Stella looked directly at her, and Mary Jean was suddenly self-conscious all over again about how much weight she'd put on, how shabby her clothes must look, how much older—despite the same unmade-up face and long, loose brown hair—she must seem.

Stella drew in a gasp and then she did something that totally bowled over Mary Jean, astonishing her far more than when Stella had been about to walk away. She threw her arms around Mary Jean and pulled her into a tight embrace. "Everything's horrible," Stella sobbed, her breath warm and wet against Mary Jean's shoulder. "I don't know what I'm going to do."

Out of the blurry corner of her vision, Mary Jean could see the photographers swarming their way.

Stella darted a look over her shoulder. "Oh, shit."

Mary Jean leaned in close. "Come on," she said, all energy and no doubt. "Let's run."

Acclaim for the novels of Pamela Redmond Satran

YOUNGER

"A funny, touching, instructive guide for the bewildered."

—*Publishers Weekly*

"Satran's tale is resonant with truths, some funny, some painful, and readers young and not so young will love this new twist on the coming-of-age theme."

—*Booklist*

"Beautifully written, *Younger* weaves a tale that will strike at the hearts of women of all ages."

—RT Bookclub

BABES IN CAPTIVITY

"Satran tells realistic and intriguing stories that will enthrall and, ultimately, surprise readers."

—*Booklist*

"Tender, hopeful, funny and engaging. . . . Don't miss it!"

—chicklitbooks.com

"This novel is a breath of fresh air. . . . It's delightful to read about women attempting to find out what really makes them happy, without throwing away their families to accomplish it. The friends' unique dilemmas make their stories fascinating."

—*BookLoons*

"It's a fast, funny read, with characters you'd love to have as friends."

—*Parenting* magazine

"Featured Book of the Week!"

—girlfriendbooks.com

"My fave chick-lit choice."

—The Book Babes, *Good Housekeeping* Online

"Joy, love, and sex in the modern suburbs—Pamela Redmond Satran gets it exactly right."

—Laurie Lico Albanese, author of *Blue Suburbia*

THE MAN I SHOULD HAVE MARRIED

"This witty first novel . . . is both completely readable and utterly charming."

—Jacquelyn Mitchard, #1 bestselling author of
The Deep End of the Ocean

"I love, love, love *The Man I Should Have Married*. Pamela Redmond Satran has captured Kennedy's dilemma with energy and wit. I couldn't put it down."

—Alice Elliott Dark

Also by Pamela Redmond Satran

The Man I Should Have Married
Babes in Captivity
Younger

Available from Downtown Press

SUBURBANISTAS

PAMELA REDMOND SATRAN

neW YORK LONDON TORONTO SYDNEY

...iginal Publication of POCKET BOOKS

 DOWNTOWN PRESS, published by Pocket Books
1230 Avenue of the Americas
New York, NY 10020

ISBN-13: 978-1-4165-0559-4
ISBN-10: 1-4165-0559-8

This Downtown Press trade paperback edition March 2006

10 9 8 7 6 5 4 3 2 1

Manufactured in the United States of America

Designed by Jaime Putorti

For information regarding special discounts for bulk purchases,
please contact Simon & Schuster Special Sales at 1-800-456-6798 or
business@simonandschuster.com.

To Rita DiMatteo,
My Stella. Or maybe my Mary Jean.

ACKNOWLEDGMENTS

Thank you to my always brilliant editor, Amy Pierpont, and my ever-fabulous agent, Deborah Schneider, for all the intelligence, insightfulness, and support they brought to this novel. Thanks also to Louise Burke, Hillary Schupf, Anne Dowling, and Megan McKeever at Pocket Books, and to Cathy Gleason and Britt Carlson at Gelfman Schneider.

My novelists' group read an early draft and provided extremely helpful criticism as well as support throughout the writing of this and all my other books. Thank you Alice Elliott Dark, Benilde Little, and Christina Baker Kline.

For an amazing retreat that allowed me to blaze through the entire first draft in a paradise of inspiration and comfort, I would like to thank the Virginia Center for the Creative Arts and the Geraldine R. Dodge Foundation. And during a week in Little Rock laboring over the revision, I was helped by the support of my friend Murry Newbern and her friend Ellison Poe, who generously loaned me her house, details of which she may recognize in this story.

I would also like to thank Jessica deKoninck, my astral twin, for great insight into local politics, real estate law, and New Jersey desegregation rules. And my friend, the wonderful Marty Beiser, for loaning me his name for a character who resembles him not at all.

And thank you to my family: my children Rory, Joe, and Owen Satran, who put up with me spending a lot of time staring into space, and my husband, Dick Satran, generous reader and partner.

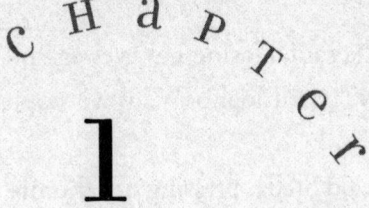

1

Stella Powers slumped in the backseat of the limo, her eyes squeezed shut in exhaustion. The midsummer sun had finally set on this endless day, which had started thirteen hours and 3,000 miles ago in L.A., and still six-year-old Idaho was bouncing in her seat and chattering.

"Are we almost there yet, Mommy? I think I can see Grandma's house just over the hill. Is that it? Is it, Mommy?"

With considerable effort, Stella lifted her eyelids to half-mast. She had felt the limo turn off the Garden State Parkway onto local streets, but it didn't look like they were in Home-wood. There was a Williams-Sonoma, a Gap, a Banana Republic, not the kind of stores that populated Stella's poky little hometown. The driver must be cutting through some other, far posher place.

"A little farther, sweetie," Stella said, closing her eyes again.

"I see a Cold Stone Creamery!" cried Idaho. "Can we stop, Mommy? Can we?"

"Grandma's waiting for us," said Stella, pressing her thumb into the spot where her head was starting to throb. "Now sssssh. Mommy needs a tiny break."

At this rate, Stella was going to be exhausted when the shoot started Monday morning, not rested as she had planned. She knew she should have brought Greta along, but her mother would have considered it scandalously indulgent, not to mention wasteful, to fly a nanny clear across the country to take care of a child whose mother and grandmother would be right there the whole time. And the truth was, there really wasn't room in her mother's little house for all of them. Besides, Stella wanted a chance to tell her mother all about Eddie without worrying that Greta was listening.

"There's the pizza place!" Idaho squealed. "The one you likeded when you were a little girl like me, Mommy! Ve- Ve- Ve- . . ."

"Vesuvio?" said Stella, coming to attention and peering out the window.

Sure enough, there was Vesuvio's neon volcano, spewing hot pink lava onto the dark sidewalk of Broad Street.

"Damn," said Stella, sitting up taller and looking around. "This *is* Homewood."

Vesuvio's looked exactly as it had when she and Mary Jean

used to go there nearly every day after school in junior high, when Pete kissed her in the pink glow of the doorway for the very first time. But almost everything around it was different, the mall stores and the fancy little boutiques and the Thai restaurants.

Had it been so long since she'd been to Homewood? She'd persuaded her mother to come out to California for Christmas, and had taken her to the Bahamas before that, and before that had been their big trip to Ireland. So it had been at least a year since she'd been here, and then it had only been for her usual quick visit, and she'd spent all her time closeted in her mother's house. As much as she would have loved going down to Vesuvio for a slice or to Cozy Corner for a milkshake, it wasn't worth getting ogled and asked for her autograph a dozen times.

"Turn right here," Stella told the driver, as they reached the corner of the block where she'd grown up.

"This is Grandma's street!" Idaho said excitedly, out of her seat now, her face pressed against the darkened glass of the limo's rear window. "It looks exactly the same!"

Indeed, Stella was relieved to see, her mother's street, at least in the dark, looked exactly as it always had, the small two-story shingled houses hunched close together beneath the towering trees, so full and lush after the relative scrubbiness of California. Her mother's house, painted white as always, glowed like a moon beyond the curve on the right, the climbing bloodred rose vine her mother had been cultivating for nearly forty years covering its lower half like knobby splayed fingers.

"It's so beautiful," Idaho breathed.

To Idaho, New Jersey was the fantasy place, fresh from the television screen. Idaho seemed to feel that this was where she really belonged, whereas Stella had always felt just the opposite, that she was meant for someplace much grander and more glamorous.

But now, as the car glided to a stop in front of her mother's house, the house where Stella grew up, she felt herself getting excited. The porch light was on, as it always was when Stella was out past dark, and as soon as Stella and Idaho stepped out of the car, her mother came out of the front door and hurried down the walk to meet them.

For so long, Stella's mother had seemed to stay the same indeterminate middle age—not young but, with her tiny figure and quick movements, certainly not old. But in the last few years, she had crossed some line, so that now Stella was always surprised to see that her mother had become an old lady, her white hair thinning, her blue eyes large and watery and vague behind her thick lenses. She was still thin, and there was still a good amount of energy in her step, but her shoulders had curled over and her hands were knotted and weak against Stella's back when Stella bent down for an embrace.

"Don't tell me this big beautiful girl is Idaho," Stella's mother said, setting off giggles in the little girl. "Why, you're practically a teenager."

"I'm six," Idaho said, grinning to show the gap where, until recently, her two front teeth had been.

Stella's mom looked over her granddaughter's head to the

limousine, where the driver was struggling with Stella's huge suitcase.

"Where's Edward?"

"Eddie," said Stella. "He wanted to be here, but he's been in the recording studio day and night with his band. We decided Idaho and I should come on our own."

"I thought I was going to get a chance to meet him finally."

"I know, Mom, he's looking forward to meeting you too. But he couldn't get away right now, and I wanted to grab the chance to see you before I start the new film. After what I went through to get this role, I can't miss even an hour on the set."

Across the street, where old Mrs. Jackson used to live with her seedy bachelor son, a young woman stepped outside and stared across at them. Stella now noticed that, a few doors down, two teenage girls were standing on the sidewalk, looking their way. Homewood's downtown may have gotten spiffed up, but seeing a movie star was still a major event.

"Come on," Stella said, taking her mother's arm and her daughter's hand. "Let's go inside."

Compared with California, where the nights always turned cool no matter how warm the days, the New Jersey evening felt hot and muggy, and even hotter once they stepped inside the cramped house. Her mother had not, apparently, spent the money Stella sent that spring for her to install central air-conditioning. Then Stella breathed in, and instantly it was evident why the house was so warm.

"Oh, Ma," Stella said, savoring the delicious aroma, her mouth watering even though, five minutes before, she hadn't felt the least bit hungry. "I can't believe you made a pot roast."

Idaho raced past both of them and tore gleefully upstairs to what Stella knew was her favorite spot in the house, the bedroom where Stella herself had slept as a child, with its same white twin beds and pink nylon flounced bedspreads that Stella had picked out when she was nine. All her old books were still on the shelves, her stuffed animals and dolls lined up at the foot of both beds. On her odd visits, she slept in this room with Idaho, with the little girl insisting on claiming the bed that had been Stella's own, and Stella taking the guest bed, which they'd always referred to as Mary Jean's.

"I thought we were having company," her mother said stiffly.

This might be the way other mothers behaved—angry, passive-aggressive—but not Stella's mother. Josephine Powers, a nice Irish Catholic girl from Queens who worked as a secretary, had gotten knocked up at forty by her married boss and been kicked out of the house by her shamed parents. Giddy with freedom, she used the money the boss gave her to buy a house in Homewood, even in the sixties known as a place that welcomed less conventional parents and their children: interracial couples, rich blacks, divorcees, blended families before the term had been invented. "You were the best thing that ever happened to me," Josephine always assured Stella, acting as if her daughter were the sun and the moon, never screaming or criticizing or demanding like so many other parents.

And so Stella had trouble believing that she was doing it now. If anything, when her mother disapproved of something

Stella did, she'd make one cutting remark and then drop the issue. But Josephine was still glaring her way.

"Mom," Stella said, lowering her voice and crossing the room to where her mother hovered on the threshold to the kitchen, taking both her mother's hands. "I want to explain about me and Eddie."

"Oh, no," her mother said, pulling her hands away. "You don't have to explain."

"No, I do. I'm sorry that we got married in Vegas that way, without inviting you or even telling you. It was kind of a spur-of-the-moment thing."

"You don't have to report to me on your actions. You never have."

"Oh, come on, Mom. It isn't like I was trying to hide anything from you. I called you five minutes afterward."

Idaho's footsteps sounded on the stairs, which seemed to be Josephine's cue to swivel and disappear into the kitchen. A moment later, the electric mixer roared to life—the potatoes were being whipped, with hot milk and melting butter and plenty of salt, the way they had been nearly every night of Stella's childhood.

"Ma!" Stella called over the whine of the mixer. "Won't you please let me do that?"

"You can set the table," came her mother's voice, still with an edge to it, from the kitchen.

Without a word, Idaho scurried to the china cupboard in the dining room and dropped to the floor, tugging at the humidity-swollen drawer until it burst open, emitting the sweetish woody smell Stella remembered from childhood. The little girl pulled out place mats and napkins, while Stella took the good dishes from behind the glass doors. Her visits were the only time her mother used the good dishes anymore.

She really did not want her mother to be mad at her. She couldn't stand it. It happened so infrequently, she could recount every single instance of her mother's anger: the time she and Mary Jean jumped from the roof of Mrs. Atanasio's garden shed, the night of the infamous pot bust that marked the end of her long romance with Pete, the day she called from Los Angeles to tell her mother she'd run away to become a movie star.

And even then, after ten minutes of fury, her mother had reverted to being loving and supportive, offering to wire money and urging the seventeen-year-old Stella to audition for only the best parts.

"Don't waste your time going out for toilet paper commercials," her mother had counseled. "Being an actress is too hard to blow your talents on that."

Now her mother appeared in the dining room, bearing the old white chipped platter with the pot roast sliced thinly and arrayed across it, ringed with caramelized carrots and covered with a river of gravy. Stella rushed to clear a place on the table for the big platter, and then sprinted into the kitchen to retrieve the bowl of steaming potatoes, the butter melting in a little crater atop the fluffy white mountain. This meal was a Hollywood trainer's nightmare—there were more fat and carb grams here than she was supposed to eat in an entire month—

but that was exactly what made it so fantastic. Mashed potatoes were the new cocaine.

Once a year in L.A., usually when the rains came and nothing seemed right with her world, Stella was roused to attempt
making a pot roast of her own. She'd call her mother each time
and ask to be walked through every step of the process, from
what cut of meat to buy to which kind of oil to use for the
browning to how much water to put in the pot. "Oh, not
enough to cover it," her mother would say. How many onions?
"A couple." How long do I cook it? "Till it's done."

Not surprisingly, Stella's pot roast never tasted half as good
as her mother's. Now, she piled her plate high and gobbled the
ambrosial meat and vegetables, thinking of nothing else, not
even the fight that had started, until she noticed that her
mother was sitting there, picking at her food.

"Aren't you hungry, Ma?" Stella asked.

"I'm fine," said her mother, propelling a carrot into the wall
of her potatoes. "I'm just not used to eating so late."

"I wish you wouldn't have waited. We could have done this
tomorrow night."

"Are you staying tomorrow night?" her mother asked, peering at her over the steel rims of her thick glasses.

"Yes, of course," Stella assured her. "We don't have to leave
until late on Sunday. I start filming Monday morning."

"Mommy is *not* going to be the mommy in the movie,"
Idaho said.

They'd offered her the role of the mother first. At thirty-
nine, she was asked to play the mother of a female character

who was supposed to be a grown-up. That would have been as good as tolling the bell for Stella's career, at least as a lead actress. Once you crossed over to playing the mother to some young hottie, you might as well move back to Kansas. Or New Jersey.

"I think this is the role, Mom," Stella said, relieved that they were on to a new topic. "The one I've been waiting for all these years."

She'd convinced them to give her the lead by showing up in the director's office dressed like the younger character, her lines already memorized. The director hadn't even recognized her at first, and then had been won over by the acting skill and enterprise she'd brought to what wasn't even an official audition. Even he had said he thought this would finally get her a nomination.

"It's just one of those women's parts that don't come along that often," Stella said. "The character is this strong woman who's engaged in a struggle between the welfare of the town where she grew up and her own ambitions."

"And she's pretty, too," Idaho piped up.

Stella smiled. "Yes, she's pretty, but also deep. I think until now, I was too young to do justice to a character like this." She laughed ruefully. "And now that I'm ready, they thought I was too old."

As her fortieth birthday approached, it seemed as if the entire industry, including her own agent, was giving her up for dead. He'd left her on her own to fight for the movie role she'd landed, though he'd been happy enough to collect his 15 percent. If she got nominated for her performance, she decided, the first thing she was going to do was find a better agent.

"Hmm," her mother said.

Stella cleared her throat. Her mother could usually be counted on to be interested in all the ups and downs of her career, but now she just sat there with her lips pressed together, a faraway look in her eyes.

She must be even more upset about the Eddie thing than Stella had guessed. Stella shot a glance at Idaho, who was crusting her potatoes with salt. It wouldn't do to reopen the Eddie discussion in front of the little girl, who'd barely calmed down herself about him moving into their lives.

"So, what's up with Mary Jean these days?" Stella asked, deciding the best tack would be to change the subject for now.

"She's busy with her children, I suppose. They say Pete might be the next police chief."

That seemed so laughable and so perfect at the same time. Pete Wright, her first bad-boy boyfriend, introducing her to cigarettes in seventh grade, to making out in eighth, to pot in ninth, and to sex in tenth. Pete Wright, whose entire life seemed constructed to stick it to his own father, who himself had been the police chief. And then one little threatened marijuana bust junior year—Stella had been the one to get caught, while Pete fled into the woods—had been enough to scare him straight. Poor Mary Jean, married to a man who'd started out as James Dean and ended up as Dudley Do-Right.

Although he'd aged well, Stella had to hand him that, judging from the pictures from the *Homewood Herald* that her mother had sent her over the years. He looked like a virtuous cop from central casting, with his neatly combed blond hair, his broad shoulders and long limbs in his sharply creased uniform—like a Ken doll with a touch of goofiness that was endearing because it made him seem more human.

"How many kids do he and Mary Jean have now?" Stella asked. "Six? Seven?" In her mind, Pete and Mary Jean's kids were like rats, twining in and out of their parents' legs in ever-multiplying numbers.

"I think it's four," said her mother. "She had the three big ones, and then she had a late one, a little boy, who must be about Idaho's age."

"Can I play with him?" asked Idaho.

"We don't really know them anymore," said Stella. "Now eat all those potatoes you put on your plate."

In L.A., she never heard her mother's voice in her own, never identified herself with her mother, feeling instead with Idaho like some together but still cool babysitter, without the heavy lifting. She had a real babysitter, Greta, for that. But here, especially here, the parallels became powerful: the single mother and the only little girl, the nonexistent father and the mom carrying all the responsibility on her shoulders.

Stella wanted to be the same kind of mother to her daughter as her own mother had been, though Idaho was already a bafflingly different child from Stella herself. Retiring where Stella had been bold, plain (it had to be said) where Stella had been arrestingly beautiful, even at Idaho's age, with her black hair and turquoise eyes and creamy skin and torso so narrow and elegant people always wondered if she was a dancer, Idaho seemed to need a more tender brand of care.

Now, for instance, following Stella's instruction to eat her potatoes, Idaho's eyes began welling up and she hung her little head, her wren-brown hair dangling straight into the potatoes, her lower lip swelling in defeat.

It had been a long day, and time difference or no, it was going on eleven at night and Idaho should be in bed.

"Never mind," Stella said hurriedly, getting up from her place, silently thanking her daughter for saving her from the hundreds of calories she'd undoubtedly have consumed if she kept sitting there. "It's time for little girls to go to sleep."

Her mother stood when she did, and started clearing the table.

"Leave the dishes, Mom," Stella said, lifting Idaho into her arms. "I'll do them when I get down."

Her mother hesitated.

"Really, Mom. I'll be down soon. We need to talk anyway."

"We certainly do," said her mother, turning away again and retreating to the TV room.

As Stella carried her daughter upstairs, as she helped the little girl retrieve her nightgown from her Barbie suitcase, as she worked her daughter's T-shirt over her head and slipped the nightgown on and smoothed back her stick-straight bangs and kissed her hot, damp forehead, all Stella could think about was her mother's anger. She was desperate to figure out what she could say or do to make her mother stop being so annoyed and be her usual sweet and supportive self.

But at the same time, Stella was angry that her mother was insisting on being angry. Eddie's not being here, them getting secretly married—all that was so much spilt milk. She had so little time to spend with her mother, she resented having to waste any of it on these pointless arguments.

She listened, half expecting to hear her mother cleaning up despite her strict orders not to, but all was silent downstairs. Interpreting this as yet more evidence of the intensity of her mother's anger, Stella blew on Idaho's neck to cool her off, singing a few lines of a lullaby and then leaning in to kiss the child, relieved to hear the little girl's breath already rhythmic and slowing into sleep.

Coming down the stairs, she saw the dishes right where they'd left them on the table. Her mother was sitting on the couch in the sunroom, staring at the dark, silent television, her hands palm up beside her on the sofa, her knees slightly apart in the way of old ladies in cartoons.

"Mom?" said Stella. "Are you okay?"

Her mother started, as if she was surprised to hear Stella's voice.

"What? Oh, oh yes. It's just the food was so heavy."

"But you hardly ate anything."

"I was nibbling before you came. I have a touch of indigestion."

Stella hesitated. "Can I get you something?"

She'd been lucky, she knew, that her mother had been mostly healthy all these years, had never really needed anything despite Stella's willingness, eagerness even, to give. Stella paid for her mother to visit the best cardiologist in New York to stay on top of her lifelong arrhythmia, tried to hire cleaning people and handymen to help manage the house. But while Josephine consented grudgingly to see the doctor, she refused all offers of outside help with the housework, just as she kept the cashmere sweaters and copper pots and down-filled comforters Stella sent stowed away in their original wrapping. With bigger things, the air-conditioning was typical: Stella would send money for her mother to paint the house or buy a new car or install air-conditioning, and her mother would leave everything exactly as it was. And when Stella asked what became of the money, Stella's mother would only say that she'd tucked it away for a rainy day, surviving, from the looks of it, on her social security.

"No, no. I'm all right."

Feeling all her own annoyance drain away, Stella crossed the room and sat heavily on the couch beside her mother. She hesitated just another moment before leaning over and resting her head on her mother's thin shoulder.

"Oh, Mommy," she said. "Don't be mad at me."

"I'm worried about you, about your future," Josephine Powers said, pulling back, speaking with more energy than Stella would have guessed her mother would have been able to muster. "Why can't you settle down with a normal man? Someone who can offer you security, a real future? This is round three for you, Stella. You can't afford to make another mistake."

Stella felt as good as slapped. She couldn't remember her mother ever talking to her this way. Ever.

"This is not a mistake, Mom. For once I feel like I married someone for the right reason."

As opposed to the first time, when she married her agent for her career, definitely a wrong reason. And the second time, when she got pregnant and married Idaho's British actor father, figuring that having a baby together might make them fall in love. Instead, marriage made him decide he was definitely gay.

"And what is the right reason?"

Stella stared at her mother, stupefied. Well, she thought, her mother had never been married. She couldn't be expected to know this.

"Love, Mom. The right reason is love."

Just thinking of Eddie now, the way he sang to her after they made love, the pressure of his lips against her neck, made her warm with pleasure. It didn't matter that they'd been together only two months; she'd known he was her sexual soul mate the first time she met him, before she even slept with him, before they'd spent so much as a single evening together.

An odd look stole across her mother's face, as if she'd never heard the word *love* before. Had Stella said something wrong? Did her mother have something against Stella falling in love, against love in general?

"I know that when you meet him, you'll agree that it was all worth it," Stella said, aware of the pleading tone in her voice. "I know you're going to love him too."

But instead of agreeing or saying something conciliatory, her mother pulled away and lurched to her feet.

"I just don't feel well," her mother said.

And then she staggered to the side.

Stella leaped up from the couch.

"Mom," she said, truly alarmed for the first time. "Mom, come here, sit down."

She tried to put her arms around her mother, who was stepping to the side, veering downward, as if she'd been punched.

Then suddenly she fell, her full weight on Stella, knocking Stella backward onto the couch, where she dropped with her mother heavy, even though she couldn't have weighed more than a hundred pounds, on top of her.

"Mom," Stella said, trying to maneuver her mother into a less awkward position, sitting beside her, or maybe lying down.

What was she doing? Stella was confused, trying to cushion her mother and move the right way, trying to talk to her mother and think about the right thing to do.

"Mom," she said, growing more frantic by the second, feeling her mother grow stiff and unmoving. "Mommy."

Her mother's eyes were closed and her breath seemed to be coming slowly but loudly, her mouth open as if she needed the widest possible passageway to accommodate the necessary air.

"I'll get help," Stella said, lifting her mother's feet onto the sofa. Though she was reluctant to leave her mother's side, even for a second, she rushed to the phone and dialed 911.

In her panic, she flashed on the night she left home, her mother upstairs asleep while she moved frenzied but determined through the half-lit downstairs. There was the same feeling that night of urgency, of heightened awareness, of how essential it was that everything go right.

And then she was only in the moment, as she described the problem to the emergency operator, as she tried to clear her mother's airway, tried to pump her mother's chest, resorted to holding her mother while she heard the sirens screaming louder and louder, closer and closer, until her house was filled with strangers and a red light pulsed in an unfamiliar rhythm against the living room wall.

It was only later, when she sat stunned and alone in the dark living room after everyone had left, Idaho slumbering on improbably above, that the memory came back to her. It *was* like that long-ago night, she thought. One minute, her entire world, everything she'd ever known, was as it had always been. And the next minute, it was gone.

CHAPTER 2

Mary Jean Atanasio Wright picked up the *Us Weekly* from the top of the pile of magazines and newspapers that littered the coffee table. Gazing at the picture of Stella on the cover—thinner and paler than ever, her long dark hair in a tangle and huge sunglasses covering half her face—all Mary Jean could do was shake her head. EDDIE GROOVES WHILE STELLA GRIEVES, read the headline.

Above Stella's sad face, in a smaller circle, was a photo of her new husband Eddie Skinner dancing in an L.A. nightclub with a young blond woman who everyone in the Western world now knew was Stella's little girl's nanny, Greta. "Greta the Homewrecka," the *New York Post* had dubbed her. The paparazzi had snapped the couple's picture last Friday night,

Mary Jean had read, when Stella first arrived in Homewood, knowing they had a juicy story. But they wouldn't realize exactly how juicy until it turned out that Stella's mother was dying at the same time her brand-new husband was getting it on with the nanny.

"Poor Stella," Mary Jean sighed.

Next to her on the blue-striped sofa, her husband Pete, who had been studying the *Homewood Municipal Code Book,* rolled his eyes and let out a grunt.

"I feel sorry for her, I really do," Mary Jean said. "First losing her mother, who was all the family she had in the world aside from her little girl. And now losing—what is it?—her third husband."

"She's a rich, famous, hot movie star," said Mary Jean's daughter Franny from across the room, where she was playing Go Fish with her six-year-old brother. "I don't feel one bit sorry for her."

"She's a human being," said Mary Jean. "Don't forget, she was my—"

"—best friend since the first day of kindergarten," chanted Franny, her twin sister Caitlin, and even little Jimmy. The kids knew this part of the story well.

"I was just wondering," Franny said. "How come you two aren't friends anymore?"

Oooops, this was the part of the story they didn't know. How their straight-arrow dad had once been Stella's boyfriend. How Stella's getting busted for pot while Pete tore off into the night broke them up. How Stella's best friend Mary Jean, always the smart good girl to Stella's wild child, had been only too happy to open her arms to Pete after Stella broke up with him. How, six months later, Stella ran away to Hollywood without a word to Mary Jean, who was already knocked up with Peter Jr. How they never saw each other or spoke again.

"We drifted apart," Mary Jean said vaguely. "But I'd love to see her now, tell her how sorry I am about her mother."

In fact, Mary Jean had kept in touch with Mrs. Powers all these years, exchanging cards and even stopping in to visit her from time to time. She used to fantasize that Mrs. Powers was *her* mother. The Powers's house was always so calm and quiet, compared to the chaos of the Atanasios', where there were eight crazy kids running around. And Mrs. Powers was the only one who ever seemed shocked that Mary Jean wasn't going to college after high school, who even seemed to notice that Mary Jean got good grades and loved to read and had the brains to do more than be a cop's wife, like her mother, like her sisters, exactly, in fact, like she became.

"I should go to the funeral," Mary Jean said, thinking of what it would be like to see Stella again after all these years. She wished that she could somehow lose thirty pounds before tomorrow. She'd always imagined that if she ever saw Stella again, she'd have time to get thin again first. It wasn't that she thought she needed to look like a movie star—ha!—in order to feel good enough to talk to Stella. She just hated the idea of Stella looking at her and thinking only one thing: FAT.

Don't be ridiculous, Mary Jean told herself. Stella's mother just died. Her new husband got caught fooling around with the babysitter. The last thing on her mind is going to be your stupid weight."

"Are you invited?" Franny asked. "Can I go too?"

"You don't have to be invited to a funeral," said Mary Jean. "You just show up. Pete, I think we should be there."

Pete looked up from his code book. "I am going to be there," he said. "I have to work it."

"You didn't tell me that."

"Practically the whole force has been assigned to it," Pete said, turning his attention back to his book.

"Why?" Mary Jean persisted, feeling her cheeks flush.

"Duh, Mom. She's like a major celebrity," said Franny. "If you don't have to be invited, I don't know why I can't go."

"I need you to watch Jimmy."

"Caitlin can watch Jimmy."

When Mary Jean found out she was having twins, and then when they turned out to be two girls, she was hoping to live out the closeness she felt she'd been denied with her own twin sister, who'd died of a staph infection when they were just toddlers. But Caitlin and Franny had never been particularly close and couldn't have been more different in looks as well as temperament. Franny was thin and energetic and red-haired and mercurial, funny and wild, a natural actress, while Caitlin was Mary Jean without the craving for love: smart and studious and happiest when she was alone with a thick book. Or, Mary Jean saw with dismay, alone with a thick book and a chocolate bar, as Caitlin also seemed to have inherited her mother's sugar addiction and consequently round figure.

Now Caitlin lifted her head from her book long enough to say, "Can't. Working."

The girls were heading into their senior year of high school, and the deal was that Mary Jean and Pete would help pay for them to go to a state college, but if they wanted to go to a private school, they had to earn part of the money. Caitlin was hoping for Princeton, and was working three jobs this summer, in addition to commuting to a Columbia summer school program for which she'd gotten a scholarship. Franny, on the other hand, dreamed of being a star and was preparing by spending as much time as possible lying on their little patch of patio in her bikini.

"So Jimmy can come with us," Franny said.

Mary Jean sighed. It was well known among her kids that she couldn't say no. So what that this was her chance to reconnect, if only to say how sorry she was, with her oldest friend. So what that a funeral was not an appropriate event for a six-year-old. So what that Jimmy, who had an ocular condition that necessitated the wearing of thick glasses that made his pale green eyes large as grapes, was painfully shy and sensitive.

"He won't know what's going on anyway," said Franny, as if anticipating her mother's objections. "Come on, Mom. This is my one and only opportunity to see a real live movie star."

"All right," Mary Jean said, eyeing Pete, who seemed now deliberately not to be looking her way. What was up with him? Why *hadn't* he mentioned that he was working the funeral? She was stunned to feel a bolt of jealousy pierce her heart, imagining her handsome husband once again in the force field of Stella Powers. And not just Stella Powers, the hottest girl at Homewood High, but Stella Powers, the famous gorgeous actress. Stella Powers, the famous, gorgeous, newly single actress.

"Come to think of it," said Mary Jean, "I *want* you to come to the funeral, Franny. Jimmy too. It would be nice if Stella met the whole family."

As it turned out, they were stuck outside the church during the funeral. While St. Kieran's refused, as a matter of policy, to close its doors during the brief service, the church had filled quickly with people trying to get a look at Stella, and the police were charged with keeping the throng of photographers and television reporters outside, along with everyone who hadn't shown up early enough to squeeze into the little wooden church.

They'd been late because Franny had been intent on blow-drying her long red hair absolutely straight, adding more and more product in an attempt to fight the 98 percent New Jersey humidity. And now her hair was frizzing anyway, which Mary Jean could have told her would happen. Not that Mary Jean, the perpetrator of the frizzy gene, was allowed to say anything. Her own long frizzy hair was still wet, slicked back in a French twist, her black linen hopefully slimming dress wrinkling in the awful heat.

For once, Franny's fury was directed at Pete, who was attempting to maintain a poker face worthy of a palace guard in the face of his daughter's harangue.

"Come on, Dad, let us in, you know you can," Franny said.

Pete stared straight ahead, refusing to meet Franny's eye, never mind let them through when he was charged with keeping all the other hundreds of onlookers out. He seemed not even to hear, though Stella could see the vein in his temple throbbing, a sure sign that he was upset.

"Okay, if you won't let me in, I'm just going to go around you," Franny said, starting to duck under the space beneath where his arm was linked with one of his fellow officer's.

"Franny, step the hell back," Pete said through clenched teeth.

"What are you going to do?" Franny said, a smile playing at her lips. "Shoot me?"

At that little Jimmy, by far the most sensitive of all the children, burst into tears.

"Don't worry, honey," Mary Jean rushed to say, drawing Jimmy close and at the same time digging her fingers into Franny's arm and yanking her back from the police line. "Daddy's not going to shoot Franny."

It was a job calming Jimmy down and at the same time letting Franny know in no uncertain terms that this was one time when she had to listen. Mary Jean found it dizzying, trying to deal with a teenager and a kindergartner at the same time. And it wasn't only the huge gap in the kids' ages that made her crazy, but how different all the kids were from each other. The oldest, Peter, who was at summer school and would be entering his senior year at Penn State in the fall, had always seemed to be wrapped in gauze, sturdy and imperturbable, an average student and a natural athlete. Caitlin was a true intellectual and oddly, for a twin, a real loner, while Franny's gift was for the dramatic, onstage and off.

And Jimmy, well, Jimmy seemed to have been born without skin, so vulnerable, every emotion bubbling on the surface, though his head was often in dreamland. Mary Jean thought that his visual problems, not diagnosed until he was nearly three, had turned him inward. His only friends tended to be the imaginary ones he chattered with endlessly; *they* never hurt his feelings the way real children so often did.

"What's wrong with you, Franny?" Mary Jean said. "Look how you upset your brother."

Jimmy was still blubbering, biting his lip and casting worried glances, his eyes even larger than usual behind his thick glasses, in the direction of Pete's holster.

"I just wanted to see what was going on in there," Franny said. "I thought, between you and Dad, I was going to have this big in, and now I'm stuck out here on the sidewalk with all the nobodies."

"We can go out to the cemetery. I'm sure not all these people are going to go out there."

"Oh, ugh. You mean like when they put the dead body in the ground?"

At that, Jimmy's mouth dropped open and his teary eyes widened in terror, as if Mrs. Powers's ghost had appeared right in front of him.

"That's what a cemetery is," Mary Jean hissed, tightening her grip on Jimmy's hand. "This is a funeral. What did you expect?"

"I expected to at least get a look at her outfit," Franny said coolly. "And with you two being best friends and all, I thought you might be nice enough to introduce me."

After all the bragging Mary Jean had done over the years about her relationship with Stella, she now felt exposed as a big outsider like everybody else in Homewood. The truth was, although she and Stella *had* been best friends for twelve years, from the first day of kindergarten until the spring of senior year, when Stella ran away to Hollywood, they hadn't seen each other in—oh, God—over twenty years.

"*If* we get close enough at the cemetery, and *if* Stella's in any kind of shape to talk to anybody, of course I'll introduce you," Mary Jean told her daughter. "But you better shape up if you expect me even to try."

That statement was like magic, instantly transforming Franny into the ideal teenager, quiet and sweet, tending to her brother, acting as lovely as she looked in her short black skirt and her neat white blouse, her body long and slender and her hair a dramatic flame against her pale skin.

Suddenly there was movement at the door of the church, and the photographers raised their cameras. The first one out the door was Cameron Dunn, Homewood's premier realtor, head of the Nokomis Elementary PTA, and first black Junior League president—a notable local personage, perhaps, but not worthy of coverage in *Us Weekly.*

"Is that Halle Berry?" Mary Jean heard one photographer ask another.

"Nah, it's nobody."

Right behind Cameron was Henry Sladowski, big-time local—wait a minute, wasn't that an oxymoron?—developer, who actually looked around as if he expected someone to take his picture. Oh, barf. As eager as Mary Jean was to get her first look at Stella along with—okay, she had to admit it—any other movie stars who might be there, she had to turn away. She hated that man, she thought in the vernacular of her tough Atanasio cousins, *wit' a passion.* She would have hated him even if he hadn't just bought the tumbledown little house that she and Pete had been renting since they first got married more than twenty years ago. Now, besides loathing and fearing him in theory, she worried about the actual power he had over her life.

A few of the camera people took Sladowski's picture, and she heard somebody ask whether he was Alec Baldwin.

Alec Baldwin! In his dreams! The only thing Henry Sladowski had in common with Alec Baldwin, from what Mary Jean could see, was a kind of squintiness around the eyes, a heaviness at the jawline. When he first moved to Homewood a year ago, Mary Jean remembered thinking—along with every divorced mother in town—that he was kind of good-looking. But that had been before she knew anything about him.

Pete and his fellow policemen moved to form a line down each side of the stairs descending from the church door, clearing a path to where the hearse stood waiting at the curb. From the dark doorway of the church, the casket emerged, glinting in the bright noonday sun, its burnished lid covered with gorily red roses. Mrs. Powers's roses! Could Stella have really cut them from the vine outside her mother's house?

At the thought of the roses, the house, of Mrs. Powers herself sitting calmly for Mary Jean's entire life and now lying unmoving in that box, on her way to the cold earth, Mary Jean was shocked to feel herself choke up, tears spilling from her eyes. She sucked down a deep shuddering breath, trying to get herself under control.

"Mom, your face is bright red," Franny whispered.

"I know," Mary Jean said, fanning herself and breathing more deeply still. "I'm just sad."

She remembered sleeping over at Stella's on summer nights, both she and Stella in their matching seersucker shortie pajamas, sitting at the kitchen table with the windows thrown open to the night air, drinking cold glasses of milk as Mrs. Powers fussed around them: "Can I get you girls some cookies? How about another glass of milk, M.J.?"

Those days were so long ago, yet it was only at this moment that they seemed irredeemably gone. Never, Mary Jean thought. We'll never sit at that table like that again.

And of course that inspired the tears to flow more freely, no matter how hard she tried to blink them back.

Franny sighed dramatically, rolling her eyes and edging away from Mary Jean. And then, all at once, as Stella appeared wan and pale amid a ring of famous faces at the door of the church, as the television lights flashed to life and as the cameras began whirring and clicking like frenzied crickets, Franny stepped forward, breaking through the line of policemen and starting up the stairs of the church directly toward Stella.

Mary Jean saw Stella pull back in alarm, heard a cry escape

from her own throat, spotted the two large men who must be Stella's bodyguards move swiftly down the stairs and grab Franny by each arm, only to have Pete move in and lift Franny from their grasp, lift her as if she were seven and refusing to do something, and carry her away.

Everything stopped, all eyes on Pete and Franny, and then Mary Jean heard the cameras start up again, shooting at an even faster pace than they had before, first in the direction of Pete and Franny and then at Stella herself, who had begun to move once again down the steps of the church. She looked as if she was about to collapse, leaning heavily on the arm of a short balding man beside her, holding the hand of her little girl Idaho.

Mary Jean had the urge to step forward and apologize for Franny, but she was afraid the bodyguards would grab her too, and there would be no Pete to rescue her from their clutches. She stared at Stella, trying to catch her eye, trying to send her psychic messages—always a favorite activity in their girlhood—but Stella was gazing at the ground, shrinking from the press of people who surrounded her. She was so thin, so much thinner even than she looked in pictures, so much thinner even than Mary Jean remembered her being in high school, and seemed frail now that they were so close, more rather than less human than she'd seemed all these years in Mary Jean's mind.

Where was Franny? Mary Jean swiveled around to see Pete talking to her over by the squad car, pointing toward their house, and Franny walking away with her shoulders slumped. Pete caught sight of Mary Jean and shrugged, and Mary Jean shrugged back, their private language for: What are you going to do? They seemed to say it more and more about Franny these days.

Franny paid more attention to Pete than she did to Mary Jean, and he had undoubtedly told her she was grounded now and sent her back to sit in the hot house, and Mary Jean was sure the girl would not defy her father. Mary Jean felt a jolt of guilt for not going after Franny, driving her home and supporting whatever it was Pete said to her. But Franny would only take out all her anger at Pete on Mary Jean, and Mary Jean didn't need that right now. She had to go watch the last of her childhood get buried.

At the cemetery, Mary Jean didn't even try to get close to Stella. She was embarrassed about what had happened with Franny, despite the fact that Stella couldn't have had any idea that Franny was her daughter. More, though, it was that seeing Stella on the church steps, with all the photographers so eager to take her picture, flanked by her famous friends, made Mary Jean realize that she didn't know Stella anymore, couldn't even pretend to be her friend. Why would Stella even be interested in being friends with her, a mom from New Jersey? She wasn't; she'd made that clear by never once getting in touch all these years. It was time for Mary Jean to let go of their long-past connection.

So she sat in the shade on a grassy hill beneath a tree looking down on the burial, as Jimmy sang to himself and hit a gravestone with a stick. From here, Mary Jean was free to stare at Stella and her daughter and to think about their friendship, and of course about Mrs. Powers. The burial at least seemed more focused on her, all of what passed for Homewood's high society as well as Stella's famous friends now gone, with only Mrs. Powers's friends from the League of Women Voters and Planned Parenthood and the soup kitchen remaining at the graveside, the photographers and the throng of persistent fans held at a distance by the police.

Mary Jean had hoped to see something of Stella in her daughter, but the little girl—Idaho, the name alone had been front-page news—was pale and plain, nothing like Stella who as a child had resembled Elizabeth Taylor in *National Velvet*.

Mary Jean had always been so proud to be Stella's friend. It made her feel like the chosen one, especially since she really had no—even she knew this—obvious qualities that marked her as the natural companion of the most beautiful, glamorous, coolest girl in school. Mary Jean was pretty enough, in a milk-maidy, overfed kind of way. She was certainly smart, but everyone knew that smart didn't make you popular. She was nice, she was fun, but maybe a little *too* nice, maybe not quite *enough* fun.

Not nearly as fun as Stella, in any case, who'd always been wild and hilarious, perfectly mimicking Father Raymond's Irish brogue and Miss McCue's nasal lectures, dancing the monkey on the balance beam in gym, and making out with Pete in the coat closet during bingo night. Always Mary Jean was there in the center front row as Stella's audience, laughing the hardest, cheering on every exploit, holding every secret close.

It was Mary Jean whom Stella had confided in when she finally lost her virginity to Pete, for instance, after years of grappling in the coat closet. "I don't know," Mary Jean remembered her saying. "It doesn't really feel like anything."

Where was Pete? Oh, there he was, in the middle of the line of officers, facing the grave. Even with his back to her, Mary Jean knew him instantly from the fringe of blond hair hanging beneath his cap, the way his shoulder strained against his sleeve. She'd stared at that back, after all, for years, secretly in love with Pete for as long as she could remember, never dreaming he could actually be hers. Even before Stella declared that she liked him, he seemed far out of Mary Jean's league; he was cute, an athlete, class flirt and class clown, the logical mate for Stella, not for Mary Jean.

It had seemed enough, for so long, to hear about him from Stella, to imagine what it might be like to be with him the way you might with, well, with a movie star, enjoying the fantasy without any expectation that it would come true. And then Stella had broken up with him, and had urged Mary Jean to go out with him so that he would quit mooning around acting so hurt, but then had been furious when they not only started going out but started sleeping together. Stella had never admitted being mad, but she wouldn't listen to any of the details of the relationship, the way Mary Jean always had. "Been there! Done that!" she'd carol, although Mary Jean knew that her romance with Pete was not the same as Stella's. Mary Jean was in love with Pete, for one thing, and the sex was always thrilling for her, the only thing missing being able to talk about it with

Stella. Stella had started spending more time with other friends, claiming Mary Jean was "an old married lady" and that she just wanted to be free. The biggest slap of all had been running away to California without saying a word to Mary Jean.

No, Mary Jean thought. The biggest slap had been never coming back.

The priest was saying something in the distance. Then the coffin, which had been poised above the hole in the ground, began moving slowly downward. Mary Jean saw Stella bend over and scoop up a handful of dust, which she threw into the grave with a faraway clatter of pebbles.

And then Mary Jean could tell, from the angle of her head and the movement of her shoulders, that Stella had started crying. She'd seen Stella cry so many times before, when someone had teased her in the playground, when she hadn't gotten the lead in the school play. Mary Jean leaned forward, instinctively wanting to comfort Stella, and then remembered that no, that wasn't her role anymore. Even if she wanted to do it, she wouldn't be allowed.

The photographers surged toward the sobbing Stella in a blaze of flashes. Stella let out a cry, and the crowd moved toward her too. Stella's bodyguards, the guys who'd grabbed Franny, put their arms out like basketball players and moved toward the crowd, and then Pete and the other cops, not to be outmaneuvered by (Mary Jean could imagine Pete saying this) a couple of private dicks, made their move too.

And then suddenly—Mary Jean did not see what tipped it from a slight shift in positions to an all-out melee—there was pandemonium. The crowd of fans rushed toward Stella, and there was a scream as somebody slipped and slid toward the open grave. Mary Jean caught a flash of Pete, taller than almost everyone else, wading into the crowd, arms working, but she couldn't see Stella anymore. The photographers who were still standing were madly taking pictures, and the priest, holding his prayer book stiffly before him, was walking with great deliberation backward.

Mary Jean swiveled around to check on Jimmy, who, oblivious, was now twirling his stick above his head and talking to himself, narrating some imaginary battle of his Yu-Gi-Oh characters. She turned back just in time to spot Pete moving away from the crowd, hunched over with his arm shielding a slight figure in a black dress. Stella.

They walked quickly, no one seeming to notice, until they were far on the other side of the crowd from where Mary Jean watched, and ducked behind a bush. The photographers, the fans, if they even noticed Stella was not among them, would not have been able to see where they were, but Mary Jean could. She saw Pete bending down, talking to Stella, who seemed still to be crying, more hysterically than before. Pete reached in his pocket and handed Stella one of the white cotton handkerchiefs that he ironed himself. Stella blotted her face, and then Mary Jean watched as Pete hesitated a moment before leaning down and putting his arms around Stella, holding her close and patting her back as she sobbed against his chest.

Mary Jean reeled around, feeling as if she might throw up,

and then her attention was distracted again by a piercing scream and a woman's voice—Stella's voice—calling, "Idaho! Idaho!"

Stella lurched out from behind the bush, Pete right after her, yelling her daughter's name, looking every which way, seemingly oblivious to the mob that was still near her mother's grave. Pete was struggling to keep up with her, though Stella also seemed oblivious to him, Mary Jean saw with satisfaction. The crowd and the photographers, for their part, stopped their fighting and just stood there quietly, looking around, though they didn't seem sure for what. This gave the cops and the bodyguards a chance to restore order, surrounding the group and moving them away from the grave, away from Stella and Pete, toward the parking lot.

Mary Jean looked around to call Jimmy to her, thinking that she had to help Stella and, she supposed, Pete, find the little girl. That's when she noticed Jimmy was gone too.

"Jimmy?" she called. "Jimmy!"

Could he have run down by Pete? But no, Pete was on his own, and there was no Jimmy anywhere between here and Pete.

"Jimmy!" Mary Jean called more urgently, moving over to the headstone where he'd been playing. His stick was there, but there was no sign of him.

"Jimmy!" she screamed, beginning to feel frightened now.

She surveyed the rolling hills of the cemetery, which had seemed so full of people just a moment ago, and all she saw was green. The full green trees, heavy under their summer burden of leaves, swayed lazily; nearby, a wasp buzzed. From far away, she could still hear Stella calling for her daughter, and then Pete's voice too—sounding self-conscious to her practiced ear; she'd heard Pete make fun of Idaho's name—but she couldn't think about them now.

Still calling Jimmy's name, she moved quickly, trying to think like a six-year-old boy. He was timid; she couldn't imagine him deliberately running away, the way Franny or Peter might have at his age. But she could imagine him going off with someone, which was even more frightening.

When Jimmy started kindergarten last year, Pete had given him the same lecture about strangers that he gave when he visited the elementary schools, and when he finished, he asked Jimmy, by way of a test, what he'd say if someone offered him candy to get in their car.

Jimmy thought about that a minute and then said, "I'd ask them what kind of candy."

Mary Jean heard herself moan aloud, remembering this, darting to look behind a tree, inside a rhododendron, around the corner of one of the small mausoleums that dotted the property. Each time there was nothing, she felt more and more frantic, looking in panic for Pete, whom she finally spotted way on the other side of the now-deserted cemetery, still trailing Stella.

"James Joseph Wright!" she cried in frustration. "If you don't come out here right this minute, you're going to be in serious trouble!"

That's when she heard it: the giggle. She couldn't tell exactly where it was coming from, but she knew it was Jimmy's. Then she heard it again, and noticed another, higher-pitched peal of laughter too.

"Jimmy?" she said, trying to make her voice sound both friendly—she didn't want to scare him, or them, away—and commanding. "Jimmy, you better tell me where you are right this minute."

Silence again.

"I have Yugi right here with me, and he says you better come out."

The giggles again, from the direction of a slim flowering tree that had seemed too narrow to shelter anyone. She moved toward it.

"What's that you say, Yugi?" she said loudly. "You want to meet Jimmy? And his friend Idaho, too?"

At that, Idaho and Jimmy, eyes glittering behind his thick glasses, stepped out from behind the tree, both smiling up at Mary Jean.

"Where did you two go to?" she said. "Don't you know that everybody's looking for you?"

From far away came the sound of Stella's voice calling Idaho's name. Idaho looked in the direction of her mother, fear on her face.

"Never mind," said Mary Jean, holding out both hands. "We'll go show them you're here."

The two children obediently took her hands and walked with her toward the speck that was Stella and, even farther away, Pete.

"Are you a stranger?" Idaho asked. *What kind of candy?*

"She's not a stranger," said Jimmy. "She's my mommy."

"And I knew your mommy when we were both little girls," Mary Jean said. "Like you."

Idaho stared up at her, breathing through her mouth. Mary Jean could see a little bit of Stella now, in the eyes.

"Did you know my grandma?" the child asked finally.

"Yes, I did know your grandma. Very well."

"She died," Idaho said.

"I know that," said Mary Jean, stifling an impulse to laugh. She was instantly ashamed of herself, but the little girl was so somber, so sweetly unconscious of what was so evident to the entire crowd at the church and in the cemetery—not to mention millions of readers of *Us Weekly* and viewers of *Entertainment Tonight*.

"Your grandma was a really nice lady," Mary Jean told the girl, which inspired the child to draw a deep sniffle in through her nose.

Stella was getting closer. She saw Idaho, Mary Jean could tell, though she seemed not to focus on Mary Jean at all. She has no idea who I am, Mary Jean thought. She thinks I'm just some fan from the crowd who found her kid. Or maybe she thinks I'm some creep who staged this whole thing so I'd get a chance to meet her.

Behind Stella, Mary Jean saw Pete take in what was happening. He stopped suddenly, wheeled around, and walked away. *Weenie,* Mary Jean thought. Though she was feeling pretty weenie herself, her heart beginning to tom-tom in her chest and her palms turning slick against the children's little hands.

"Mommy!" Idaho cried, letting go of Mary Jean's hand and hurtling across the grass straight into her mother.

"I found them playing together behind a tree," Mary Jean explained. "I don't know how they both got away from us."

Stella didn't look up from where she was bent over embracing her daughter, talking urgently to the little girl and then finally taking her hand and half turning as if to walk away.

"Stella!" Mary Jean found herself aghast that after all this time, after all her angst, Stella might walk away without even acknowledging her. Did she think Mary Jean had deliberately spirited Idaho away? Did she not *recognize* Mary Jean, even now that it was just the two of them, face-to-face? Mary Jean, after all, had had the advantage of watching Stella through the years in photographs and in movies, whereas Stella hadn't seen her at all.

"Stella," she said, taking one step closer. "It's me. Mary Jean."

"It's your friend, Mommy!" cried Idaho in obvious delight.

For the first time, Stella looked directly at her, and Mary Jean was suddenly self-conscious all over again about how much weight she'd put on, how shabby her clothes must look, how much older—despite the same unmade-up face and long, loose brown hair—she must seem.

Stella drew in a gasp, and then she did something that totally bowled over Mary Jean, astonishing her far more than when Stella had been about to walk away. She threw her arms around Mary Jean and pulled her into a tight embrace.

Mary Jean stood there for a moment, feeling the strangeness of Stella's slight body—she was far smaller than either of the twins—leaning into the softness of her own, and then she put her arms around her old friend, hugging her back as warmly as she was being hugged. Soon they were both crying and laughing at the same time, as Jimmy and Idaho gazed up at them, mesmerized. Out of the blurry corner of her vision, Mary Jean could see the photographers begin to swarm their way.

"Everything's horrible," Stella sobbed, her breath warm and wet against Mary Jean's shoulder. "I don't know what I'm going to do."

"I know," said Mary Jean, smoothing Stella's hair, feeling at once how odd it was to be thrown into such intimacy with someone who was an icon, and how natural it felt to be finally talking like this again with her old friend. "My mother died right after the twins were born, and between the grief and exhaustion, I really thought I was going to die. I understand how awful you must feel right now."

"But it's my fault," Stella said. "I killed her."

Mary Jean reared back. "Stella! What are you saying?"

"She was mad at me," Stella said, her face wild. "We were fighting. That's what made her heart give out. I killed her."

"No," Mary Jean said, gripping Stella's arms, surprisingly muscular despite their slender appearance. "She had that heart problem for years. And she was eighty years old, Stell."

"She was healthy," Stella said, her eyes darting crazily, not resting on anything. "I had to give her a hard time about

Eddie, that scum-sucking son of a bitch, even though she tried to tell me—"

Over Stella's shoulder, Mary Jean spotted the camera people heading toward them, raising their telephoto lenses to shoot. She tightened her grip on her friend's arms.

"They're coming," Mary Jean breathed.

Stella darted a look over her shoulder. "Oh, shit."

Mary Jean leaned in close, beckoning the kids to listen, too. "Come on, everybody," she said, feeling suddenly like her eleven-year-old self, all energy and no doubt. "Let's run."

"You shouldn't have taken matters into your own hands like that," Pete told her. "Just the two of you and the kids—anything could have happened."

"But it didn't," Mary Jean said happily. "The car was right there, and I brought Stella home and put her to bed and then I straightened up and let the kids play until the old ladies showed up with more food with them than it looks like Stella eats in an entire year."

Pete exhaled noisily and shook his head, his lips pursed. It had been a breach of security; that's what bothered him, Mary Jean knew. Even though, once the public event of the funeral was over, Stella was no longer the responsibility of the Homewood Police Department, Pete took his responsibilities very seriously. He was annoyed at Mary Jean for grabbing control of what he saw as his turf.

"Come on," Mary Jean said, rolling toward him and giving him a squeeze. In bed, with the lights off, late at night after all the kids were asleep, was the only time they could talk in the little house they'd rented since right after Peter was born, always trying to save enough money to buy a house but never quite making it. "Don't be mad."

He stiffened, but didn't respond. Mary Jean hooked a leg over Pete's hip. A lot of her girlfriends joked about sex, about how they never wanted it, how they were always trying to avoid it, but she was still as turned on by Pete as she'd been back in high school. Maybe after the girls were first born, when she had three little kids and was exhausted all the time, she'd stopped wanting it. But now she found herself daydreaming about sex a lot of the time, looking forward to being with her husband in bed.

It was Pete who seemed less interested, claiming he had to study his goddamn police manual, or complaining that his back hurt, or that he was worn out after working a double shift. Usually Mary Jean took him at his word, but now she felt the old insecurity rearing up.

"Do you think I'm fat?" she asked.

He hesitated, which was all it took to make her feel terrible.

"You do think I'm fat. I'm going back to Weight Watchers, as soon as the kids are back in school. I bet you wish I was skinny, like Stella."

Pete drew in a deep breath. "I don't wish you were skinny. I think you look great."

"You do not. I saw those pictures from vacation, in my bathing suit. You look like a goddamned Ken doll, and I look like Fatso Barbie."

She rolled over onto her back, bereft at the memory of the image, and at the memory of the needle on the scale that morning: 174 pounds, to Pete's trim 168. He stayed thin by lifting weights and also by continuing to smoke, although never around her or the kids. She pretended she didn't know, even though she could smell the smoke on him right now.

"No, you don't," Pete said, pulling her back to him, kissing her cheek. "You look fine."

"Fine," mimicked Mary Jean. "Thank you very much."

Mary Jean was still in love with her husband, she liked her husband, she had great sex with her husband, she rarely felt anything but safe and happy with him. But Stella's return somehow catapulted her back to feeling like her own teenage self, worried that she was Pete's consolation prize.

"Stella looks so amazing," Mary Jean said, summoning the vision of her lithe, creamy-skinned, lush-haired old friend. "Do you wish you were with her instead of me?"

Pete pulled back to study her. "Why are you saying these things, Mar?"

Mary Jean sighed so deeply, it felt as if she was exhaling twenty years' worth of air. "I just . . . usually I think I'm okay. I think . . . we're good, you know? But then I see her, and it reminds me of everything I didn't do with my life."

"I bet she feels the same way seeing you," said Pete.

"Oh, yeah, right," laughed Mary Jean, sitting up. "I bet right now she's wishing she lived in a rented shack in New Jersey and had four kids and got fat and married the local cop."

It was only when Pete looked stricken that Mary Jean realized her blunder.

"I'm sorry. I didn't mean that part about you," she rushed to assure him. "I'm sure she really does wish she married you. Look at you: you're hot, you're devoted, you're a million times better than any of those creepy guys in Hollywood. I'd rather have you than Brad Pitt any day."

Pete grinned, obviously buying every word. Like most men she knew, Pete had that bedrock of confidence that trumped all evidence to the contrary and helped him weather any threat to his ego. Mary Jean wished her own self-doubt could be so easily assuaged.

"And the kid part," Mary Jean went on, remembering how needy Stella's daughter had seemed for the company of another child. "Only children always seem kind of sad to me. I'm really happy we had four."

Though what she'd always wanted was two, a quiet little household like the make-believe one she'd enjoyed with Stella and Mrs. Powers. Having twins, of course, had changed all that, and then ten years later she'd gotten pregnant with little Jimmy, when she and Pete went away for the weekend without the kids for the very first time on their fifteenth anniversary and, giddy with unaccustomed freedom, got a little careless with the birth control.

"It's not her family situation I'm jealous of," said Mary Jean with renewed conviction. "It's how great she looks. And how much money she has. And—oh, not her career, exactly—but her, I don't know, power. Or independence. Or not independence, but her ability to make things happen in her life, to buy a beautiful house and nice things."

Mary Jean felt her shoulders sag as she looked around their own tiny bedroom, the shapes of discarded clothes littering every surface. She worked so hard to make the house look cute, trolling Homewood's juicy yard sales for bargain treasures, re-upholstering furniture she found on the curb on Bulky Waste day and painting the walls Veuve Clicquot orange and Tiffany blue. But with no money and four children in such a tiny space, it was a constant battle to maintain any sense of style and order.

This was the first place they'd rented when they saved enough money to move out from Pete's parents' house, early in their marriage. They were only supposed to stay here for a few years, until Pete got out of college and little Peter started school and they were both working. But then she'd gotten pregnant with the twins, and as soon as the girls started school, Mary Jean's mother had gotten sick with breast cancer, which had consumed two or three years in caregiving and grief, and then finally Mary Jean had had *her* chance to go to college, only to be derailed by the surprise appearance of little Jimmy. Now finally, with Jimmy starting full-time school this fall, she was going to start working on her degree.

Pete cleared his throat. "There was a letter from Sladowski," he said.

"Oh, God!" Mary Jean said, remembering the sight of Henry Sladowski's smarmy face on the church steps. "I couldn't believe he had the nerve to show up at Mrs. Powers's funeral."

"He's tearing down the house," Pete said.

"As if he or Cameron Dunn or any of the rest of them ever would have given Mrs. Powers the time of day when she was alive," Mary Jean said, shaking her head. "Those people are *happy* when someone like Mrs. Powers dies. They can make another easy half million by renovating and flipping her house."

Pete set his strong hands on her shoulders. "Mary Jean, you're not listening to me. Sladowski is tearing down our house."

Mary Jean finally focused on Pete. "Why would he tear down our house?" she asked dumbly.

"He owns it, Mary Jean. He's going to knock it down and put up a new bigger one he can sell for a lot of money."

"But we were worried about him raising our rent."

"I know, but that's not what's happening."

"When?" Mary Jean said, her mind racing to calculate how much time they had left until the school year started again, how much money they could scrape together for a down payment. There was the nearly $6,000 she had set aside for her tuition and books; that could go. And $5,000 in the girls' college fund, but they were going to need that in a year. Peter would be graduating next spring, so they could use the money they'd been spending on him. And maybe instead of going to college, Mary Jean could get a job as an aide at Jimmy's school, cover expenses that way.

"We have three months," Pete said.

"Three months!" She counted on her fingers. "November. Right before the holidays. That shithead."

"Maybe we can get him to give us until January 1," Pete said. "Find something else cheap to rent."

"Do you know how much rents are in Homewood now? A two-bedroom is like $2,000 a month." Mary Jean had taken to reading the real estate ads in awe and mounting horror, aware that their own $800 rent, which they had long considered outrageous, had in fact fast become an amazing bargain.

"So we won't stay in Homewood," said Pete. "We'll move a little farther out."

"Pete, are you crazy? The girls are going into their last year in high school. Jimmy's about to start school, and he's going to need every last service this school system has to offer. We can't leave Homewood."

"We might have to, Mary Jean."

Mary Jean was now kneeling upright on the bed, waving her arms around. "I am not going to let that carpetbagger kick us out of *our* town. What is wrong with this place when people who are protecting the town can't afford to live here? When the only people who can buy a house are stockbrokers from New York or developers who want to tear them down?"

Pete shrugged. "What are you going to do, Mary Jean? That's just the way it is."

"But I'm not," said Mary Jean, "going to let it be that way."

CHAPTER 3

Stella lay in her mother's pink bathtub, tepid water up to her chin, bubbles long since dissolved. Her Cosmo glass was nearly empty, and she debated her options. Ask Idaho to bring the vodka, the limes, the cranberry juice, the ice, and the cocktail shaker into the bathroom so she could mix herself another drink? Nix. Even an inexpert mother like her knew you couldn't ask your six-year-old to do something like that. It was bad enough that she'd laid in every animated DVD ever created, along with the complete works of Mary-Kate and Ashley, and let Idaho watch them from morning till night. It was bad enough that every day they ate doughnuts for breakfast, pizza ordered in from Vesuvio's for lunch, and pizza again for dinner. It was bad enough that she spent all her time lying in the tub, or lying with the shades down and the fan blasting in her mother's bed, or sobbing over dusty boxes in the attic, sipping Cosmos through it all. She couldn't now ask her child to act as her bartender.

The phone started ringing. The phone rang all the time. Because her mother had no answering machine and no voice mail, it would keep ringing for a very long time. Some, a few, of the calls were probably from people who were worried about her and Idaho. More were from her agent, her lawyer, or the producers of the movie she was supposed to have started filming ten days ago. And most were undoubtedly from the press, wanting her reaction to Eddie and Greta, to her mother's death. How does it feel, Ms. Powers, to have your entire life fall apart? But there was no caller ID, so she never had a clue who was calling, and couldn't take the risk of lifting the phone to find out.

The phone stopped ringing. Stella relaxed, slipping deeper into the tub, but then she heard something that made her tense up again. Idaho's voice. Idaho's voice having what sounded alarmingly like a phone conversation. Then there came the sound of little footsteps on the stairs, and then the bathroom door creaked open.

Idaho stood there, wearing panties and a pink-sequined Dora the Explorer T-shirt, staring at Stella.

"What is it, sweetheart?" Stella said.

Idaho pointed at Stella's breasts.

"What's that?" she asked.

She gestured toward Stella's thick dark pubic hair.

"And that?"

"You know what that is, honey. That's Mommy's body. Did you come up here to tell me something?"

Idaho thought for a minute. "There's a man on the phone."

"Didn't Mommy tell you that you weren't supposed to answer the phone?"

Idaho blinked. "But *Cinderella* was over."

Stella sighed. "What man?"

"He said to come get you."

"Tell him I can't come to the phone right now."

"I know," said Idaho. "I already told him that. He said I had to come get you right now."

Stella sighed again, but now she was getting mad.

"I told you I don't want to talk to anyone on the phone. Just go down there and hang up."

Idaho's eyes filled with tears. "He said if you didn't come to the phone, he was going to call the police." She started crying for real.

Stella, suddenly filled with rage, leaped up in the bathtub, water cascading off her body and over the sides of the tub. She grabbed a towel and sloshed out into the bathroom.

"That shithead," she said. "Excuse my language, sweetheart. Whoever that bad man is, he shouldn't have said that to you, and Mommy's going to go tell him so."

She hadn't been spending much time downstairs, and was stunned to see what a wreck it was, pizza boxes everywhere, dirty glasses and half-empty soda cans strewn about, Idaho's toys and dirty clothes and discarded DVDs littering the floor and the furniture and all the tables—with thousands of dead flowers forming a macabre backdrop to the chaos. She imagined the police really coming—Jesus, maybe Pete!—and finding the house like this, the photographers swarming in, taking pictures of the housekeeping disaster that would land on the cover of next week's *Star* and *Us Weekly,* leading her away in handcuffs and a towel as Idaho stood there sobbing.

Her anger rising again, she snatched up the phone.

"Whoever you are, I'm going to sue your ass off for threatening my little girl."

There was a silence so long that she began to think maybe the caller was another of Idaho's imaginary friends, but then finally she heard the deep voice of her agent, Marty Beiserman.

"I was worried about you, Stella."

"Worried, Marty, does not warrant scaring my kid half to death by threatening to sic the cops on us."

"Okay, okay," he said. "I'm sorry."

Wow, she thought, an apology from the guy whose motto is "A contract means never having to say you're sorry." She felt gratified for half a second, but then suspicion honed by two decades in the jungles of Hollywood kicked in.

"What's going on, Marty?"

Another long silence. This guy used silences the way other people used tantrums.

"They're dropping you, Stella."

Stella felt her entire body flush hot.

"What do you mean, they're dropping me?"

"From the movie. You're out."

"They can't do that, Marty. I have a contract. You negotiated it yourself."

"But there's a start date in that contract. A start date you didn't make."

"But they know what happened. If immediate family dies, you always get a week. Shit, the caterer gets a week."

"It's been ten days."

"But they know about Eddie, too. They know I'm stuck here in New Jersey alone with my kid. Show a little humanity, for God's sake."

In the ensuing gulf of silence, Stella pulled the towel more tightly around herself and half turned to see Idaho gazing solemnly in her direction.

"They called," Marty said. "I called. We were sending a great deal of human love and kindness your way, Stella, and you wouldn't pick up the fucking phone."

Stella tried to breathe to get her bearings, like they told you in yoga. But it was as much bullshit as Lamaze had been. Too bad that now, there was nobody nearby who could give her an epidural of the heart.

"I've been falling apart, Marty," she said, lowering her voice and curling away in hopes that Idaho wouldn't hear. To really make the whole thing even more horribly difficult, she was tethered to her mother's old-fashioned dial phone, which was bolted to the wall. "But I'm getting better now. I could be there on Monday. Or tomorrow, if they're really going to be hardasses about it. As long as you find me a place to stay, somebody to take care of Idaho—"

"You're not listening, Stella. This is not a threat; this is done. You're out."

"Maybe if I call them—"

"They're already shooting it with Katie Holmes."

Now it was her turn to sink into silence. Katie Holmes. Katie Holmes was a lot like her, minus fifteen years.

"How could you let this happen to me, Marty?" she whispered.

"I did everything I could," her agent said, back to his old no-apologies total-aggression self. "Take it as a sign. You need a rest; you got it."

She could hear the rhythm of his voice quicken, recognized that he was downshifting into good-bye mode. But she wasn't going to let him get away this quickly, or this easily. She remembered now how little he'd done to get her the role in the first place, her decision that if this part panned out as she hoped it would, the first thing she was going to do was dump him.

"You're happy, aren't you, Marty?" she said.

"What?"

She felt a flush of satisfaction at landing a blow he hadn't expected.

"You didn't back me up when I wanted this role, and I bet you didn't go to bat for me when they wanted to dump me."

"You're obviously not in your right mind," he said. "I'm going to hang up now, and we'll talk when you've pulled yourself together."

But Stella suddenly felt saner than she had in years. She believed that, despite the mess in the house and the towel she was wearing, she couldn't possibly be more pulled together. Besides, she was down so far, nothing she could say or do could possibly make things any worse.

"No, we're talking now, Marty. I wasn't going to do this until after the movie wrapped, but now there isn't any reason to wait. I'm moving on, Marty. I've decided to make some changes in my career, and I won't be needing your representation anymore."

The silence again. She'd never fired anybody before: as an actress, her role was to stand around waiting for somebody to want her. But after losing first her mother, and then Eddie, and now the part, she felt it was necessary for her to do some rejecting. If she'd known how good it would feel, she would have started a long time ago.

"This isn't the time," Marty was saying. "Consider your options. I'll be there when you're ready."

"I'm ready now," Stella said. "Good-bye."

"So what are we going to do, Mommy?" Idaho said.

Stella had mustered the energy to clear the kitchen table, and they were sitting there now, eating their lunch pizza.

Stella munched thoughtfully. She'd gotten dressed, finally, and combed her hair, though makeup and crunches seemed like things she'd done in a former life.

"I don't know," she said. "We could go to France."

"What's France?"

"A place. Across the ocean. They speak French there and wear really pretty dresses."

Idaho wrinkled her nose. "I don't want to go across the ocean. I like it here."

"Here?" Stella said in surprise. "You mean at Grandma's house?"

"At Grandma's house, and at New Jersey."

"Well, we can't live in New Jersey," Stella said.

"Why not?"

Stella had never considered that before, the answer seemed so self-evident. Because it's a tacky boring pit that no one who could afford to live elsewhere would ever voluntarily stay in?

But that was just how she'd felt about it when she was seventeen or twenty-five, or from the perspective of L.A. Now that she was here every day—so green, so quiet, watching cardinals lighting on the rosebushes and bees buzzing against the window screens—it actually seemed quite idyllic. And during the few forays she'd taken in her mother's ancient Rambler, with its push-button transmission, she'd been amazed at how hip and upscale the town had become.

"You know, Idaho," she said. "We're free now. We can do anything we want."

She'd sold her house in Malibu when she married Eddie, had gotten rid of everything and owned barely more than what was in her suitcase. Even the bulk of her clothes were in storage, waiting for the huge new walk-in closet that would now never be finished. Most of her money, of course, was frozen in bank and brokerage accounts until the divorce was settled. But from the time she was in high school and had started secretly socking away money for her flight to L.A., she'd always kept an account at Homewood Savings & Loan that no one else on earth knew about—and she had nearly $100,000 in that now to finance her latest getaway.

"Well, I want to live in New Jersey," Idaho said, setting her little face into a stony mask.

"How about New York?" said Stella.

As a grown-up, she hadn't spent much time in the city, preferring to devote what few precious days she had on the East Coast to her mother, but when she was a teenager she'd loved New York, always cutting school to ride the bus into the city, saving her babysitting money to shop at Barney's and have tea for one at the Plaza, rarefied tastes that none of her suburban friends, not even Mary Jean, shared. She and Idaho could get a townhouse there, or a loft. She could do theater. Become friends with Sarah Jessica Parker.

Idaho wrinkled her nose. "New York smells."

Idaho was remembering, Stella guessed, their outing with her mother to see *Beauty and the Beast* on Broadway last summer, on a day when the temperature soared into the nineties and the streets were redolent of traffic fumes and dog shit.

"Mary-Kate and Ashley live there."

Idaho's eyes lit up. "Could I meet them?"

"I don't know," Stella said, wondering whether she still had any strings to pull, and if so, whether she wanted to use them on meeting the Olsen twins. It was unlikely to do anything for her moribund career; on the other hand, if it would unstick Idaho's attachment to New Jersey, it might be worth it. "Maybe."

"But if I could meet them," said Idaho, "I wouldn't have to live in New York. We could just go there and see them and then come right back home."

Stella looked around. It had been a long time since she'd thought of this as home, though the place looked exactly as it had when she was a kid, not a single wall color or curtain or piece of furniture updated from that time. The only difference was that it was messier now—a lot messier—though she had at least gotten rid of the rotting flowers. As if that could exorcise the ghost of her mother or the sadness that haunted every corner of the little house.

"Maybe we should just take a little day trip into the city and look around," Stella suggested. She could wear her biggest dark glasses; the clothes she had with her were so ordinary, she could blend right into any crowd.

"Maybe we should go to a playground," Idaho said. "Eat our dinner pizza at Vesuvio's today."

"You mean go out in Homewood?" Stella said, now truly alarmed. It was one thing to wander around among a million strangers, quite another to bump into somebody she knew. Strangers would either not recognize her or be too afraid to talk to her or, at worst, ask for her autograph. People she knew would actually want to talk.

Her mother's do-gooder friends and some of the neighbors had been ringing the doorbell, knocking at the window, depositing cakes and disgusting frozen hamburger casseroles on the front porch with notes in tidy Palmer penmanship: "We hope you're all right! Let us know if you need anything!"

Mary Jean had pushed a few notes through the front door. "Are you still here? Call me!" But Stella had thrown them away along with the food. It had been unexpectedly nice to see Mary Jean at the cemetery. She'd found herself, more than once, longing to talk to Mary Jean about all that had happened. In all the years that had passed since they'd been friends, she'd never been a tenth as close to anybody—all those husbands and lovers and assistants and costars and directors and hairdressers and handlers who pretended that what they had with her was friendship. But Stella, thanks to her long and real friendship with Mary Jean, knew better.

But what was the point in starting that up again, when she was just going to leave? She would have left already, if only there were somewhere for her to go. There was no point in pouring out her heart to Mary Jean, reigniting their intimacy, only to disappear once again.

"Come on, Mommy," Idaho said, already on her feet, tugging at Stella's hand. "Come on, let's just go for a walk."

Stella realized she looked faintly ridiculous walking through downtown Homewood wearing a huge pair of dark sunglasses and her mother's wide-brimmed straw gardening hat with her shorts and T-shirt, but the alternative—getting recognized, being mobbed the way she had been at her mother's funeral—was worse. But now, with the town emptied out for August and no one on alert that she was even here, she felt free to walk at Idaho's dillydallying pace, even to look in all the shop windows.

If she'd been dropped here blindfolded, she might not have even recognized that she was in her hometown. There were a few holdouts from her childhood—Vesuvio's, of course, and the big old secondhand bookstore, along with the dusty stores that somehow managed to struggle on: the shoemaker's and the uniform shop and the old-fashioned department store that had had the same powder-blue blazer hanging in the window since 1989.

But more and more of the stores, Stella saw now, were the same chain stores as could be found on the main street in downtown Santa Monica or Silver Lake, in any Orange County—or New Jersey, for that matter—mall. There was a Gap and a Kids' Gap, a Williams-Sonoma and a Pottery Barn. Where the model train store had been was a sign announcing that a Banana Republic would be coming soon, and a J. Crew was slated to take over the newsstand where they used to buy their rolling papers in high school.

And then there were the new places that actually made Stella want to go inside. There was an exotic home furnishings store, with a painted Asian cupboard and pretty glass hanging lights in the window. Then there was a shop that seemed to be totally filled with pretty things, from an antique pine table to a white pottery pitcher full of heavy pink roses, and a clothing shop with cozy-looking fall cashmeres and even a Prada bag in the window. There was a really cute Thai restaurant and a sushi bar, a groovy-looking trattoria on the site of the old Nino's, where her mother had taken her for veal parmigiana once or twice, along with a Starbucks and a more eclectic coffeehouse.

This procession of new food places made Stella think of the old Cozy Corner, and her heart nearly stopped as she looked around, afraid that it had vanished along with so many other of the old places. But no, there it was up ahead, its silver sides shiny as ever.

"Want to go get a milkshake?" she asked Idaho. She hadn't had a milkshake since probably the last time she was at the Cozy Corner, in 1984. "That place up there has the best milkshakes ever. They serve them right in the silver container they mix them in. I'm going to have chocolate. What kind are you going to have?"

Idaho announced that she was going to have vanilla, then decided that no, she thought she would have strawberry, and was veering back to vanilla when they reached the restaurant and Stella saw with dismay that it was closed. She checked her watch. It was one in the afternoon, which should have been the Corner's prime time. Cupping her hands around her eyes, she peered through the glass. Inside, all looked as it always had, and there was evidence—a pyramid of little cereal boxes on the counter, sundae glasses filled with green Jell-O protected by plastic wrap in the refrigerator case—that the restaurant was still open. But not today.

"I'm sorry, sweetie, but it's closed," said Stella.

Idaho shrugged. "That's okay."

"I think I saw some ice cream in the freezer. Maybe we could make milkshakes at home."

The word slipped from her lips before she even realized it. It didn't mean anything, she immediately told herself. When she was shooting a film, she called the trailer home. When they went on a trip, the hotel room became home.

She took Idaho's hand as they turned onto Beech Street. This town was not the home of her memories anymore. It was more like the Homewood of her dreams, literally, which had always featured some aspects of reality mixed with things from her imagination—a denser wood, a steeper hill, a field where there had always been a house.

Beech Street had always been an avenue of grand old houses, three-quarters of the way up the hill that crested at Homewood's western border, which was marked by thick forest and a spectacular view of Manhattan. From here, huge leafy trees and even bigger houses blocked whatever view might theoretically lie beyond. This had always been one of Stella's favorite streets in town, where she had walked with her own mother, fantasizing about which house they'd buy if they, as her mother put it, "struck it rich." Now, like the rest of the town, Beech Street looked even shinier: all the houses freshly painted, the landscaping lush and well tended. Even the grass seemed greener.

Stella had the eerie sense that she was in some upside-down version of *It's a Wonderful Life*—not merely acting in the movie, actually *living* it—where she died and came back to find her town totally transformed, but in this case for the better. Where in the old movie, Jimmy Stewart discovered that his hometown without him had become seedy and tawdry, Stella felt that in her absence Homewood had blossomed into a beautiful place. A place where she belonged.

This was where she could start over, Stella suddenly felt. If she wanted to relive her life, make better choices, listen to what her dying mother had been trying to tell her, this was the best place to do it. Instead of some fantasyland—some Hollywood equivalent like Paris or a tropical island or even New York—this was a real town where she and Idaho could have a real life. And it wouldn't even take forever to create one; they already had friends here, roots, love and support.

Stella gestured to a house ahead to the right, a Victorian with gingerbread and turrets that had always been painted pink and purple, but was now rehabbed in tasteful green tones, with big pots of ferns hanging along the front porch.

"Should we buy that house?" said Stella, keeping her voice light, testing out the line, the concept.

"It's not for sale," Idaho said.

Her child, Stella was learning, took everything literally. Stella's memory of being this age was of living in a perpetual fairyland, never being quite sure where she was or what was real. She had always assumed that Idaho, that all small children, were the same. But now that she was spending enough time with her daughter to really get to know her, Stella was realizing that Idaho was her own individual little person—one with an appetite for reality and stability that seemed positively middle-aged.

"Wouldn't you like to have a house that pretty?" Stella said.

She was pleased to see that Idaho nodded seriously. "I want a pretty house," she said. "Grandma's house. Right here."

"I lived here when I was a little girl, Idaho," Stella said, try-

ing to summon her long-held negative beliefs about Homewood to balance out the frightening rush of positive feelings.
"It's kind of boring here. It gets really cold in the winter.
There's no ocean or mountains. And everybody's just . . .
normal."

"You're not normal, Mommy. You're special. I want to be
just like you. That's why I want to live here."

Stella sighed. How could she argue with that? There would
come a time, she knew only too well, when Idaho would want
to be nothing like her, would want to get as far away from her
as possible. Here in Homewood, she thought, they could be
close—as close as Stella had been with her own mother.

Up ahead on the left, where High Street dead-ended into
Beech, was another relic from her childhood, the place where
she used to go and dream of her own future. It was the Tree
House, so called because of the enormous copper beech that
dominated the long sloped front lawn. The tree was still there,
Stella was delighted to see, so huge now that no grass at all
grew beneath it in an area big as a circus ring. From the road,
the tree totally blocked the view of the big stone house she
knew lay up the hill.

"Oh, that's a cool place," she told Idaho, her breath and her
step quickening. "I used to come here when I was a little girl;
I'd sit right under that big tree."

She'd sit on the lowest branch and gaze at the castlelike
house, dreaming that a prince lived there, a prince who would
host an elaborate ball where they would dance, after which
they'd get married and live in the house happily ever after.

She'd always dreamed of getting a glimpse inside, and still found the idea tantalizing, even though at this point in her life she'd visited—even *owned*—houses far bigger and grander than this one.

She led Idaho across a patch of lawn and through the reddish leaves, more purple than copper, dense as a forest, inside to where the branches were gray and bare and thick as an elephant's limb. She took off her dark glasses and looked around. It had always been like another world in here, sheltered and private, except now the solitude was punctured by the whine of a distant saw and the pounding of hammers

"Why is that house so dusty?" Idaho said, gesturing toward the stucco house, with its archways and its little turret. Now, though, what looked to be construction dust was billowing from the open leaded-glass windows and French doors.

"It looks like somebody's fixing it up," said Stella.

An old lady had lived here all alone, Stella remembered, or at least she had seemed old back then. Once, when they were teenagers, Stella had taken Pete here beneath this tree, with a contraband bottle of wine. The old woman's dog had sniffed them out, barking and howling, and they'd had to scramble to fasten their clothes and run out into the night, dog at their heels, as they watched the police cruiser heading toward them up Beech.

Now, she and Idaho stood in the cool shade of the tree, gazing silently toward the house. A few workmen, caked in white dust and carrying tools or boards on their shoulders, moved in and out through the open doors, and then another man, taller and cleaner-looking than the others, stepped out, stood on the lawn for a moment looking over the property, and then began walking toward them.

"He's coming this way!" Idaho whispered.

"Sssssh," said Stella, laying a steadying hand on her daughter's thin shoulder. "He can't see us in here."

But still the man kept coming. He was turning his head this way and that as if he were trying to puzzle something out about the tree: its height in feet or how many large branches grew from the trunk or whether its leaves were more red or green. Stella stood stiffly the way she remembered doing as a child, playing hide-and-seek, and signaled with the pressure of her fingers on her daughter's shoulder for Idaho to do the same. She barely breathed. The man was lean but looked well fed, as if he never skimped on a meal, Stella thought: eggs and toast for every breakfast, cream in his coffee, dessert at lunch, and steak for dinner, washed down by an excellent wine—red Bordeaux, she guessed. He was wearing work boots and denim, but except for a powdering of construction dust on his shoulders, he might have just stepped out of the shower. If this were a movie, Stella thought, the audience would be trying to guess whether he was the hero or the villain.

She could feel her daughter trembling beneath her hand. The man took one last long look at the tree and finally turned away, and Stella exhaled in relief. But then, after he'd taken only two steps, he swung back around and seemed to peer into the tree.

"Hello?" he said.

Stella held her breath.

"May I help you?"

Obviously, the jig was up. Stella sighed and stepped forward, brushing the leaves clear of her face.

"I was just showing my daughter the tree," she said, finally moving onto the lawn. "I used to come here when I was a kid."

He nodded, and then all at once his face, which had seemed until that moment hard and calculating, broke into a delighted smile.

"You're Stella Powers," he said.

Stella's hand flew to her face before she remembered she'd taken off her sunglasses.

"Yes," she said. "I guess so."

He continued to grin. "You guess so?"

"Listen, I don't know what you think you know about me," she said. "But right now, I'm just a mom with her kid."

She turned around to look for Idaho, who was still standing in the shadows of the tree.

"She's scared," Stella said, gesturing toward her daughter. "She thinks . . ."

What *did* Idaho think? What had Stella herself been thinking, for that matter, when she was hiding under the tree, nervous about being discovered by this man?

She'd been feeling, she realized, exactly as she'd felt as a girl, when she'd hidden in there and gazed dreamily at the house, when she'd retreated there to make out with Pete. She'd felt that she'd gone to a magical place, but that it was not strictly a place where she belonged or felt thoroughly protected and safe, that she was trespassing and could be discovered and cast out at any moment. And that this man, like the old lady's barking dog, might be the one to do that.

"It's all right," the man said, laughing, saving her the embarrassment of trying to explain any of that.

She expected him to crouch down and tell Idaho it was okay, she could come out, there was nothing to be afraid of. But he didn't do that, instead keeping his focus on Stella.

He put out his hand.

"I'm Henry Sladowski," he said. "I'm the owner of this property. I was at your mother's funeral."

His hands were surprisingly soft and slender, almost womanly. He smelled lightly of cologne. Stella's heart rose at his mention of her mother.

"You knew my mother?" she asked.

He frowned. "Sadly, no. I'm relatively new in town, and I hadn't had the pleasure. But I'd heard about all the wonderful things she'd done for the community, and I wanted to pay my respects."

"Yes, she was amazing," Stella said, feeling herself tear up. She'd always been faintly embarrassed by her mother's do-gooder zeal, donating money—that money, her mother happily accepted—but never really wanting to hear the details.

"It must be so difficult for you," Henry Sladowski said, still holding Stella's hand. "Are you here settling your mother's estate?"

Stella smiled and shook her head. "There isn't really an

estate to speak of, unless you count a hundred boxes filled with every picture I drew when I was a kid."

"I'm sure they were worth saving," Henry said.

Finally Idaho emerged from beneath the tree, giving Stella an excuse to withdraw her hand and put it around Idaho's shoulder, drawing her close.

"And so this is your house?" Stella asked, turning her attention to the house.

"For the moment." Henry smiled. "I'm renovating it. I'm a real estate developer. Once I get it fixed up, I'll sell it."

"This has always been my favorite house in Homewood."

"Well, maybe you should consider buying it," Henry Sladowski said. "You have the inside track, and I'd give you a special price, seeing as how—"

He stopped, and Stella met his eyes, which looked, for the first time in their conversation, uncertain.

"Seeing as how what?" she asked, imagining that he'd been about to say something he realized would be impolitic: Seeing as how you're a celebrity. Seeing as how you have plenty of money. Seeing as how, along with most other men on the planet, I'd love to have sex with you.

But again, he surprised her.

"Seeing as how you love this tree. It was going to be very expensive to cut it down. In fact, if you want to save this tree, you better buy this house."

CHAPTER 4

Mary Jean pulled the old Taurus wagon to the curb in front of Mrs. Powers's house, her heart rising in excitement. Stella was back. She was really back to stay.

At first, Mary Jean had felt hurt when Stella didn't return her calls or respond to her note, but she'd told herself that Stella had been through so much, she'd be in touch when she was ready. Then she'd grown concerned about Stella, especially after all the stories in the newspapers and magazines. There were rumors that Homewood Liquors was delivering something to Mrs. Powers's house nearly every day, although no one ever saw Stella or her little girl outside the house.

And then, soon after her brother Billy the fireman's wife

Teresa, who was the receptionist at Cameron Dunn's real estate office, said that Stella was buying the Tree House up on Beech Street, Stella called. Told Mary Jean herself that she was moving back to Homewood to stay, and invited Mary Jean and Jimmy to come over for an afternoon visit. Franny, of course, had insisted on accompanying them, even offering to watch the kids so Mary Jean and Stella could talk.

It was silly, but Mary Jean had dressed up in a linen tank and long flowing skirt that Franny said made her look thinner. And she'd baked a cake, her special apple crumb, even though it made the kitchen unbearable in the August humidity. The cake rode beside her in the front seat, while the kids were strapped in the back.

"Now, behave," Mary Jean said to the kids, lifting the cake and turning to look at them over the back of the seat.

"I AM have," said Jimmy.

Franny rolled her eyes. "Mom means be cool."

"How do you be cool?" Jimmy asked, his eyes wide on Franny as he waited for the answer.

"Never mind," Franny said. "Just don't drool on yourself or anything." She smirked. "You either, Mom."

Mary Jean tried to shoot Franny a withering look, but she knew she was busted. Franny could see how nervous she was, how much she wanted this visit to go well. Well, why shouldn't she? She'd never stopped missing Stella, and she'd never really gotten over feeling badly that Stella hadn't tried to get in touch all those years. Maybe, she worried more and more as time went on, it was something *she'd* done to drive Stella away. This was her chance to make up for any inadvertent sins she'd committed against their friendship in the past.

A new crop of dark roses had bloomed on the climber, and their scent hung heavy in the hot afternoon air, reminding Mary Jean of the funeral. She pressed the buzzer and waited, and then pressed again.

The door flew open, and there stood Stella, looking more like her old self, her *young* self, than she had at the funeral, certainly than she ever had beaming up from the glossy pages of some magazine, her face slathered with makeup, dressed in some ridiculous designer gown. Now Stella looked as she had at seventeen, in her torn jeans and her tiny T-shirt, with her hair loose and her pale face bare.

"How *great!*" Stella cried, throwing her arms around Mary Jean's neck. "I'm so excited that you're here!"

"I'm excited too," said Mary Jean, attempting to balance the cake plate on one hand. Feeling relief wash over her at Stella's warm greeting, she pulled back and studied her old friend, "You look better than you did the last time I saw you. A lot better."

"I feel a lot better. God, for a couple of weeks there, I thought I was going to lose my mind."

"I know," Mary Jean said. "It's horrible. Listen—here."

She extended the cake.

"Wow," Stella said, examining it. "Now that I live here, am I going to have to learn how to bake a cake?"

"Absolutely. At least, if you expect to be a PTA member in good standing."

"You're going to teach me."

"Oh, come on. Your mother was a great cook. I'm sure she taught you all her secrets."

"She tried, but I was standing there with my eyes closed and my fingers in my ears, trying to block it out."

The children, the two little ones and the one big one, were standing at the perimeter of the conversation, listening.

"Oh, I'm sorry," Mary Jean said. "Stella and Idaho, you already know Jimmy. And this is my daughter Franny."

Franny stepped forward, smiling brightly and extending her hand, a more businesslike Franny than Mary Jean had ever seen.

"I'm really happy to meet you, Miss Powers," she said.

"Oh, really," laughed Stella. "Call me Stella."

Franny blushed and lowered her eyes.

"Okay, Miss . . . Stella."

Stella kept holding Franny's hand, peering at the girl.

"Have we met?" she asked. "Or have I seen you before, somewhere around town?"

"I think we've passed each other on the street," Franny said quickly.

"Franny was with me at your mother's funeral—" Mary Jean began.

"At the cemetery?" Stella asked, still holding Franny's hand, her brows drawn together in confusion.

"No," Mary Jean said. "Outside the church. When you were coming down the steps—"

But then Franny shot her a look so dark and furious, she stopped speaking.

"I said hello," Franny told Stella. "Because I knew who you were. I mean, through my mom."

At least, Mary Jean thought, Franny was still blushing.

"Amazing hair," Stella said, finally letting go of Franny's hand, addressing the remark to Mary Jean, as if Mary Jean had personally selected her daughter's hair color.

"You remember my mother's hair." Mary Jean's Irish mother had worn her bright red hair long and curly.

"Do all the kids have it?"

"No. Peter—he's the oldest—is blond, like Pete. And Caitlin, that's Franny's twin, has my boring brown. And Jimmy's, well, you know, is reddish, but not like Franny's. Hers was even brighter when she was his age."

"I know actresses who would kill for your color," Stella said. "And I mean that literally."

"Really?" said Franny. "I was thinking that if I, you know, ever went out there, I might have to go blond, like Lilo did that time, or even dark."

"Who's Lilo?" said Mary Jean.

"Lindsay Lohan," Franny and Stella said in unison, looking at each other and laughing, their private joke.

"Oh, no," said Stella. "I think the entire industry agrees the blond was a huge mistake for her. Jessica Alba too."

"You never went lighter," Franny said.

"I was asked to a few times, but it was one thing I would never change." She hesitated. "How do you know that?"

"Oh, I know everything about you," Franny said. "My

whole family does, because my mom always talked about you nonstop."

Mary Jean shot her daughter a look. She wanted Stella to see her as a friend, as an equal—not as some crazed stalker.

"Franny, weren't you going to take the kids out to the playground?"

"Oh," Franny said. "Oh, right. Listen, Miss, um, Powers, if you ever need a babysitter"—she drew a slip of paper with their phone number already scribbled on it from the pocket of her jeans—"just call me, anytime."

"Franny's going to be busy with school soon."

"Not that busy," Franny said, pressing the phone number into Stella's hand and finally rounding up the children and leaving the house.

Once they were alone together, Mary Jean found herself gripped by shyness, convinced she wouldn't be able to relax enough to talk with Stella until she was eating a piece of cake. Ducking away, she went into the kitchen and retrieved two of the same small plates from the same shelf where they'd always been, took two forks and a cake knife from their usual resting place in the drawer beside the sink, and carried them into the dining room, where Stella had set the cake. Then she cut into the cake and handed Stella a piece, finally cutting a sliver for herself. She'd been looking forward to eating this for hours, since she first cracked an egg into her favorite spongeware cake bowl, and she looked around the living room for a place to sit.

Every chair was filled with mail or newspapers or clothes. Stella had set down her cake plate and was standing with her back turned, fiddling with the ancient cassette player. Mary Jean finally dumped a pile of newspapers, still in their plastic wrappers, onto the floor and flung herself into the chair, raising a forkful of the ambrosial cake to her lips.

And then, as Stella turned around with a grin on face her, she stopped. From the cassette player came a compelling rhythm, as familiar and as distant to Mary Jean as one of her baby's heartbeats.

"Is that—"

Stella nodded, her grin widening. "Prince."

"I *love* this song!" Mary Jean set down her cake and leaped to her feet, feeling herself bounce in time to the music. It was "When Doves Cry," hugely popular when they were seniors in high school, always Mary Jean's favorite song. She danced to it alone in her bedroom; she remembered dancing with Stella to it right here in this very room, the two of them laughing and singing the lyrics.

"Maybe you're just like my mother," Mary Jean sang to Stella now, all her inhibitions gone. "She's never satisfied."

"Tell it, Mama!" Stella cried.

When they were young, the song reminded them of *their* parents, but now it made Mary Jean think of Franny and the other kids, of how they viewed her and Pete. Oh, fuck it, she didn't want to think about her children, about being a mother, about getting older, about anything at all. She just wanted to feel the music and dance, the way she never did anymore. If she and Pete even tried, the kids hooted and teased them till they'd wrung all the pleasure from the process.

But Stella had been her first and always her best dancing partner, and somehow it was easier here, with her. The two of them bobbed and twirled, moving around each other and across the room in their familiar way, all the steps and the feelings effortlessly returning. They both had their eyes half closed and were mouthing the words—the words they remembered, anyway—to themselves, laughing anew when they caught sight of each other. When the song was done, they collapsed into each other's arms and stood there, panting.

"God, I remember you were the one who discovered Prince," Mary Jean said, when she finally caught her breath.

Stella grinned. "I wouldn't wear anything but purple for three months."

"We made those shiny purple dresses."

"Oh, Jesus, those were hideous. We went to that fabric store—"

"—right down from Port Authority."

"I wonder if it's still there. I haven't sewn anything in years."

"I still have that sewing machine. Do you remember the one?"

"The one you got for eighth-grade graduation."

"And then my mother expected me to make all my own clothes all the way through high school," Mary Jean groaned. But she was smiling despite that awful memory, with the pleasure she felt at picking up with Stella seemingly right where they'd left off more than twenty years ago. She'd never talked to anyone else so easily, not her brothers, not even Pete, and she was surprised and pleased that she and Stella were able to find their old rhythm again so easily.

"Do you still sew?" Stella asked.

"Only curtains and pillows and slipcovers," Mary Jean said. "All the passion I used to put into making my own clothes, I now put into fixing up my house."

My house that's not really my house, she thought. But she didn't want to dump that on Stella's lap. It made her look too pathetic, made them seem too unequal. She couldn't afford that. With any luck, they'd figure out a way to stay in the house before anyone found out what was going on.

"I can't wait to show you my house," Stella said, leaning forward, eyes shining.

"The Tree House," Mary Jean said. "I remember how much you always loved that place."

"I've never had a house before that was really me. In L.A. I had a decorator; everybody did. But I want to do this place by myself."

"I went to an estate sale at the Tree House, and I remember it was really in original shape. There was lots of dark paneling and great old tile in the bathrooms. And it had these awesome mantels on all the fireplaces. How many fireplaces are there?"

"I have to admit, I'm not really sure," Stella said. "There's so much construction going on inside, it hasn't been safe for me to poke around."

"What are they doing?"

"Mainly structural stuff. Henry says they still have weeks left of shoring up walls and straightening floors and replacing old wiring and pipes before I'll be able to get in there and do the fun stuff."

Mary Jean felt her breath stop. "Henry?"

"The guy who's fixing up the house," Stella said happily. "The guy I'm buying it from. Henry Sladowski."

"Oh, God, not him," Mary Jean blurted.

"What do you mean?" Stella said, her brow creasing. "Why not?"

Mary Jean sat there with her mouth open but no words coming out. She'd already said too much, but she wasn't sure how to fix it. Tell Stella every reason she didn't like Sladowski? Or try to pull her foot out of her mouth? She so wanted everything to go well with Stella.

"It's just . . . ," Mary Jean said. Maybe it was best to proceed with the truth. Which of course meant confessing that they were getting kicked out of their house, which she hadn't wanted to do. But she had to be able to be herself with Stella, she thought, if they were truly going to be friends.

"It's just that Sladowski is our landlord," she said in a rush. "He bought the little house we've been renting for years, and he's kicking us out so he can tear it down."

"He's kicking . . ." Stella shook her head in confusion. "But why would he do that?"

"So he can put up a McMansion that he can sell for a lot more money. I thought this kind of thing originated in California. Now Sladowski is doing the same thing here."

"Are you sure we're talking about the same person?" Stella said. "The Henry Sladowski I know is really into preserving that old Homewood architectural character."

There was only one Henry Sladowski, as far as Mary Jean knew, and from what she'd seen of his work, she doubted he was into preserving any kind of character at all. Once he bought a place, he usually gutted it, refacing plaster walls with drywall and replacing old ceramic baths with marble and investing hundreds of thousands of dollars in kitchens that were temples to granite and stainless steel. The people who moved to Homewood from the city, with their new babies and bank accounts fat from selling their co-ops, couldn't tell authentic architectural detail from reproduction charm and only wanted a place that looked like the Pottery Barn catalog ideal of suburbia. Which Sladowski delivered with overpriced cookie-cutter perfection.

But she couldn't say that to Stella. She wanted Stella to be happy here, not so scared of what was happening that she'd run away. That had happened before, leaving too big a hole in the center of Mary Jean's life.

"I'm sure he's doing a great job on your house," Mary Jean said, trying to convince herself along with Stella. "I mean, that place has to be protected by at least some of the historic preservation rules. That tree is a local treasure."

"All I know is that Henry has really been fantastic to me," Stella said.

I bet, thought Mary Jean. A movie star, rich and white and beautiful, was his ideal home buyer. If Sladowski and his friends had their way, Homewood would be totally populated by movie stars.

"He even cut me this special deal so I could buy the house. Most of my money is tied up in California until this fucking divorce is settled, so he let me put down this little bit of money I had in an account here—not much, just a hundred thousand—and then he said we can close whenever I have access to the rest."

Mary Jean zoned out contemplating the phrase "not much, just a hundred thousand," and when she focused again, Stella was saying, "I actually think he's kind of cute."

"Who?" Mary Jean asked, figuring she'd missed a complete change of subject.

"Henry, of course!"

This time, it was no use trying to hide her feelings. A sputter of astonished laughter escaped her lips. She supposed, if you saw a picture of Henry Sladowski without actually encountering him, you might think he was good-looking. But she would sooner stick her tongue down the throat of a frog than get within two feet of that man.

"It's easy for you to laugh," Stella said, obviously not amused. "You found the love of your life early. You've been happily married all these years, you have this stable family life, this place where you feel rooted. I want that too."

Stella Powers wanted to be more like *her*? That was pretty amazing. And ironic, considering that Mary Jean was wishing she were more like Stella, more of a risk-taker, someone who did things instead of just sitting around thinking about them. Or being afraid of doing them.

"I feel like I owe it to my mother to try and make a more settled life for me and Idaho," Stella said. "That's what she was trying to tell me when she died. I just wish she was around to share it with."

"She would have loved that," Mary Jean said, softening. "I know she always hoped you would move back here, though I don't think she ever expected it would happen. I felt the same way, Stella. I just don't like Henry Sladowski."

"I think if you really knew him, you'd like him," Stella burst out. "If you knew him personally, I mean. I understand why you're upset about what's going on with your house, but that's business. I know he and Pete are friendly."

It was Mary Jean's turn to be confused. "*My* Pete?"

"Henry's mentioned his name a couple of times. And I saw them talking together once up at the house."

Mary Jean shook her head. "Maybe they've met in passing, on some police business. But I don't think Pete actually knows him."

What Stella didn't seem to understand about the new Homewood was that people like her and Pete—and like Stella's own mother—didn't socialize with people like Henry Sladowski. They might all pretend that they were fellow citizens of the same cozy little community, but Sladowski's world revolved around the golf club and museum benefits and expensive dinners at the cool new restaurants in town, while Mary Jean's and Pete's life was centered on trying to keep the house picked up and getting the kids through school. Mary Jean had assumed, when Stella moved back, that she was moving to the same

Homewood where Mary Jean lived, because that's the way it had always been. But she saw now that money and fame trumped history, and that meant that Stella was moving to Henry Sladowski's Homewood.

"I'm sure Pete and Henry know each other pretty well," Stella was insisting. "In fact, Henry told me he's talked to Pete about whether he should run for mayor. Whether Henry should run, I mean."

"Whether he should *what*?" Mary Jean cried, hoping she'd heard wrong.

"Run for mayor. It's still up in the air. In fact, I guess I wasn't supposed to say anything. But maybe the four of us could get together and . . ."

But Mary Jean didn't hear the rest of what Stella said. She was too focused on figuring out how she was going to murder her husband.

Mary Jean drove by the playground to check that the kids were there, but she turned onto a side street before they could see her. She wanted time to confront Pete while they were out of the house.

It was Pete's week to work nights, so he was just waking up, sitting in bed with their bedroom air conditioner—the only one in the house—blasting, drinking coffee and watching a Mets game.

"So," said Mary Jean, standing in the doorway, watching him, trying to formulate exactly how she was going to do this. Pounce? Or tease the details out of him, and then pounce?

"Hey," Pete said, a surprised look on his face. "Where are the kids?"

"We stopped over at Stella's. Franny took Jimmy and Stella's little girl to the playground. Stella and I had a long talk."

"Oh," Pete said, not picking up on her ominous tone. "That's nice. Caitlin?"

"This is one of her Columbia days." And Peter, their oldest, had already returned to Penn State for lacrosse practice. She suddenly saw where this was going, definitely not where she'd intended it to.

"So I guess we're alone," he said, a grin beginning to spread over his face.

"It looks like it."

His grin widened. He set down his coffee mug, threw back the sheet that covered his legs, and patted the side of the bed, raising his eyebrows.

They were never alone, and on the rare occasions they were, they immediately had sex. It didn't matter whether they were fighting, whether Mary Jean had her period or Pete had a cold, whether they had only ten minutes. Being alone was just too good an opportunity to pass up, no matter how great the countervailing pressure.

Until now. Until she found out her own husband knew that Henry Sladowski was plotting to take over not only their home but their entire town, and hadn't told her. What else was he hiding from her?

"God, you look gorgeous," he said.

This definitely was not going according to plan.

"Stop trying to butter me up," Mary Jean snapped.

"Do I have to butter you up?" Pete said, still smiling. "Okay, then."

He set down his coffee cup, flicked off the TV, got out of bed, and crossed the room to where Mary Jean now stood with her arms crossed over her chest. Very softly, he brushed her hair back from her brow.

"I know it's hot outside," he said, kissing her brow. "Let me help you relax."

He cleared the hair from her neck and bent to kiss the back of it, using his tongue to lap up a drop of sweat. She felt her knees go weak. Then he slipped one loose linen strap from her shoulder.

"Pete," she groaned. "Don't."

"I have to," he whispered, bending into her and cupping her bottom with his large hands, pulling her close.

He was wearing only his boxers and he was hard, as he always seemed to be near-instantly, so excited he was running his hands up and down her body, tugging at her clothes, pulling her tank over her head and unhooking her bra.

Could she really have sex with him before she eviscerated him? Wasn't that a tad . . . callous?

Oh, Jesus, he was down on his knees now, lifting her linen skirt, running his tongue up her thigh.

"Pete," she said, digging her fingers into his scalp.

He looked up at her, his eyes glassy with lust.

"We can use the bed," he said, misunderstanding.

He danced her over there and threw her down, pulling her

elastic-waist skirt off with one yank and then going for her panties.

"I have to talk to you," she gasped.

"Can't it wait?" he said breathlessly, kneeling on the bed, diving again between her legs.

Oh, God, now he really had her. She felt her eyelids flutter as a deep purr escaped her throat. He was putting in extra effort, too, taking care to do it exactly the way she loved, the way he'd taught her to love. This had always been his favorite, even when he was a teenager. Had Stella demanded it, or was it a natural predilection? She had been a virgin the first time she had sex with Pete, and he of course had been doing it with Stella for nearly two years. Although they were the same age, he seemed like a man to her, vastly knowledgeable and practiced. She was so thrilled to be with Pete, to be his girlfriend, to hear him murmur "I love you" as his penis edged inside her, as his pace quickened and he began to come, that she would have and in fact did let him do whatever he wanted. Make love without a rubber, for instance, which is how she got pregnant with Peter. Come in her mouth, on her breasts, on her face; do it naked outside on the ground, or on his boyhood bed as his family watched TV downstairs.

She had long ago gotten over any shame she felt at any of this, had learned instead to use it to up the excitement and make the sex even better, but now she found these old thoughts of Pete with Stella competing with her pleasure, brain versus body. She tried relaxing her muscles and concentrating only on the flick of his tongue, but it was no good, she kept coming back to her conversation with Stella, Stella staying in Homewood, Stella's new house, Stella and Sladowski.

Mary Jean bolted upright and pushed her husband away. "You *jerk*!" she cried.

"What?" He looked shocked, as if she'd pinched him awake from a beautiful dream.

"Why didn't you tell me about Sladowski?" she said, realizing immediately what a non sequitur this must seem to Pete.

But very quickly, his look shaded from baffled to guilty, and she knew she had him.

"What about Sladowski?" he asked, suddenly wary, a cop and not just a husband.

"You know what. That you and he have suddenly become big buddies. That he's thinking of running for mayor. That you know all about it."

"Who told you that?" Pete asked, eyes narrowing.

"Never mind who told me that," Mary Jean said, shoving him again. "I want to hear it from you. The truth."

"This is privileged information."

She reached out and clamped her fingers onto his nipple. "Spill."

And then, inexplicably, maddeningly, his big goofy smile was back.

"Isn't it *great*?" he gushed.

"Great?!?" She hopped out of bed and began pacing what little space there was in the bedroom. "How can you say Henry Sladowski running for mayor of Homewood is great?"

"It's my big chance, Mary Jean. *Our* big chance. If Slad-owski wins, he says he'll make me police chief."

She stopped in her tracks. Police chief. Of course. Becom-ing chief had always been Pete's dream, but as long as Francis X. Fitzgerald, Homewood's longtime mayor, was still in office, George Barnes would remain chief. A new regime was Pete's only shot.

"I know how much you want this . . . ," she began softly.

"But don't you see?" he said, sitting up in bed, his muscles lean and hard as they were twenty years ago. "I don't just want it for me, I want it for us. If Sladowski becomes mayor and I become chief, then, A, he won't be so quick to kick us out of this place, and B, you won't have to worry about working be-cause I'll actually be making enough money for us to buy a house here."

The way prices were going, maybe not, Mary Jean thought of saying, though she bit her tongue. She wanted to be happy for Pete, wanted him to be chief as he had always dreamed. But at this price, to her and to the town she loved?

"Pete, first of all, I want to go to work. And I'd love you to become chief. But you *can't* endorse Sladowski. You can't really want him to be mayor."

"I know what I want for myself," Pete said, setting his mouth in a line. "I know what I want for our family. If I have to support Sladowski to get it, I'm there. Fuck, Mary Jean, if I have to lick his shoes to get it, I'm there."

Mary Jean shook her head. "No, Pete. You're too good for that. You're too good for him."

"So what should I do instead?" Pete asked. "Become sheriff of fucking Stroudsberg, Pennsylvania?"

Over the whine of the air conditioner, through the closed door, Mary Jean heard the front door slam, heard Jimmy call for her and then the sound of his feet banging up the stairs.

"Mom?" he screamed. "Are you here?"

She rushed to lean back against the bedroom door so he couldn't push it open. Pete pulled a pillow over his groin.

"Yes, honey," Mary Jean sang through the door. "I'll be there in a minute. Go downstairs now."

"Mom? Me and Idaho had a lot of fun."

"That's great, honey. Go watch TV, and I'll be right down."

There was a moment's hesitation, and then the little boy's feet retreated down the stairs.

Pete dropped the pillow and walked over so that his face was right in front of Mary Jean's.

"I want you to be with me on this," he whispered, his breath rich with coffee and sex.

Mary Jean set her chin. "I can't."

"Try, Mary Jean. You have to."

"Why do I have to?"

"You have to," said Pete, "because it's our only chance."

CHAPTER 5

"Idaho. Idaho!"

This was happening more and more lately. It would be time to go to the store, or even to eat dinner or go to bed, and Idaho would disappear. Stella would find her hiding under the bed or in the closet, but lately she'd gotten more adventurous in her hiding places, squeezing into the cupboard beneath the sink, and the other day even going up to the attic. Stella tried to tell her these places weren't safe, that it was terrifying for Stella when she couldn't find her, but here was Idaho, hiding again.

"Idaho! If you don't come out, I'm going to have to tell Jimmy's sister to go home instead of staying to babysit you. And then the two of you won't get to watch *Cinderella* together."

That did it. Slowly Idaho emerged from behind the sofa. "Look, you're all dusty from being back there," said Stella, brushing off her daughter's tiny butt, trying to avoid getting her own white dress dirty. The boxes with all her good clothes had just arrived from storage, and she'd found this Balenciaga that she'd never even worn, steaming it to perfection in her mother's pink-tiled shower.

It felt so strange to be going out not only in Homewood, but on an actual formal date. Henry Sladowski was a different kind of man from any she'd ever been involved with—so *normal*—and she was determined to proceed in a different way than usual. Instead of going to some hot club in the city until four in the morning, they were going out to dinner right here in town. She was planning to drive herself to the restaurant; she was in no way ready to introduce another man into Idaho's life, not after putting her daughter through her instant marriage and breakup with Eddie. And she definitely would not have sex with him tonight, no matter how much either of them might want to.

The doorbell rang: Franny, who swooped in bearing board games and a cache of old Barbies, sending Idaho into a starry-eyed swoon. What a gorgeous girl, with Pete's tall, lean body and Mary Jean's soft features and creamy skin and that fabulous hair. In a few years, she'd be ripe to get all the parts that used to go to Stella; looking at her, it was easier for Stella to accept that by comparison she really was over the hill. But that didn't matter anymore, because now she had a whole new life, a life that didn't depend on some baby director deciding whether she was thin or pretty or young-looking enough. A real life with a real future.

"Be good for Franny," Stella said, kissing Idaho. And then, to Franny: "Help yourself to anything you want. I won't be late."

"You look awesome," Franny said.

"Really?"

"Amazing. I love those earrings."

These were a remnant from her L.A. days, long gold fili-greed chandeliers dripping pink crystals. She'd worn them on an *InStyle* shoot, and the designer had been only too happy to give them to her.

"Not too slutty?" Stella said, fingering them. She'd been wearing them when she met Eddie, and while she now hated him and every minute of their relationship, she couldn't forget how they'd mesmerized him

Franny looked startled. "N-not at all," she stammered.

The poor sheltered thing had probably never heard the term before, at least not from someone her mother's age. Stella smiled, feeling more confident. "Okay, then. Have fun, girls."

Idaho was already twining herself around Franny, talking excitedly about Barbie and pulling the older girl into the living room, where her own dolls were waiting. Stella's heart lifted at the sight of her little daughter so happy. If she sometimes worried, lying awake in her mother's bed in the middle of the night, about whether she was doing the right thing moving here, she had no doubt that it was great for Idaho.

Downtown Homewood was bustling on Saturday night,

even in late August, the time Stella remembered everyone went away because the camps closed down but school wouldn't start until after Labor Day. It was so refreshing to see people out walking, the sidewalks filled with couples strolling to one of the new restaurants that lined Broad Street, or to one of the two downtown movie theaters, or whole families parading, holding hands or licking ice cream cones.

This was it, Stella thought, her heart rising: real America, the kind of place she'd come to think existed only in movies. The rural towns everyone idealized were often boarded up now, populated only by evangelical churches and methamphetamine labs. Small cities, places she'd visited for gratefully brief location shoots—Rochester and Appleton, Sacramento and Memphis—were tangles of chain stores and run-down neighborhoods.

How ironic that once-faceless suburbs like Homewood had become the cradle of wholesome, idyllic small-town American life. And how wonderful for Stella and Idaho that they found themselves in the middle of all this splendor because of her mother's sudden death. She felt, since losing her mother, more spiritual, more willing to believe that everything happened for a reason, and in life after death. Though she hated to think that her mother had suffered a fatal heart attack in order to create a happier life for Stella and Idaho, she liked the idea of her mother smiling down peacefully from heaven. "I love you, Mom," Stella whispered, before she straightened her tight dress—much tighter and shorter and whiter than anything anyone else in Homewood seemed to be wearing, she realized now—and pulled open the door of Thai King restaurant.

It was so dark inside, Stella had to stand blinking in the foyer, breathing in the icy air-conditioning, for a long minute before her eyes adjusted well enough to take in the layout of the place. Blond wood chairs and tables were clustered close together, and Asian waitresses were dressed in navy and white kimonos. Wait a minute, weren't kimonos Japanese? But before Stella could dwell on that question for too long, Henry Sladowski rose to his full height from a chair in the center of the room and crossed to greet her.

He was man-sized, not like one of those Hollywood men, who always really *were* smaller than you thought they were going to be. And not only, Stella mused, in terms of height. Sladowski by contrast was tall and broad-shouldered, clean-shaven and dressed in an expensive-looking suit and a starched white shirt, so confidence-inspiring compared with the sweaty T-shirts Eddie usually wore. True, he'd looked sexier in the jeans he was wearing the first time she saw him, but they were together as grown-ups now, not as lust-crazed kids. The scent of his cologne was stronger now, its spiciness harmonizing with the smell of the food. He took her elbow—the last time a man did that to her, she was playing a role in a Jane Austen movie—and steered her to his table.

"I hope you don't mind," he said smoothly, "but I've taken the liberty of ordering for both of us. I know the chef here, and he makes special things just for me."

Actually, Stella *did* mind. She was used to being the one in charge, and besides, she'd spent the past two decades honing what she could and couldn't eat if she was going to stay at movie-worthy weight. Given the amount of pizza and Cold Stone Creamery ice cream concoctions she'd been consuming, she was definitely going to have to be more vigilant than ever.

But maybe, she thought, if she was going out with a different kind of man, she had to try to be a different kind of woman. More pliable, more supportive of what *he* wanted. While she couldn't imagine her mother counseling subjugation, exactly, she knew Mom would consider this more of the kind of "normal" relationship she wanted for her daughter. And if Stella was going to give up her career and move back to New Jersey, if she was finally going to put family before work in her life, shouldn't she think about becoming a wife, rather than a movie star with a husband?

"That sounds amazing," she said, casting a longing glance at the empty table in a dark corner where she would have preferred to sit, but instead allowing him to pull out a chair for her at the ringside table he'd already commandeered.

He sat opposite her and pulled a bottle of Cristal from an ice bucket she only then spotted near the table.

"What's this for?" she said, raising her eyebrows.

He raised his eyebrows back at her. "For you," he said. "In celebration of our first date."

Hmmm, a little slick, and definitely uncool. But maybe she was just confusing warmth with uncoolness? Maybe she'd spent so long dealing with sharks like Eddie Skinner that she'd forgotten how to appreciate a genuine nice guy? Why not let herself be with someone who unashamedly wanted her, who was capable of taking care of her—and of Idaho, she reminded herself—and would love to be given the chance?

"Thank you," she said, raising her glass to him as the first steaming dishes arrived.

Don't get ahead of yourself, she thought, you're just going out with the guy, not marrying him. Though the truth was, she probably had more experience with getting married than with dating. What she and Pete had done in high school couldn't have been called dating—they never went anywhere—and most of her early dates in California had been other struggling actors, writers, musicians, the occasional director or producer looking to get in her pants. Then she'd married her agent—not her last agent, Marty, but the guy who was three agents before him—who worked so much that they never had time to go out to dinner, just the two of them, and do nothing but talk. Then she'd married Idaho's father, which had been a mess of tears (his) and anger (hers). And finally she'd married Eddie, which had been all about sex, until it was all about cheating.

And now here she was at almost forty (although she'd already told Henry Sladowski thirty-five), going out on one of her first bona fide dates. The kind of date people went on in every romantic movie, every television show, she'd ever been in.

"Here's to us," he said, tapping glasses with her. "And to your house."

"To the house," she agreed.

"You're going to love living in this town," Henry said,

spooning shrimp and noodles onto her plate. "I mean, I know you lived here as a child, but you're going to be amazed by how much it's changed. Now that Manhattan has become so insane, with even Park Slope and Williamsburg and Hoboken going through the roof, places like Flatbush and Riverdale and Homewood are the new SoHo."

Stella laughed, but Henry looked completely serious.

"Where else can truly creative people afford to live?" he said. "Raise their families? And still find a sophisticated environment and community? This is the best place to live in America."

"Wow," said Stella. Even Cameron Dunn, who'd managed her real estate transaction with Henry, hadn't spoken of it so glowingly. Of course Mary Jean loved living here, but that was because she'd always lived here, not because she'd actively chosen it. Henry made her feel as if this was a place where she *wanted* to live.

"I lived in Manhattan for nearly twenty years," he told Stella, refilling her champagne glass, "and spent a lot of time in London, L.A.—big cities. But now that I'm here, I can't imagine ever going back to urban life."

"But why would a single man move to a town like this?" asked Stella, fishing for what she figured was the inevitable tale of the ex-wife across town, the kids he shared custody of.

"I came to a party out near here, at Bobbi Brown's," he said. "The makeup mogul Bobbi Brown, not the rap star Bobby Brown. And I just thought, I want this. I want grass, flowers, trees, real life. Correction: I don't want it. I *need* it."

"But it's so family-oriented," Stella said. "Everybody's married—"

"Not everybody," said Henry, raising his champagne glass to her. "I believe everything happens for a reason. Maybe the reason I moved here is so I could meet you."

Stella felt herself pull back, literally, until she slammed into the chair behind her. Stop it!, she scolded herself. Take a deep breath and let the evening unfold. Pretend you're in a movie about two unlikely people who fall in love.

"I've heard things about you," she confessed to Henry, feeling that since their relationship was starting out on such a serious note, she should lay all her cards on the table. "Some people think what you're doing with your real estate business is not so good for this town."

Henry sighed. "You know, Stella," he said, "there are people in this town who don't understand me—who don't understand you, either. They think because I've lived other places, because I've made all this money and done all these things, I'm not like them. But I want the same things they want. I want to make this town a great place to live, to raise my children. I want to make it the kind of place where a kid with a dream can thrive, not that they have to run away from."

Did he know that about her, that she'd felt as if the only way to make her dreams come true was to leave? She narrowed her eyes at him, but he was happily munching on a shrimp, seemingly oblivious to how directly he'd nailed her.

"The truth is," he said, "my life in New York was wild. All I did was work and party, party and work. I'm ready to settle down now. I want a nice home, marriage, family, a pot roast in the oven."

Stella laughed, a real laugh this time. "I love pot roast."

"Well, see then. I knew we had a lot in common."

Maybe her childhood dream would come true, she thought. She imagined her big new house all fixed up, as beautiful as she'd remembered it being in her childhood visions. But now along with her and Idaho gliding across the lawn, Henry was there too, and a little boy, tumbling in the grass, and maybe a baby in her arms, and a dog, plus a procession of servants behind them. They'd be like Marilyn Monroe and Arthur Miller, the beautiful movie star and her intelligent, powerful husband. Without the divorce, of course.

Suddenly Henry dropped his shrimp tail and beamed in on her with a shine in his eye.

"I have an idea," he said. "I want to show you Homewood the way I see it. Come on, let's get out of here."

He wiped his hands, hurling his napkin down so decisively it tumbled to the floor, then stumbled to his feet, reaching across the table to help her up.

"But . . . ," she said, gesturing to the waitress who was approaching their table, a sizzling dish in each hand.

"We'll take the food with us," Henry said, gesturing wildly. "The champagne too. We have to get out there before it's too dark."

An hour later, Stella sat parked with Henry on a wooded section of High Street, looking over the lights of the city. The open champagne bottle sat between them, and Henry was eating now-cold chicken with chopsticks from a plastic container. He was still talking.

Stella had stopped listening. It wasn't that he was boring, exactly, or that she didn't like the sound of his voice. It was just that the ground he was covering was beginning to sound awfully familiar—the history of the housing stock, the tax base rate and the need for revaluation, what Henry saw as the absurdly high expenditure on education. Property taxes were way too high, he was saying, and the town needed a hands-on mayor who would manage its finances for the present population and not for the way things had been in 1978.

Stella stifled a yawn and reached for the open champagne bottle. It was, unfortunately, nearly empty. Half an hour ago, she might have offered to share it with him, but now she just raised it to her own lips and drained it. Screw it. If they were going to talk about property taxes, she deserved to be a teensy bit drunk.

At first, when he'd parked the car, she'd stiffened, bracing herself for an onslaught of hands and lips. This spot had been a favorite parking place in high school; she and Pete—she and a lot of other boys, too—had often come here. But no, Henry seemed in no hurry to attack her. Because he's a grown-up, she reminded herself. Instead, he suggested a picnic with their still-uneaten food and half-finished champagne. Then they spotted lightning on the horizon, dramatically lighting up the skyline of the city, and realized the humid day was turning into a drizzly evening. So they settled for eating and drinking in the car—or rather, Henry ate while Stella drank.

She had just felt the last of the champagne bubble onto her tongue when a spotlight shone bright as the midday sun into the car. She and Henry both gasped and swung around, only to have the spotlight switch off and another, much smaller light go on. Henry rolled down his window, and Stella was stunned to see Pete's face appear.

"Oh, I'm sorry, Mr. Sladowski," Pete said. "I didn't recognize your car."

"That's all right, Pete," said Henry. "The Jag's in the shop. I guess I got so caught up in talking to my friend here, I lost sight of what it looked like, us parked here like this."

Pete peered into the car, and it was impossible for Stella to shrink far enough into the seat for him not to notice her.

"Hey, Stella," Pete said. His blond hair had grown a tiny bit too long, and was sticking out awkwardly from the bottom of his policeman's cap, tipping him from handsome toward dorky. He smiled, and he tipped back toward handsome again.

"Hey, Pete."

Henry looked surprised. "You two know each other?"

"We went to school together," Stella said.

At the same moment Pete said, "We used to go out."

There was an awkward silence, and then Stella said, "A long time ago."

"A really long time ago," Pete agreed.

Henry cleared his throat. "So, Pete," he said. "Can I count on you at the Labor Day gathering at Mrs. Dunn's?"

"Sure, Mr. Sladowski," Pete said.

Mr. Sladowski? Mrs. Dunn? Especially since Henry was

calling Pete "Pete"? Stella registered surprise, but neither of the men seemed to notice.

"You'll be there," Henry said to Stella. "I hope."

"It's a party?"

"Yes, a party. And more." Henry winked at Pete.

"So Mary Jean will be there too?" Stella said to Pete. "And your kids?"

Pete looked as if this possibility hadn't occurred to him. "I'm not sure," he said. "Maybe."

"Mary Jean, Pete's wife, is my oldest friend," Stella told Henry. "I'd love you to meet her. I think you two would really hit it off."

Pete stood up so precipitously he half fell against the car. He righted himself and then swayed there, his face out of sight, for a moment, before he leaned back down.

"Just in case someone else comes by," he said, "there's an ordinance against having an open alcohol bottle in a vehicle."

"It's empty," said Stella, lifting it toward him.

"Even so. You'll want to dispose of that."

"Yes, sir," Stella said, saluting and grinning, thinking of all the nights they'd sat up here together, opening contraband beers one after the other.

Pete didn't smile back.

"All right," he said finally, touching the bill of his cap. "You folks have a good night now."

"We were just leaving," Henry said, turning the key in the ignition.

"No hurry," said Pete.

But as soon as the police car pulled away, Henry put the car in gear and pulled into the road too, and Stella was glad he had. Neither of them spoke, and they hadn't touched the whole time they'd been sitting there. So why, Stella wondered, did she feel as if she'd been caught with her panties around her ankles?

"Now, what are you going to do for landscaping at the new house?" Cameron Dunn asked.

The other four women—Stella was embarrassed that she couldn't remember any of their names—sitting around the wrought-iron table on the patio beside Cameron's glittering pool all leaned in to listen.

"I'm not sure," Stella stammered. "I really haven't thought about it yet."

In Hollywood, most people she knew didn't think about this kind of thing at all. Sure, a couple of people like Courteney and Brad had well-publicized passions for decorating, but most of the industry people she knew were too busy working to manage the design of their gardens or decoration of their houses, beyond setting forth their basic tastes—if they even had any.

But the upscale women of Homewood, Stella was discovering over the course of this lunch that Cameron very nicely had thrown so she could meet some of "the girls," lavished as much attention on their houses and yards as the women of Hollywood did on their looks. They may have hired decorators and stylists and landscape designers to do the heavy lifting for them, but they were intimately involved in every aspect of their homes—for better or worse.

"I use Fanucci and Sons," said the only redhead in the group. All of the women were in their thirties and well toned, two were blond—though one had paler hair and was taller—and one looked Italian or Jewish, much more ethnic, in any case, than Cameron herself. "They're fabulous."

"Do they do all the seasonal plantings for you?" one of the blondes asked.

"Yes." The redhead, who had breasts so large they had to be fake, turned to Stella. "I have daffodils and tulips in the spring, then they plant in white impatiens for the summer, the golden mums for the fall, and fairy lights on all the evergreens for Christmas and on through the winter."

"Complete with matching wreaths," the darker blonde added, with, Stella thought she detected, an ever-so-slight roll of her blue eyes.

"Your first order of business," Cameron said, focusing on Stella, "will probably be getting rid of that tree."

Stella shook her head. "I'm not getting rid of the tree."

"It's going to be difficult to do landscaping," said Cameron, "if you keep that tree."

"Then I won't do landscaping," said Stella.

There was silence around the table, as if she'd just said, "Then I won't wear deodorant" or "Then I won't take care of my child."

She felt the same way she had when she first walked in here, wearing her gold sandals and little Juicy white dress over her bikini—Cameron had called it a pool luncheon, after all, and she was dying after the summer in her mother's sweltering house—only to find the other women in their flowered capris and little pastel polo shirts, their pearl earrings and tortoise headbands. Nothing that could get wet.

"I mean," said Stella, "I'll just have to find a way to landscape around the tree."

Everyone started to breathe again.

"When the time comes," Cameron said, "I'll be happy to give you some names."

"I'll recommend you to Fanucci," said the redhead.

"Thanks," said Stella. She tasted a spoonful of her gazpacho, eager for a way to change the subject. "Mmmm, this is delicious."

"Thank you," said Cameron.

"You made it yourself?"

Cameron nodded, and then the dark-haired woman piped up. "She even grows her own tomatoes. She even makes her own crème fraiche. She's a regular Martha."

"It's nothing," said Cameron.

"Nothing," said the dark-haired woman, "when you have a six-burner Viking stove and honed granite countertops and two Sub-Zero refrigerators and two dishwashers."

"Well," said Cameron, waving her perfect pink-painted fingernails dismissively. "Who doesn't?"

"I don't," said Stella.

They all stared at her.

"Don't worry," Cameron said finally, recovering. "You will."

"The only thing I know how to cook is my mother's pot roast," said Stella. "And I don't even really know how to cook that."

"What do you eat?" asked the paler blonde, utterly serious.

"Restaurant food. Takeout. In L.A., I'm embarrassed to admit this, but we had a cook."

"A cook," said the blonde. "I'd love to have a cook."

Cameron shot her a disapproving look. "Then how would you keep on top of the nutritional value and fat content of the food your family ate?"

"Everybody had a cook in L.A.," Stella rushed to say, wanting to avoid another conflict. "I guess because most of my friends were working moms."

Actresses, was what she meant. Actresses who made several million dollars a year and were chained to the set from five in the morning until eight or nine at night.

"I just have to ask you," one of the blondes burst out. "What is Brad Pitt really like?"

Stella opened her mouth. Until this moment, none of the women had acted as if they thought Stella was anyone but another mom new in town. And now this.

"I don't really know," she said, trying to stifle a smile. "I never met the guy."

"Well, who *did* you meet? Come on, tell us some real dirt."

They all leaned in, even more attuned to her words now than when they were discussing landscaping.

"I don't know," Stella said, frozen. Most of the people she

knew well enough to have "real dirt" on were not big names this group would recognize—they were character actors or musicians or producers or writers. And she wasn't about to dish out the insider gossip she'd heard to this group like so many hors d'oeuvres.

"I hear Meg Ryan's a really good mom," she offered.

"She *lost* weight after she had her son," said the dark-haired woman approvingly.

"*That's* not dirt!" said the blonde. "I mean, what was it like to sleep with Russell Crowe!?"

"Gee, I never did that," Stella said. "But I hear that when he comes he likes to scream, 'Go, Russ, go!'"

Five faces stared openmouthed at her.

"I'm kidding!" she cried. "Kidding!"

"Oh," Cameron said. "Ha ha. Now on to something more important. Where are you sending Idaho to school?"

Another collective exhale. At this point, she would never tell them that the story about Russell Crowe was actually true.

"I signed her up for Nokomis Elementary," Stella said. "I went there, and I love the idea of her going to the same school as me. My friend Mary Jean Wright says—"

Stella hesitated, Mary Jean's name provoking a spasm of guilt. She had planned to go with Mary Jean and the kids on a picnic in the county park today. Then, when Cameron invited her to this lunch, Stella begged off, claiming she had to talk to the mortgage people about her house. Mary Jean had gone to the park alone with the kids, and now Stella felt doubly awful.

Not only had she lied to her friend, but she was glad she was here eating this fabulous food by this pool instead of sitting on the grass with tuna fish dripping onto her legs.

"Who's this Mary Jean?" asked Dark Hair. "Do we know Mary Jean?"

"She was my best friend growing up," said Stella.

"Have I seen her at the Beach Club?"

"She's not in the Beach Club," Cameron said. "Her husband's that cop. She does a lot of work in the schools. You know."

"Oh, right," said the paler, taller blonde. "Heavyset girl?"

"She's not really—" Stella began.

"The one with the redheaded kids," said the redhead.

"I know her from the schools," said Cameron. "You know, I'm PTA president at Nokomis next year."

"You have to ask for Mrs. West as a teacher," said the dark-haired woman. "Ben had her, and she was amazing."

"I'll talk to the principal for you," said Cameron.

"That would be great. Mary Jean says the schools here are wonderful." Talking about Mary Jean was making her feel less guilty, as if she were somehow including her friend in the luncheon.

"Oh, they are," said the darker of the blondes. "Now."

"Now?" Stella raised her eyebrows. "They were good when I was growing up. Did they get not-so-good at some point?"

"When we first moved here," the blonde said, "before the population started changing, we were afraid the balance in the schools was going to tip."

Cameron looked up sharply. "Tip?"

"You know," said the blonde. "Every year it seemed like there were more black faces in the class picture, and we were just afraid that the whites were all going to pull their kids out, and the racial balance was going to tip."

"You mean the schools were going to be predominantly black," Cameron said, gazing steadily at the woman, "and then you wouldn't want to send your children there."

"Oh, Cameron," said the blonde, looking horrified. "I'm not talking about *you*."

"Yes, you are," Cameron said coolly.

The women's voices were quiet, but Stella felt she'd never been anywhere more tense than this idyllic garden.

"But Cameron," interrupted the redhead. "This is not really a race issue, it's a class issue."

"No, it's not," said Cameron, standing up and lifting the empty gazpacho terrine. "I may live in this house and have plenty of money, but I'm still a black woman, and you'd do well to remember that."

She disappeared into the house, and the other women sat there not looking at each other until a maid appeared and began clearing the table. Stella found herself wishing that Mary Jean were there for real. She'd know how to defuse the situation, or at the very least, she'd be able to help Stella make sense of this strange new suburban world.

Mary Jean did not want to go to the Labor Day party for Henry Sladowski at Cameron Dunn's.

"I already said yes," said Pete. "We have to go."

"*You* have to go," Mary Jean corrected him. "I wasn't invited. And I have no interest in spending my holiday afternoon with a bunch of stiffs."

"Stella invited you. Mr. Sladowski was sitting right there."

At this, Mary Jean faltered. In fact, though Cameron Dunn hadn't sent an invitation to the party, Stella had called and urged Mary Jean to come. Mary Jean didn't want to let down her friend, and she wanted to be supportive of Pete. And she didn't want to embarrass anybody in front of Sladowski, who did after all hold the keys—literally—to their future.

"I don't have anything to wear."

"They have a pool. You could wear your bathing suit."

"Ha! I'd rather be shot at dawn."

"All right, so wear whatever. It's a barbeque. Casual. You'll look great in whatever you put on."

The man may have been clueless, but it was such a sweet kind of clueless.

"I doubt that," she said sullenly, though they both knew from long experience with the tone of her voice that she had decided she was going to go. "Not compared with all those babes in size four white linen pants."

"You'll be the biggest babe there," Pete said, kissing her loudly.

"Yeah, biggest is right," she muttered as soon as she'd turned away, so he couldn't hear.

The day of the barbeque was mercifully cool, so at least she could wear long loose black linen pants and a sweater without sweltering or looking like an idiot. Franny was so excited about the party—Pete insisted the entire family was welcome—that she volunteered to do Mary Jean's makeup.

"I don't wear makeup," said Mary Jean.

"Well," said Franny, "you should."

Mary Jean submitted, closing her eyes and turning her face up toward the sun filtering in the kitchen window, trying to hold still while Franny's brushes fluttered like insects against her skin. Even Caitlin got in on the act, brushing her mother's hair and smoothing it back into a chignon. When the girls were finished, and Mary Jean peered in the mirror, she thought she looked like a clown, but Pete and even Jimmy assured her she looked great.

"You look almost as pretty as Idaho's mom," Jimmy said admiringly.

Mary Jean leveled a look at him, but he just gazed back at her with those huge magnified eyes as if he were in awe at her newfound beauty.

"Thank you, sweetheart," she said, pulling him into a hug.

As they left their house, Mary Jean grabbed a bumper sticker she'd ordered that read GREED KILLS, thinking she'd stick it on the back of their car after they parked, when Pete wasn't looking, and at least make a statement passive-aggressively. But once she shooed the family ahead of her up Cameron Dunn's driveway, claiming she needed to make a quick call, she had a better idea. There was the car she recognized as Sladowski's obnoxious gold Jaguar, looking all shiny and pristine. Walking casually over to it, her heart pounding so hard it seemed to be trying to leap out of her throat, she slipped the bumper sticker from her purse. Without looking she peeled off the backing and slapped it on Sladowski's chrome as nervously as if she were hurling a bomb. Oh, God, she felt like such a delinquent, but satisfied too. If she was ultimately powerless against Sladowski, at least she could annoy him, like a wasp in his ear.

When she finally made her way up the steep driveway, breathing hard at the entrance to the stately brick house, she found Pete had disappeared with Jimmy to the garden where the party was taking place, but the girls were still standing in the cool, pale foyer, gazing around the living room.

Cameron Dunn's house, it was immediately apparent, was gorgeous. A little too done for Mary Jean's taste, perhaps, not quite as funky or eclectic as she would have made it, but a study in subtle stylishness. All the walls—no, make that all the surfaces she could see in the entire house—were white or beige or some indefinable pale blue-gray-green that was the color of seawater. The wood floors were dark, the art was real, the books in the shelves looked as if they'd actually been read. Silver-framed family photos sat discreetly on end tables, in contrast to one mansion Mary Jean had visited for a school fund-raiser where you walked in the front door to be smacked in the eye by a six-foot-high family photograph mounted on the wall. French doors at the far end of the living room opened onto a flagstone patio, bordered in lush hydrangeas, where the party was in full swing.

"I want to live here," Franny said, gazing around the living room.

"Me too," Mary Jean agreed.

"Come on, Mom. I thought you were against bourgeois materialism," said Caitlin, who'd insisted on wearing jeans to the party.

"I'm not against it," Mary Jean said miserably, feeling all her high-minded principles evaporate in the beauty of the house. "I just don't have enough money to be for it."

"Hypocrite," Caitlin muttered, stalking away.

Mary Jean felt torn. She would have liked to have followed Caitlin outside into the more democratic open air. After all, she reminded herself, with a fresh pang of guilt, greed kills. But for once, she found herself more in league with her other daughter, who was still transfixed by the prettiness of the room.

"This is how my house is going to look when I'm a movie star," Franny told her.

Mary Jean raised her eyebrows. "Oh, really? I hope you'll invite me to visit."

"If you're good," Franny said, smirking and heading after her sister out into the crowd.

Mary Jean needed a moment to work up her nerve. She wasn't at ease at big parties where she didn't know anyone, especially when she felt intimidated. And she didn't want to admit it, but that's how she felt here. She may have been scornful of these people, of their money and their hypocritical values and their provincialism. But they also made her feel self-conscious and even, goddamn them, inferior.

She squared her shoulders. She was *not* going to let that happen today. Drawing in a deep breath, she willed a smile to her lips and marched out onto the patio.

At first, she didn't see Stella anywhere, but then she realized that was because Stella was hidden in the center of a knot of people, all clamoring to be her new best friend. Figures, thought Mary Jean. A movie star was exactly the kind of social feather in their caps that the Mean Housewives of Homewood craved, right up there alongside the rich black real estate agent slash PTA power broker slash Junior League honcho.

Mary Jean liked Cameron Dunn, she really did, even admired her, though she hated the way all the rich white liberals in Homewood had adopted her as their patron saint, dropping her name whenever possible to broadcast that they had a black friend. At least Cameron guilted them into keeping their kids in public school and volunteering their time and money to help the education system. Without Cameron Dunn, Mary Jean sometimes feared, the rich new Homewoodians would abandon the public schools en masse, and then the school system in general would sink, and then Homewood would no longer be such a desirable place to live, and the property values would plummet. See how they liked *that*.

Rather than join the throng—she refused to make herself into one of Stella's fans—Mary Jean sidled up to the bar to get herself a drink.

The bartender, she was surprised to see, was an off-duty fireman who worked with her brother Billy. A *black* off-duty fireman, where all the other help she could identify were white.

"Hey, Ray," she said. "I didn't know you did this on the side."

"Got to," he said. "The way the taxes are going in this town."

"I just wish we could afford to buy a house and pay some taxes," she told him.

"Our place has gone up $300,000 in the three years we've had it. I wish we could get the money out, but then where are we going to go?"

"Bartender," someone called from the other end of the bar, holding up a wineglass.

"What can I get you?" Ray asked Mary Jean, ignoring the wine drinker.

"White wine, I guess."

"Don't want something frostier? I could make you my special."

"What's in it?"

Ray winked. "Only good stuff. Just for you."

Mary Jean surveyed the crowd as she listened to the whir of Ray's blender. There were probably 150 people here, with plenty of lawn to spare. A few kids were splashing in the pool, but mostly, people were standing around, talking and drinking, eating the shrimp and filet mignon hors d'oeuvres passed by uniformed waitstaff. Mary Jean recognized a few women she'd worked with on school benefits, some parents she'd met over the years when the girls played soccer and from swim classes at the Y. There was Pete across the lawn, talking to Henry Sladowski, who was wearing a long-sleeved dark gray linen shirt, black pants, and dark sunglasses like some suburban Darth Vader.

Stop that, Mary Jean told herself. You're supposed to be trying to like this guy.

"Here you go," said Ray, handing her a tall glass filled with something pink and frozen, complete with a straw and an umbrella on top.

The drink tasted like raspberries and lime and went down alarmingly quickly. Mary Jean was still standing near the bar, gazing at the crowd and the gorgeous garden, when she realized she'd already finished it.

"Another one?" asked Ray.

"Oh, I don't know."

It was already evident that there was something a lot more powerful than raspberries and lime in the drink.

"You could use it," said Ray, in a low voice, "dealing with this group."

She grinned at him. "Maybe you're right."

By the time she was nearing the bottom of the second drink, her mood was distinctly lighter, and she had worked her way through a dozen hors d'oeuvres and clear across the patio. Every time she'd head toward a knot of people, with the idea of joining their conversation, she'd hear something that would make her veer away again: "Botox" or "size zero" or "housing prices." Finally she just pretended to be absorbed in Cameron Dunn's blue-and-white garden, which she hoped would keep her from looking totally pathetic.

"Campanula," a voice said.

It was the only African-American guest Mary Jean had seen at the party—besides Cameron herself, that was—an older woman sitting on a wrought-iron chair at the edge of the garden.

"It means 'bells,'" the woman said. "Very delicate."

"It's beautiful. The whole garden is amazing."

"My daughter's quite a gardener," the woman said, holding out a thin hand. "I'm Mrs. Dunn, Cameron's mother."

Mary Jean introduced herself and shook the woman's hand.

"Oh. Great to meet you. I know your daughter from the schools."

"I was a teacher at Nokomis," said Mrs. Dunn, "before Cameron and her sister were born."

"I didn't know that," said Mary Jean happily. "I went to Nokomis. All my kids went there, and my youngest is just starting."

"Cameron went there too. It was a wonderful school, even back in my day."

"Oh, I know. My youngest, Jimmy, has some learning issues, and I know Nokomis is going to be perfect for him. My husband and I can't afford private school—"

"Mary Jean."

Mary Jean felt a hand on her arm and swung around, surprised to see Stella standing there, her ring of admirers looking on as if a performance were about to begin. Mary Jean couldn't help but feel pleased that Stella had sought her out.

"Stella!" said Mary Jean, hesitating only a moment before hugging her friend. "Do you know Cameron's mother? This is Mrs. Dunn."

The two women shook hands, and Stella turned as if to introduce the women she'd been talking with to Mary Jean and Mrs. Dunn, but they'd all turned away.

"Oh," Stella said, shrugging. "I was going to introduce you to my new friends."

"That's okay," Mary Jean said. "I already know them."

"Really?" said Stella. "How?"

Though the women seemed to be pretending she wasn't even there, Mary Jean had met the redhead in the playground one day, where they'd struck up a conversation about the kids' hair color. The woman had been very friendly until the first time she saw Mary Jean's little house; then she'd never called again. The tall, very blond woman had graciously allowed Mary Jean to host her son on several play dates, but had never invited Jimmy back to her house. And the dark-haired woman had met Mary Jean at least a dozen times at school events, but always looked at her blankly, as if she were an utter stranger.

"Just around town," Mary Jean said. She leaned in close to Stella and lowered her voice. "They're not really your friends, are they?"

Stella looked shaken. "Why not?"

They were the kind of shallow, unimaginative people that, in high school, Stella would have disliked even more than Mary Jean had. But Stella's taste in friends seemed to have changed as much as her taste in men.

"Never mind," Mary Jean said. "How are you doing?"

The two of them saw each other when they dropped off or picked up Jimmy and Idaho, who played together nearly every day. But they hadn't had a substantial conversation or actually gotten together since that day at Stella's mother's place. Though Stella hadn't reintroduced the subject of Sladowski, Pete said they were officially going out now. Mary Jean supposed Stella was busy with her new relationship, and she didn't want to hear about it.

"I'm great," Stella said. "Just so happy. I've been meeting all these fantastic people, and things are going really well with Henry."

"Oh," Mary Jean said, trying to sound enthusiastic. "That's great."

"I'm so glad you came today. I really want to introduce you to Henry. Now where did he go?"

Mary Jean knew exactly where Henry Sladowski was, standing near the doors to the living room, conferring with Cameron. But she was in no hurry to get close to him. In fact, she'd been hoping that if she could avoid him long enough, Stella's infatuation with him would just go away and she could at least have her friend back. Though Stella seemed to prefer the company of Henry and Cameron's crowd to being with Mary Jean.

There was the sound of a spoon tapping against glass, and then a male voice boomed, "Attention. Attention, friends."

It was Henry Sladowski, who had climbed onto a chair, his arms raised until the whole crowd was quiet and staring up at him. Behind him and to the right, Mary Jean spotted Pete, standing with his legs apart and his hands folded over his groin, looking like Sladowski's Secret Service agent.

"Welcome," he said, "on this beautiful Labor Day, a day of rest for all of us poor working stiffs."

A ripple of laughter went through the crowd. Mary Jean rolled her eyes, but no one else seemed to find any irony in Sladowski's statement, including Stella, who was laughing harder than anyone else. Well, Mary Jean supposed that millionaire developers and Wall Street lawyers and even retired movie stars worked hard too. The difference was they were well rewarded for their efforts.

"We're here today," Sladowski continued, "thanks to our

good fortune at living in this glorious suburb, the best America has to offer. I truly believe that, and I'm dedicated, as I know are all of you, into making the best even better. That's why I've chosen this time and place to announce my intention of becoming the next mayor of Homewood, New Jersey."

A roar went up from the crowd. So it was really happening. Mary Jean felt herself shiver. Had Pete known that it was definite, and that the announcement would be made today? She tried to catch his eye but he stared forward as resolutely as a palace guard. Beside her, Stella clapped enthusiastically, a Laura Bush gleam in her eye.

Well, Mary Jean consoled herself, this is far from a done deal. Sladowski still had to beat Francis X. Fitzgerald, who'd been mayor of Homewood for as long as Mary Jean could remember.

But then, as if reading her thoughts, Sladowski said, "And I'm happy to announce that Mayor Fitzgerald, who will be retiring, has been kind enough to honor me with his endorsement."

Fitzgerald retiring, she thought in panic. Endorsing Sladowski. Already September, and not a whisper of anyone else even thinking of running. She felt like a serf in a medieval kingdom with a new and malevolent ruler.

Emboldened by the alcohol in Ray's frosty drinks, Mary Jean shot her arm into the air. Sladowski looked startled at the interruption.

"So can we assume," Mary Jean said, "that since you have Mayor Fitzgerald's endorsement, you'll be continuing all his policies?"

Stella looked at her curiously, and she saw Pete frown. A reporter from the *Homewood Herald,* the short guy who looked about twelve, was there writing everything down, though he obviously wasn't too swift about asking questions.

"I mean to continue Mayor Fitzgerald's work, while putting my own individual stamp on the office of mayor," Sladowski said, smiling, as if that were an answer.

"But how would you define your own individual stamp?" Mary Jean persisted. She could tell, even from this far away and without much actual evidence, that Pete was growing uncomfortable with her questions. But if the reporter from the local paper was there, this meant that Sladowski's announcement that he was running was planned, which meant that Pete knew about it, which meant that he'd hidden it from her. Which just fueled her drive to be as provocative as possible.

"One example: I'm for safety for all our citizens," Sladowski said. "I think we all in this community remember nine/eleven, the horrible specter that had a very personal and tragic impact on Homewood."

Homewood, like many prosperous communities in New Jersey, had lost several citizens when the World Trade Center was hit. And the attack unfolded within view, literally, of the town. From this very garden, at this very moment, Mary Jean could see the Manhattan skyline. But some wannabe mayor using 9/11 to further his own political aims? That was much lower than Mary Jean thought he was capable of sinking.

"And to help guarantee the security of our town," he went on, "I'm already assembling my team should I be elected, headed by Pete Wright, longtime member of the Homewood police force, who will be my chief of police."

Pete stepped forward, smiling and looking shy, and Mary Jean couldn't help but clap for him. But she was still boiling at Sladowski's hauling out 9/11 for his own aims, never mind suggesting that Pete or any police chief in the world could keep a terrorist attack from happening again.

"I would also," said Henry Sladowski, "like to introduce one of Homewood's most illustrious new citizens, and a special friend of mine, Miss Stella Powers. Come up here, Stella."

Stella turned to Mary Jean and made a face, but she was smiling, and she strode forward to stand beside Henry and Pete. Henry rested a proprietorial hand on top of Stella's head as everyone cheered. Stella looked at Mary Jean and crossed her eyes, but Mary Jean couldn't bring herself to smile back.

"Stella is a new homeowner in our town," Sladowski continued, "and like many of us, feels the weight of Homewood's exorbitant property taxes."

There was a smattering of applause at that, a shouted "Hear, hear!"

How could Stella let that creep use her like window dressing? Rather than softening toward Sladowski, Mary Jean found herself disliking him even more. And she suspected that he chose that moment to invoke the names of Pete and Stella in hopes that it would silence her. You don't know me very well, buddy, she thought, shooting her hand into the air.

"Mr. Sladowski," she said, not waiting for him to acknowledge her, "are you saying you're planning to *lower* property taxes?"

"Lower taxes," Sladowski said, smiling and nodding as he surveyed the crowd, seeming to make eye contact with everyone except Mary Jean. "Now there's an idea I think everyone can get behind!"

A cheer went up, and there was a burst of applause. Mary Jean could see Pete and Stella and even Franny and Jimmy clapping. The only person who didn't seem to be putting her hands together was Caitlin, who was examining her split ends. And Mary Jean herself.

"So lower taxes would mean less income for Homewood?" Mary Jean continued. "And lower spending?"

"That is correct." Sladowski issued a tight smile.

"I'd love to hear what you're going to cut from the budget. Mayor Fitzgerald and the town council revisited this issue every four years and never found anything they could cut while maintaining the level of services Homewood offers."

"I'm a businessman, not a politician, Mrs. Wright, and as a businessman, I know there are always meaningful ways to save money by spending where it's warranted and cutting what's wasteful. Our school budget, for instance—"

Now he was getting warmer.

"—contains many expenditures that are not relevant in the Homewood of today. What's important for our children now is competency on state-mandated tests, and I intend to focus school spending on preparing our children in reading and math. And an enormous portion of our school budget is being spent on outmoded busing and magnet programs that can be retired in favor of neighborhood schools."

It was as if someone had stuck a live wire down Mary Jean's throat. Her entire body started to buzz, and she felt herself moving forward to where Sladowski was standing without feeling her feet hit the ground. Was he actually saying he was going to cut the music and arts programs in the schools? Do away with magnet schools and freedom of choice for parents, go back to the kind of neighborhood schools that had been dismantled even before she went to kindergarten? Then Idaho would go to school with all the rich kids, and Jimmy with all the poor kids. Plus she could only imagine how her sensitive, artistic son would fare strapped in a seat studying addition and spelling all day.

"Everything can't be measured by numbers," someone else said.

Mary Jean looked around, startled. Was someone in the crowd actually agreeing with her? Not only were they, but Mary Jean was further astonished to see that it was Cameron Dunn.

"Homewood has one of the most advanced school systems in the country," Cameron said, catching Mary Jean's eye. "It's been developed over decades to serve the needs of a diverse range of kids."

"Diversity is to be valued, of course," Sladowski said, finally sounding shaken. "But the Homewood of today is not the Homewood of yesterday. Our population has changed, our state testing standards have changed, and our town has changed. And I think we can all agree that most of these changes are great ones."

A cheer, the loudest yet, went up.

"What if we don't?" said Mary Jean.

She spoke more loudly now, so that everyone could hear.

"Mary Jean—" Pete began.

"No," said Mary Jean. "It's like this one man is taking over our town, and everyone seems willing to lie down and let him do what he wants. Is that really true?"

She looked around the beautiful garden, glistening on this sunny breezy day, and everyone gazed off into some middle distance. The only person who looked directly at her was Cameron Dunn.

"Well, I'm not," said Mary Jean. "I don't want these changes for our schools, I don't want these policies for our town. And I'm sorry if this sounds rude, but I don't want this man for our mayor."

"Love it or leave it, baby!" a male voice shouted.

"Yeah," someone else mumbled. "It's not like there's anybody else."

"There is someone else," Mary Jean said aloud, as if the person had been speaking directly to her. "There's someone else running for mayor. And that person is me."

They drove home without speaking. They cooked dinner and cleaned the kitchen without speaking.

When Franny said, "You weren't really serious about running for mayor, were you?" they both said, in unison, "Quiet, Franny."

When Caitlin joked, "So Mom, would you say you're more

of a liberal feminist or a radical Democrat?" they both said, "Drop it, Caitlin."

When Franny later said, "It's even more embarrassing than when you got pregnant with Jimmy," they said, "Time for you kids to go to bed."

Once they were alone in their bedroom, though, Pete turned on her.

"I want you to drop this idea, Mary Jean, right now."

She'd known, of course, that Pete was mad at her. But it was so unlike him to shout, especially at her. He'd usually just give her the silent treatment until she couldn't stand it anymore and did what he wanted, the customary outcome. But that wasn't going to happen this time.

"I'm not dropping out of the race, Pete. If Sladowski becomes mayor, he's going to ruin this town the way he's ruining all those old houses."

"Yeah, and if you run against him, he's going to kick us out of this place, and then we won't be able to live here anymore."

"If he becomes mayor, I won't *want* to live here anymore."

That was a dramatic statement, and once it was out of her mouth, Mary Jean had to consider whether she really meant it. She did, she realized. That was how much defeating him meant to her.

"And what about me?" Pete asked, beginning to pace the carpet in their tiny room. "You know that all I've ever wanted to do is become police chief, and now I finally have that chance. And you're ruining it."

"How am I ruining it?" Mary Jean said. "In fact, maybe this

is better for you. If Sladowski wins, you can still become chief. And if I win, you can become chief too."

"Oh-ho! That's how qualified you are to be mayor of this town, Mrs. Smartypants! Local code number 7832, paragraph B, also known as the Homewood Anti-Nepotism Act, *prohibits* any mayor of this town from naming any first-degree relative to the post of deputy mayor, fire chief, or police chief. And first-degree relative includes your mother, your father, your brothers and sisters, your children, AND your spouse. Not that I would want you to be my boss even if you could!"

Mary Jean stifled a laugh. She was upset that Pete was so angry, of course; she hated it when anyone got angry at her, especially him. But at the same time, he looked so ridiculous waving his arms and ranting, his blond hair flying and spit spraying from his mouth. Over code 7832, paragraph B!

"Come on, Pete," she began, crossing to him and laying her hand on his arm.

"*Don't* you touch me!" he cried, snatching his arm away. "How exactly do you plan to find the time to run for mayor, Mary Jean, much less *be* mayor? I thought you were going back to school this fall. I thought we were finally looking forward to having two incomes in this family. You're not going to have time for any of that being mayor of Homewood."

For the first time since she thrust her hand in the air, Mary Jean was seized by doubt. Being mayor of Homewood may have been nearly a full-time job, but it paid next to nothing. Maybe she couldn't afford to do this.

But then she thought of Jimmy's future, of the future of the town, how she'd feel if she sat back and let Sladowski take over, and thought, I can't afford not to.

"If Sladowski can run a business and be mayor, I can go to school and be mayor."

"You're a mother, too, Mary Jean, and a wife," said Pete. "What happens now when the family needs you? I'm supposed to be going to all these campaign events with Sladowski. Many of the same events, need I point out, that you'll have to go to also, along with a hundred other places you'll have to go and people you'll have to meet. Who's supposed to take care of Jimmy then?"

"I suppose the girls will have to pitch in," Mary Jean said. "And I may have to put off school for another semester or two."

"Caitlin's too busy with work and studies, and Franny's pretty busy babysitting for your friend Stella. Or did you forget that too?"

"Then maybe we'll need to hire our own babysitter."

Pete opened his mouth and closed it, and then opened it again. "Maybe you'll need to stay home and take care of your family."

"Maybe *you* will," Mary Jean shot back. Now she was the one who was pacing in an ellipse around Pete, which seemed to paralyze him. "For twenty-two years, Pete Wright, every time there was a sacrifice to be made for the sake of this family, *I* was the one who made it. I was the one who worked when we had Peter so you could go to college, I was the one who dropped out when the twins were born so you could start your career on the force, I stepped back again when we had Jimmy. Now it's my turn, Pete."

She kept pacing, expecting him to respond. But he didn't.

And then him pulling back, quieting down, allowed her own fears and uncertainties to rise up. What *am* I doing? she wondered. I haven't even considered this carefully. I have no idea what's involved. This is already a disaster for my family.

"Pete," she said, stopping, again reaching out for him.

"I'm not going to change my mind, Mary Jean."

That did it. "I'm not going to change my mind either."

She grabbed the afghan off the foot of the bed and flounced out of the bedroom, down the stairs, and into the living room. Then she stopped short. She wished she could keep going—she was so worked up, she needed to burn off some energy, and she wanted to make a statement to Pete, too. But where was she going to go? Nothing in Homewood was open after ten p.m., especially not on Labor Day, and she wasn't about to go stalking through the dark deserted suburban streets. She had a flash fantasy of going over to Stella's house, the way she did when she was a teenager and they had some burning issue to discuss, but she didn't think Stella would be too receptive to *this* burning issue. Besides, what if Sladowski was there?

Mary Jean moaned, collapsing onto the sofa. So did this really mean that she and Stella were going to have to stop being friends, just when they'd finally started again? Was she going to lose her best friend *and* her husband over this stupid election? The town could go down in flames before she'd let that happen.

But she couldn't believe that Stella and even Pete wouldn't

come to see her viewpoint on this. The better they got to know Sladowski, the more public his policies became, the more likely it was they would see things her way and come over to her side.

It was stifling down here with no air-conditioning, but when she got up and opened a window, she could hear all the traffic sounds from MLK Drive. There was no hope of sleeping either with the window closed *or* open. She'd just have to wait until she figured Pete was safely unconscious, and she could go back into the bedroom and get back in bed without him noticing she'd caved.

In the meantime, she crossed to the kitchen, where she opened the refrigerator and, far in the back, retrieved a foil package labeled "Dried Prunes." Inside was her stash of chocolate kisses. Taking a handful, she settled back onto the couch and began eating them in the dark. Summer was over; in a few days school would begin again and the kids would be out of the house. She'd be so busy it would be easier not to eat, she'd feel more like exercising as the weather got cooler, she would definitely and finally lose all this weight. All the more reason to finish the chocolate tonight, when it seemed, in relative terms, like the only reliably good thing in the world.

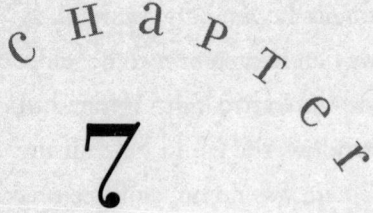

CHAPTER 7

Stella stood in the corner of yet another overdecorated living room, her smile plastered in place and her eyes fixed in what she hoped was a fascinated gaze. This experience was going to come in handy, she thought, if she ever had to play a first lady. At least, she'd discovered, she didn't really have to listen. He said the same thing over and over anyway, like an actor in a play. When everyone else clapped, she clapped; when Henry said it was time to leave, they left. And went on to the next event and did it all over again.

She was getting very tired of this, and the campaign had only been going on a couple of weeks. At first, she'd been excited: this was real politics, not some bullshit Hollywood cause for which she wrote a check and had her picture taken and never really got involved. Here, she was in the trenches, making a difference. Or so she told herself. She was happy, in any case, to be meeting so many people. Everyone in Homewood was so nice; they all wanted to be her friend. And Henry made her feel so important, right at the center of his world. This was what her mother had meant by finding someone who could offer her security, a real future. She was only sorry her mother wasn't here to see that Stella was finally taking her advice. She would have been so proud.

A cheer went up, her cue to put her hands together and clap. At the center of the room, Henry was immediately mobbed, and Stella turned toward the bar, figuring she'd squeeze in one more glass of wine.

But the path to the wine was barred by a young woman who wanted to know the real diet secrets of the stars ("Drugs," Stella felt like telling her) and an older man extolling the high points of his church ("Plus, every spring there's a women's fellowship campout!") and a mom who wanted to discuss the strengths and weaknesses of every teacher in the entire Homewood school system. If only Mary Jean were there to throw out a wisecrack or grab her hand and pull her outside for an illicit cigarette.

It was bad enough that Henry was running for mayor, but Stella could not for the life of her understand why Mary Jean was insisting on doing it too. Stella could hardly think of anything more boring and meaningless, any bigger waste of time. What did small-town politics matter to real life?

Through the crowd, Stella saw Henry, still absorbed in con-

versation with his constituents. He never seemed more animated, or more attractive, than when she glimpsed him from a
distance like this. Being onstage seemed to fill him with power,
the way, come to think of it, it did for some actors. This was
something she could understand: the seductiveness of the spotlight, the way it could make real life seem comparatively pale.
She was turned on watching Henry take command of a room.

"Excuse me," Stella said to the mom, who was now on to
an analysis of the middle-school teachers. Leaving the woman
standing there with her mouth open, Stella drifted across the
room, ignoring everyone who approached her, focused only on
Henry's back, his broad shoulders tapering down to his narrow
hips. She reached out and pinched what she was pleased to
find was his very firm butt.

"Whoa!" he cried, startling and whipping around.

She giggled.

Without a word, he grasped her elbow and turned her toward the door, steering her outside with his fingers firmly on
the middle of her back as if he were pressing a button. They
got into his Jaguar without speaking. He pulled from the curb
and drove through the quiet streets, eyes straight ahead, still
saying nothing. Stella imagined that he was finally taking her
to his house, the sleek glass-and-cedar ranch built into the top
reaches of Homewood's highest ridge, beyond which stretched
the plains of New Jersey, to make wild passionate love away
from the crush of the crowds. But instead, he turned into the
dark driveway of her Tree House, yanking the emergency brake
and finally turning to her.

"What the hell do you think you were doing back there?" he spat.

She was utterly stupefied. "Wh-what?"

"Touching me like that where everyone could see. What were you thinking?"

"I was bored," she said. "I saw you across the room, and you looked so good—"

She bit back the rest of the sentence, not wanting to give him the satisfaction of hearing her say anything nice about him when he was being such a jerk.

He slumped in the seat. "I'm sorry," he said. "I just . . . I have to think about my image, Stella."

She let out a laugh. "I know all about image, Henry."

"I know you do," he said. "But this is different. Homewood isn't Hollywood. People are very conservative here."

"Are you kidding? You're the politician. Haven't you noticed that Homewood is one of the liberal bastions of the New York suburbs?"

"People here might claim to be liberals. They might give a couple of hundred dollars to National Public Radio and the local soup kitchen. They might say African-American instead of black and vote for gay marriage and against the death penalty. But you know, Stella, that people here are mostly middle-aged and middle-class, they're mostly married with children and big mortgages and not-so-big salaries. As liberal as they'd like to seem, where they live, they're really conservatives."

"Come on, Henry. People here may be married with houses and kids, but a lot of them are also Jewish or black or gay. My mother moved here because it was one of the few places she felt she could be a single working mother without being stigmatized—and this was forty years ago."

"This town might have been more genuinely liberal forty years ago, or even ten years ago, before the housing prices started going up," Henry said. "Don't get me wrong. My heart is in the same place as yours. Hey, I hosted a fund-raiser for John Edwards. It's just that I have to be pragmatic if I want to get elected."

"Maybe it would be more pragmatic for you not to go out with me at all," she said, leaning back against her door, crossing her arms over her chest.

"No!" he cried, finally reaching for her. She was so hungry for his touch—maybe for anybody's touch—that she didn't pull her arm away even though she wanted to let him know how awful he'd made her feel.

"That's not what I want, Stella. That's not what I meant. You're right, I am being ridiculous about this. Everybody knows we're together anyway. I *want* them to know."

"Well, then come inside with me," she said. "Inside this house."

"What?"

"Why not? It's private, it's romantic, and I own it. I mean, I guess, technically, *you* own it."

"Stella, there aren't even any lights in there."

"All the better. We'll bring a flashlight. And there's a full moon. You never let me go in during the day, when all the guys are working. You can give me a moonlit tour."

She imagined, despite the tarps and the still-open walls and dangling wires of heavy construction, that the place would look beautiful at night. The few times Henry had arranged for her to make her way through, she'd seen gorgeous carved mantels and great old white subway tile, marble sinks with nickel faucets and showerheads as big as pie plates, toilets with real wooden seats and flushers that pulled from the ceiling. There were crystal doorknobs and solid porcelain sinks and tubs, and in the kitchen, huge egg-shaped hanging lights and a chrome-detailed stove fit for a museum.

But now, he was shaking his head. "It's too dangerous, Stella," he said. "There are missing floorboards, live wires—you could kill yourself. I promise we'll go through one day soon."

"All right," she said. "Then why don't we go over to my place? I mean my mother's place."

"You mean tonight? But don't you have that girl babysitting for you?"

Franny.

"Stella, you know I can't give my political opponent anything to use against me."

"Mary Jean isn't just your political opponent," Stella said. "She's also my friend."

"Is she really?" Henry said, with more heat than he was usually able to muster for a subject that did not involve politics or business. "I don't think Mary Jean Wright has been a very good friend to you at all."

"What do you mean?" asked Stella, shaken.

"Her insistence on running against me, for one thing. That's inconsiderate not only to you but to her own husband."

"Mary Jean is passionate about Homewood," said Stella. "She believes in that old-style liberal town, just like my mother did."

"I don't think she's running because of political conviction. I think she's running because she wants to hurt me. And because she's jealous of you."

"What do you mean?"

"She's envious of your money, your career, your beauty. And if you're with me, you have the home and the social position in town that she'll never have."

"I really don't think Mary Jean feels that way."

"No? I hope you're right. But I'd feel better if you promised me you wouldn't see Mary Jean Wright while this election was going on."

"She's my oldest friend," Stella stammered. "Our kids play together. Her daughter is my babysitter."

"I don't mean you have to stop speaking to her entirely. But it just makes me too uncomfortable, worrying about what might slip if the two of you are spending substantial time together. And I really have your own best interests at heart, Stella."

"I don't know."

"It's just two months. And when this is all over, we can all be friends."

"You really think that's possible?"

"Absolutely! Her husband will be my police chief, I'll find

some solution to their housing issue, you and I will be together, we'll welcome her into the fold."

"I'd like to believe it will work out like that. But, Henry—"

"Yes?"

He had started the car and turned to her impatiently, like an executive who'd already gathered his papers at the end of a meeting.

"If you and I are going to be together, some things have to change."

He narrowed his eyes. "Like what?"

"I'd like you to get to know my daughter, for one thing."

He hesitated just a second before saying, "All right."

"And we need to spend more time together. Without the voting public around."

"All right," he said, putting the car in gear.

She laid her hand on his forearm. "So, Henry," she said. "How about coming over Sunday night? I could make you my mother's famous pot roast."

"Mmmmm," Henry said. "That sounds good."

"All right," she said. "Great."

He put the car back in park and leaned over then and finally kissed her, softly, sweetly, and with his lips chastely closed. Stella thought of slipping him some tongue, the way George Clooney did when they made a movie together, just to try to get her to laugh, but then decided against it. It probably wouldn't make Henry laugh, and there would be time for that down the road. All the time in the world.

*   *   *

Why oh why had she never written down her mother's pot roast recipe? She knew why. Not writing it down gave her an opportunity to call her mother each time she wanted to make it, to let her mother take care of her by walking her through every step of the preparation. Not writing it down made it necessary, in some small way, for her mother to stay alive. As if that actually had anything to do with it.

Standing before the meat case in Whole Foods, trying to summon her mother's voice pronouncing the correct cut of beef, filled Stella with a vast emptiness. The sadness came and went, best when she was busy doing something else, worst when she was lying in her mother's bed trying to fall asleep, but instead getting hit by wave after wave of longing for her mom.

Who would have expected it, after all this time away? Of course, she'd always been aware that when her mother died, she would mourn. But she realized now she'd never understood what this meant, this descent to this dark place where no one could join her and from which it sometimes felt she would never emerge.

"Come on, Mom," she whispered. "What kind of meat do you use for pot roast?"

She listened, but no voice came to her. Top round? Bottom round? Eye round? Something round, she was pretty sure, though none of the pieces of organic beef in the case looked appropriate. At least she had the meat section pretty much to herself, the other shoppers giving her a wide berth as if she might be tainted along with the beef. The fish counter down the way was, by comparison, mobbed, the vegetable aisles packed with aggressive herbivores. Finally, she chose a piece of meat more for its shape than anything else, five times as expensive as any she'd remembered her mother ever buying, hiding it under the big bunch of romaine lettuce in her cart.

On Sunday morning, Idaho wanted to help her cook, so she covered the little girl in one of her mother's aprons, an apron edged in rickrack she remembered from childhood, and tied on an apron herself.

"Okay," she said to Idaho, hoping that maybe by talking through the recipe out loud, her mother's instructions would come to her. "I'm pretty sure the first thing Grandma did was brown the meat."

"*Brown* it?" Idaho giggled.

"That means kind of fry it so the outside gets all nice and brown. I think we need a big pot for that."

The pots her mother used were all blackened and dented with age—Stella figured she'd move the still-new copper pots with her to the Tree House—and Stella retrieved one that looked familiar and poured some vegetable oil in the bottom.

"I think she used oil," she said to Idaho, turning on the flame and lowering the heavy piece of meat into the pot, where it dropped with a dramatic sizzle, a lick of hot oil burning Stella's arm.

"Ouch!" Stella cried.

"Are you okay, Mommy?"

"I'm okay, though I'm starting to think maybe she put something on it before she browned it. Maybe flour? Flour and salt?"

She hunted around in the cupboard until she came upon a crinkled paper package with a bit of flour left in the bottom. She let Idaho stand on a chair and help her shake the flour over the uncooked side of the meat, then used a big fork to turn it, shaking out the rest of the flour over the browned side. Then they shook on some salt and pepper, except now the oil seemed to have dried up, so Stella had to shoo Idaho out of the way while she pried the meat from where it was stuck to the bottom of the pot and then added more oil, which leaped with a dangerous sound against the hot metal.

"Oh, God," Stella said.

"Are you okay, Mommy?"

Her daughter was so sensitive, Stella was discovering, much more intuitive than the imaginative but relatively out-to-lunch Jimmy. Was it a boy-girl thing? A function of their tight little relationship? She wasn't sure, but Idaho seemed more in tune with her thoughts and feelings than most kids were.

"I'm fine, sweetheart. We just have to find the pot Grandma used to use to cook the pot roast in the oven. It was oval—you know, like a stretched-out circle—and dark blue with white speckles."

Stella had remembered noticing the pot, in fact, sitting dirty on top of the stove the night her mother died, but then couldn't remember seeing it again. One of the Historical Society ladies must have come in and washed it along with the rest of the dishes from that night, but where had she put it? Stella and Idaho searched in all the cupboards to no avail, until Stella finally decided she'd have to cook the meat on top of the stove rather than in the oven, as she remembered her mother saying you could do.

She poured the water—not wine, not beer, and not too much—into the pot with the meat, and then remembered the onions. So she took the meat out of the pot, poured out the liquid, chopped and sauteed the onions, added the meat and water back in, and then thought she could have just fried the onions in a different pan and added them to the pot with the meat and liquid. Oh, well, that wasn't the way her mother had done it. Then she realized she'd forgotten the carrots, so she and Idaho walked to the store, returning to find the water boiled away and the meat scorched on the bottom. She added more water to the pot, scraped and chopped the carrots, added them too, made sure the water was on a low boil, covered the pot, uncovered it, and then covered it again, with the lid slightly askew to let steam escape the way she seemed to remember her mother doing. Then she felt like going back to bed.

But she had to clean up the house, which she'd let slide, especially now that she was so busy doing things like shopping for bathroom tiles she never found. And not just pick up the clothes and shoes and toys and newspapers and books that were scattered everywhere, but really clean, actual dusting and vacuuming, sink wiping and toilet scrubbing, in which Idaho quickly lost interest. She should have called Cameron Dunn's cleaning lady to get the place in shape for this dinner with Henry, but she somehow felt uneasy letting anybody know she was unable to take care of this little house by herself.

The cleaning took so long that she found she had only an hour to get ready before Henry arrived, and then she remembered, when she went downstairs twenty minutes before he was supposed to get there, that she hadn't even started the potatoes. She managed to peel them, cut them into pieces, and get them into the cold water, calling up to Idaho that she'd have to put her dress on by herself. She had just enough time to dry off her hands before he rang the doorbell.

"Very cute," he said, smiling down at her apron.

He was dressed, she was disappointed but not surprised to see, in a beautifully cut, tightly buttoned suit.

"You could have worn jeans," she said, tugging at his jacket. She had worn jeans herself, with a floaty top she hoped was somewhere between domestic goddess and slut. "It's just us."

"I wanted it to be special," he said, stepping across the threshold and holding out a French Bordeaux and a dense bouquet of creamy roses. "It smells great in here."

"Sit down," she said, untying the apron. "Can I make you a martini?"

"Very dry," he said, sitting in the middle of the living room sofa and looking around.

Stella mixed the drinks, checking to make sure the pot roast wasn't burning, and joined Henry in the living room.

"Just a minute," she said, handing him his drink. "Idaho?"

There was no sound from above, and her daughter did not appear.

"Idaho?" Stella called again.

Still nothing.

"Excuse me," she said, setting down her drink.

She climbed the stairs and went into Idaho's room, calling her daughter's name. Finally, she heard a giggle from the direction of the closet. She pulled open the door and peered inside. "Idaho?"

Another giggle, and Stella pushed the hanging clothes— twenty years of her own girlhood wardrobe—to one side. Idaho's eyes beamed up at her like a night animal's from the bottom of the closet.

"What are you doing down there, honey?" Stella said. "Mr. Sladowski's downstairs."

Idaho covered her cheeks with her hands and shook her head.

"He's our guest," Stella said, bending over so she was closer to her daughter. "I want you to come down and meet him."

Still, Idaho refused.

Stella sighed.

"All right," she said finally. "You come down when you're ready. But we'd really like you to join us."

When she went back down into the living room, she said to Henry, "I'm sorry. She does that sometimes."

"Does what?"

"Hides. She'll get tired of it eventually."

Henry seemed unperturbed. "It's nice just to be here with you," he said, unbuttoning his jacket. "Good drink."

"Thanks. This is the first-ever martini I've made."

"I hope you'll do some entertaining for me," Henry said.

Stella was confused for a moment—wasn't she entertaining him now?—but then she realized he meant entertaining for his campaign, for his friends and associates.

"Oh," she said. "That sounds great."

Did it sound great? She admired the ease with which people like Cameron Dunn opened their homes, the food and drink happening in the background as if self-prepared. But Stella knew, from the time she was married to the agent, that entertaining took a lot of effort, though it had never been effort she'd expended herself. Even if you had a caterer and a bartender, cleaners and florists and servers, you had to devote an enormous amount of energy to planning the party and inviting the guests and making sure they had a good time. Her husband had always taken care of all that, claiming she was far too selfish to do it well.

But she'd changed now, she thought, she hoped. At least she could *act* as if she'd changed, and see if reality caught up. As she hopped up to refresh Henry's drink, to whip the potatoes, to slice the pot roast and to lay it out on the chipped white platter her mother had used, she kept a character in mind, the sophisticated yet loving wife and mother, kind of a Nigella Lawson type, or the wife in *A Beautiful Mind,* but with food.

Of course, she had to ignore the pieces of potato that sprayed all over the kitchen, even in her hair, when she failed to sink the electric mixer deep enough in the bowl. She had to forget that the carrots, instead of caramelizing as her mother's always had, had disappeared entirely, and that she'd completely spaced out on the gravy. But pretending had always been one of her specialties.

"Idaho!" she called again as they sat down to eat. But although she heard her daughter's little feet scurry across the floorboards, and suspected Idaho was listening to everything her mother and Henry said, the little girl didn't come down.

Stella opened Henry's wine—he did seem disturbingly content to sit there doing nothing—and then sat down across from him.

The pot roast was not good. It was tough, even after spending all those hours in the pot, and stringy, and tasteless.

"I'm sorry," she told him, dropping her fork with a dramatic clatter. "I don't know what I did wrong."

"It's all right," he said. "It's good."

But she knew he was just being nice, sitting silently across from her, chewing and chewing his meat.

This is reality, she reminded herself, not a movie. The dinner might not turn out. The man might not have anything to say.

"It's nice anyway," she said, "having a little time together."

"It is nice," he said.

From upstairs there was a thump. Stella rolled her eyes and laughed. "I'm sorry about my daughter too. She's shy. She's been through a lot."

"I'm sure we'll get to know each other," he said. "At some point."

"I know it's crazy with the election," she said, wondering if she sounded like the understanding down-to-earth woman she wanted to be, rather than the diva she was trying to leave behind. "I hope the three of us will have more time to do things together once that's over."

"I was thinking we could go away," he said. "To St. John. At Christmas."

Stella frowned, thinking of all the presents that would have to be wrapped and—secretly—transported; the hotel room that looked sad, no matter how luxurious it was, without a Christmas tree. "I think with a small child, it works better to do Christmas at home."

"I was thinking just the two of us could go."

Stella opened her mouth, intending to ask him why he thought, if she wasn't willing to cart her child away at Christmas, she'd be willing to leave her behind. But then she just decided, forget it, he couldn't possibly understand, he wasn't a parent. God knew she'd probably be having the same conversation with Eddie if they were still married.

"Idaho and I will be staying here for the holidays," she said firmly. "I was thinking more along the lines of us going to a local park."

"Hmmm," he said. "Park. That's kind of like playing outdoors, correct?"

"That's right," Stella said, stifling a smile.

"Well, Cameron's friend Jennifer is hosting a campaign event for families, a pumpkin-carving kind of thing. We could do that."

Them and a hundred other people, Stella thought. Why was Henry so dense about spending time alone with her, or with her and Idaho? Didn't he *want* to be with her?

"Henry, what exactly is going on here?" she exploded. "Are we having a relationship or aren't we?"

For once, his smoothness failed him. He began blinking and twitching, and suddenly, because they were jiggling, she noticed he had jowls. He smoothed his tie, unbuttoned and re-buttoned his jacket, cleared his throat, and finally thrust his hand forward as if heading into the high point of his speech.

"Of *course* we're having a relationship!" he said. "You're ex-tremely important to me, Stella. In fact, we're together *constantly.*"

"But we're never alone!"

Suddenly, though, she had the sense that they weren't alone right now either. She heard a scuttling over near the staircase, then a muffled giggle, and knew that Idaho had somehow crept down the stairs without her hearing and was watching them from the shadows of this very room.

"Henry," Stella said loudly, raising her eyebrows at him in an exaggerated way. "Did you hear something strange?"

"Huh?" he said, swinging around. "No, I didn't hear any-thing."

"No, there's definitely something strange in this room," said Stella, standing up and looking around as if she were in a play for children. "I think it might be a large mouse. Or maybe a fairy flying around near the ceiling?"

"Mouse?" said Henry, swiveling his head but still not get-ting it.

"Yes!" cried Stella, rushing across the room and pouncing on the now wildly giggling Idaho. "And here she is!"

It felt so great to hold her sweaty squirming laughing child in her arms. She loved the salty scent of Idaho's skin, the heat and the unpredictability of her. But she needed physical closeness with someone other than her child, she knew. She needed it with Henry, sooner rather than later, if they were going to move forward.

"Idaho," Stella said more calmly, holding her child upright. "There's someone important here I want you to meet."

"Who?" Idaho said, gazing solemnly at Henry.

"This is Mr. Sladowski. Henry."

Idaho kept looking, her face very serious, and Henry looked back with the same poker face.

"Are you my daddy?" the child asked finally.

"Idaho!" Stella cried, aghast. "No, honey, no! Mr. Sladowski is Mommy's friend. Mommy's boyfriend."

Henry cleared his throat. "I don't have any children," he said, though Stella couldn't quite tell whether he was talking to her or to Idaho.

"I don't have any daddy," Idaho said. "Jimmy has a daddy, but I don't."

"You have a daddy," Stella told her. "We just don't see him."

"I want a daddy I can see," Idaho said, addressing Henry directly. "That's the kind Jimmy has."

Stella was about to apologize again, when Henry surprised her by getting up and walking over to where she stood with Idaho still in her arms.

"I knew I was going to meet you tonight," Henry said to the little girl, reaching inside his suit jacket, "and so I brought you this present."

He held out a tiny box, wrapped in pink and tied with an enormous golden ribbon. Idaho's eyes widened as she looked at the beautiful package, then up at Henry, and then at her mother.

"It's okay," said Stella, smiling and casting Henry an appreciative glance. "You can take it."

Idaho took the gift and wiggled out of Stella's arms, dropping onto the floor as she tugged at the ribbon and ripped off the paper.

Inside the box was a lovely and infinitely delicate child's necklace, its thin and sparkling gold chain threaded through a pink crystal locket. Stella heard Idaho draw in her breath as she looked up in wonder at her mother and her benefactor.

"It's so beautiful," she said.

"Here, honey," said Stella. "I'll help you put it on."

Idaho hopped to her feet, and Stella clasped the necklace around her daughter's neck. For a moment, Idaho just stood there, holding the locket out from her chest and peering down at it, and then suddenly she thrust herself against Henry, wrapping her arms around his hips and pressing her ear against his stomach. From where Stella stood, she could see that Idaho's eyes were squeezed closed, and her expression was ecstatic.

Feeling herself melt, Stella squeezed Henry's arm. "Thank you," she said. "That was so thoughtful."

Without letting go, Idaho leaned back and looked up at him. "Thank you," she said.

"You're most welcome." He patted Idaho's head, but seemed unsure about whether he should hug her back. Finally, the little girl let go and twirled around to Stella.

"Can I go upstairs and look in the mirror, Mommy?"

"Of course, darling."

When Idaho had skipped away, Stella moved closer and, without deliberating, slipped her arms around Henry.

"She's in heaven," she said. "I really appreciate that."

"Well, good."

She put her lips close to his ear. Once their relationship had moved to another level, she'd definitely have to get him to downshift on the cologne.

"Let's get together next weekend, just the two of us," she murmured. "Maybe we could go to your place?"

"Okay," he said.

She kissed him on the neck and whispered, "I want your body."

He started, as if she'd said she wanted to sink her teeth into his neck and take a good long drink of his blood.

"Come on, Henry." She laughed. "Don't you think it's time we made love?"

He nodded, still mute, looking even more terrified than he had when Idaho asked if he were her father. His entire body was rigid, except, as far as she could tell, the one part she might have wanted that way.

A mental alarm starting buzzing, but Stella wasn't sure what had set it off. Did she think Henry was gay, like Idaho's real father? Married, with a secret wife stashed up in his hilltop house in the highest reaches of Homewood? Or just terrified, the way more than a few men she'd dated had been, of making love with a real live movie star? Whatever the truth, she was ready to find it out.

CHAPTER 8

"I wish the J. Crew was open," sighed Franny, flipping through the neatly folded jeans at the Gap.

"There's a J. Crew at the mall," Mary Jean reminded her, "but we can't afford J. Crew."

"I can," said Franny.

Mary Jean took a deep breath, cautioning herself to stay calm. Shopping for clothes was the only way she could still connect with Franny, and she didn't want to be the one to ruin the outing with a blowup. She'd gone so far as to leave Jimmy at home with Caitlin, who said instead of new school clothes, she wanted her parents to put the $100 they said they'd spend into her college account. Franny, on the other hand, was already complaining that $100 wasn't nearly enough to cover the clothes she needed for school. She planned to supplement her parents' budget with the money she'd earned babysitting for Stella, and while Mary Jean thought that should go toward college savings, she'd promised herself not to say anything.

"Look at this sweater," Mary Jean said, holding up a slim orange V-neck. "It's 50 percent off."

Franny wrinkled her nose. "Not my style."

If Mary Jean picked it out, it seemed, Franny automatically didn't like it. Slipping the sweater back into the sale rack, she wandered away on her own, deciding the only thing to do was leave her daughter alone and not say anything. Maybe she could find something for herself, though most of the Gap clothes ended at size 14, and she was now a 16 or even bigger. It was so depressing, going shopping when nothing fit, and her only criterion for buying something was whether it made her look slimmer. Or rather, less fat. She shouldn't even buy anything now, until she lost weight. Maybe that could be a way to motivate herself to stick with her diet and go to the gym: she wouldn't buy any clothes until she could fit into a size 10.

Mary Jean drifted over to the men's sale rack, figuring she might find something for Pete. There were big cotton shirts, left over from summer, in pink and lavender and a bright blue and white stripe, for only $5.99, size XXL. She pulled one out. It would definitely fit her. She could wear it to more casual campaign events, like the coffee at the preschool she'd been to this morning, and it would hide all the wobbly bits around the middle. And here was a pair of drawstring cotton pants marked way down that might also work.

"Don't you think this is nice?" Mary Jean asked Franny, holding up the lavender shirt. "Only $5.99."

"It's nice," Franny said coolly, turning her attention back to her own shopping. "For you."

Locked behind the door of the fitting room, Mary Jean tried on the lavender shirt first, open over the T-shirt she was wearing. It looked good. But then she tried to button it, and found that from the waist down, the buttons didn't really close. How could this be? It was size XXL. It was big at the shoulders, even at the bust, where Mary Jean usually had trouble. But it must be cut slim, for a man, at the bottom.

Reluctantly setting the shirt aside, Mary Jean stepped into the pants and found to her horror that she couldn't pull them up over her hips. They'd looked positively voluminous on the hanger, and here they were stuck on her butt. How mortifying. The biggest clothes in the entire Homewood Gap, and she couldn't find a single thing to fit her body.

She quickly got back into her own clothes, leaving the too-snug items in the dressing room, and went outside, only to find Franny heading in, arms loaded, to try things on.

"I'm finished," Mary Jean told her. "I'll just wait here, in case you want to show me anything."

Franny gave her a look that said she was about as likely to want to show her mother anything as to want to hang out with her on Saturday night, but sure enough, after a few minutes of lurking outside the dressing room door, Franny called, "Mom?"

Franny was standing in front of the mirror in her dressing room, looking at herself in a short, tight suede jacket.

"What do you think?" she asked.

"It's cute," said Mary Jean, automatically going for the price tag. Oh, my God: $299.

"I think it's too expensive for what it is," she told Franny carefully.

"I don't," snapped Franny, still turning this way and that. "It's something I'd wear every day. I'm going to get it."

"Do you really have that much money?"

"With the $100 from you, I do."

"But that was supposed to be for things you needed: jeans, shirts."

Franny's mouth dropped open. "You mean that $100 was supposed to cover *everything?* You and Dad are not even buying me the clothes I *need* anymore? Am I going to have to start paying for my own socks and underwear?"

"That is not the point, Franny. Your father and I said we'd spend $100 for you on new school clothes, not $100 on something frivolous and then another however many hundred dollars on basics."

"If you won't give me the money, *fine,*" said Franny. "I'll just buy this now, and I'll buy the other things I want later, when I have more babysitting money."

"You're not going to have as much time for babysitting now," Mary Jean said. "You're going to have field hockey, and play practice, not to mention schoolwork. I'm going to need you to watch Jimmy for me, but what money you earn at this point should be put away for college."

"I'm not so sure I want to go to college," said Franny.

"Stella says there's not much point, if you want to be an actress. Look at Kirsten Dunst: she didn't go to college. And Gwyneth Paltrow only went one semester."

"Gwyneth Paltrow's *mother* is an actress," Mary Jean said, horrified. "Her father was a director. Kirsten Dunst has been in movies since she was a child. You can't compare yourself to them."

"But Stella's mother was a mom, right here in Homewood, just like you," Franny said. "Stella didn't even finish high school, and she became a star."

"Quitting high school and going out there the way she did caused a lot of problems for Stella," Mary Jean said, feeling her face turn red. "I hope she told you how difficult it was. Because I know Stella had to pay a lot of dues—"

"Actually, she didn't," Franny said, tossing her bright hair. "I think I know her a lot better than you do at this point. And she said it's actually easier going out there if you're really young and pretty like"—here at least Franny blushed—"you know, she was, and she thinks I am."

"I think you're pretty too," Mary Jean said defensively. "And there are things about Stella you don't know, things I remember from that time—"

"Like what?" Franny asked.

"I know it hurt her mother's feelings terribly," Mary Jean said. "I know that, no matter what Stella says now, it can't have been that easy for her, being all alone out there at seventeen, with not even a high school education."

Mary Jean felt as if sirens were going off in her head, but

she was afraid if she moved too precipitously or spoke without thinking hard enough, she might set Franny off and find her vanished from her bed the next morning, gone to Hollywood the way Stella had.

"I think you're really talented," Mary Jean said carefully. "I understand that if you want to make it in the movies, you're going to have to move to L.A. at some point. But I know what a disadvantage it is not to have gone to college, Franny. It will make it so much easier to earn a living, whether you go into acting or not."

"I could always work as a waitress," Franny said. "Or a nanny."

Mary Jean took a deep breath. "Franny, please," she said. "I don't want you to end up like me, forty years old with no college degree and no career."

"I would never end up like you," Franny spit out. "And what makes you so high and mighty about going to college? You just quit before you even started because of your stupid mayoral race."

Mary Jean felt her temper rocket off the charts. Usually she managed to stay calm with the kids, even Franny, no matter what, but this was too much.

"That does it," she said to Franny. "You're grounded. You can go to school, and you can come home, but you can forget about going out with your friends, and you can sure as hell forget about babysitting for Stella."

At that last pronouncement, Franny's face finally crumpled.

"I can't babysit for Stella?"

"It's taking away from your schoolwork anyway. And I don't like the things she's telling you."

Franny burst into tears, huge racking sobs that soon had her doubled over in the dressing room.

"You're the most horrible mother ever," she managed to choke out. "I'm going to call the *Homewood Herald* and tell them what a monster you are. Then you can see how many precious votes you get."

"Franny," Mary Jean hissed, looking around. "Get a hold on yourself."

"Babysitting for Stella Powers is the only interesting thing that's happened to me in my entire life," Franny said. "It's the only thing that's keeping me in this stupid town. That's how much you know."

"Oh, come on, Franny," said Mary Jean. "Don't you think you're being a little overdramatic?"

"I'm an *actress*," Franny said. "That's what I *do*. I don't know why you're so determined to take that away from me."

"I don't want to take that away from you," Mary Jean said, softening. "I think you're a very good actress. I just want you to finish school."

"If you make me stop babysitting for Stella, you might as well take it away from me. She's the only person I'll ever meet in this stupid town who can tell me anything about Hollywood."

Mary Jean shook her head. "You just have to promise me you'll finish high school. You can't do anything crazy. I know what I'm talking about here, Franny."

Franny hung her head. "Okay," she said. "I promise."

Mary Jean felt herself relaxing now that it seemed she'd at least negotiated one final year with her daughter at home.

"That jacket looks really cute on you," she said, moving to embrace the girl, kissing her on the cheek. "I'll buy it for you."

"Oh, no," Franny said. "It's too much."

"It will be the only thing you'll get until Christmas," Mary Jean warned, though both she and Franny knew she could never stick to these strictures. She was already feeling the pinch of what she'd have to trim—her rare night out with Pete, the winter coat she desperately needed—to afford the jacket, but holding her daughter close again was worth any price. "I want you to have it."

Maybe I'm just burned out on all this motherhood crap, Mary Jean thought.

It was Back-to-School Night, and she stood in the farthest corner of the classroom, having sneaked in late after handing out leaflets in the school's entryway for her mayoral campaign. The teacher, Mrs. West, who looked to be the same age as Franny and Caitlin, was pointing out the self-portraits on the wall the children had done. Even from here, Mary Jean could pick out Jimmy's: a corona of bright red hair, a huge red smile, stick limbs, and a flamboyantly ruffly purple-and-blue garment that might be a clown's collar, might be a dress. Oh, well, Mary Jean thought. Whatever.

At this point, though, Mary Jean had been through, Jesus, forty Back-to-School Nights, forty-one including this one—

and she wasn't even counting nursery school. Peter had started school here in 1989, so now she was in her third decade of Back-to-School Nights at Nokomis Elementary. There ought to be a statute of limitations—and surely she'd exceeded it.

Mrs. West called for questions, and Mary Jean's heart rose in anticipation of being able to slip out into the hallway, grab some coffee and maybe one of those brownies one of the more industrious mothers had baked, before it was time to once again station herself in the school's entryway and thrust election pamphlets at people who would immediately throw them away.

But she wasn't going to get a break; some eager parent in the front of the room was raising her hand to ask a question. Oh, no, it was Stella. Mary Jean had forgotten that she was going to see Stella here tonight. Seeing Stella instantly reminded Mary Jean of what Franny had said in the dressing room, how Stella had advised her to head straight to Hollywood instead of going to college. She knew she had to talk to Stella about that, let her know how much influence she had over the girl and ask her to be more responsible with her words of wisdom.

But did she have to do it here? Tonight? When all she really wanted to do was grab a brownie and sneak home early to bed?

Stella was asking something about what was being done in the classroom to challenge the children who were learning at a faster pace. Mary Jean had certainly heard that one before. If you judged from the questions at Back-to-School Night, Homewood was the place where all the children were *above* above average. What was wrong with cute but not too swift?

Mary Jean wondered. Or works hard, though not really all that imaginative?

When Stella's question and those of the other parents had been answered, they all rose and began moving slowly to the door. The hallways were already filled, and Mary Jean was sure the brownies would be gone by the time they got to the bake-sale table. She definitely could use some sugar to help give her courage for her talk with Stella, but she doubted the store-bought oatmeal cookies that were always the last thing left at any bake sale would be worth the calories.

"Mary Jean. Mary Jean!"

Mary Jean swung around. No more time to debate the cookie issue: that was Cameron Dunn, She Who Must Not Be Ignored, with Stella scrambling to keep up by her side.

"I just wanted to say I'm really interested in what you've been saying about the school issue," Cameron said.

Mary Jean took a step backward. She couldn't have been more astonished had Cameron fallen to her knees and kissed her hand.

"Well . . . thank you," she said, hoping that was the correct response.

"It's good for Henry Sladowski to be on notice that someone's paying attention to these things," Cameron said, swinging around and heading in the direction of the auditorium, where she was scheduled to deliver the PTA's welcome address for new parents. "Ta-ta, now!"

Mary Jean stared after her, hoping her mouth wasn't hanging open too far.

"If I didn't know better," Mary Jean said to Stella, "I'd think she was on my side."

"She loves this school," Stella said. "Everybody does."

"That's terrific," Mary Jean said. "But Nokomis isn't going to exist anymore if your boyfriend gets elected."

"It's too bad the arts programs have to be cut. But there are so many other arts resources in town, kids can take outside lessons if they're interested."

"Not everyone can afford outside lessons," Mary Jean said. "And it's not just a few art classes he's getting rid of. He's looking to dismantle the entire magnet school system that was created to satisfy the state desegregation order forty years ago."

"How can he do that?" said Stella.

"He just does it. I found out that a lot of the original paperwork has been lost in Trenton, so if a mayor wants to negate one of these old desegregation orders, he just goes ahead. The only way you can stop him is to sue him."

And nobody seemed willing to sue him, at least not in the new, improved Homewood. Say words like *desegregation order* and *tax rate* and *diversity,* she'd discovered, and people's eyes glazed over. Neighborhood schools and lower property taxes, meanwhile, were attractive easy-to-grasp concepts that everyone was willing to get behind.

"Nokomis is our neighborhood school," said Stella, echoing the sentiments of a lot of parents in town. "I think it would be nice if everybody walked to school with the kids on their block, like they did when we went to school."

"Yes, that is nice," said Mary Jean sarcastically. "That way

Idaho can be with all the rich little children from Beech Street, and Jimmy can be with all the poor little children from wherever we end up living."

Stella pressed her lips together and shook her head. "That's not what I meant," she said. "Plus, it's not like Homewood actually has any bad neighborhoods or poor families anymore. Not even yours, Mary Jean, though you certainly like to act like it."

"It's not just about money, Stella, though if Henry has his way this will be a town where only thirty-five-year-old corporate lawyers and investment bankers can afford to live. What about people with less conventional careers and families? Single mothers like your own mother, for instance. Or artists. Homewood has always been a town that welcomed those kinds of people, which is part of what made it an attractive place to live."

"I'm a single mother," Stella said. "I'm an artist."

"But you're also a millionaire," Mary Jean pointed out, exasperated.

"All my money is tied up in that house," Stella said. "And I don't have a career anymore. Acting is the only thing I've ever done."

Which reminded Mary Jean of Franny.

"Listen, Stella," Mary Jean said. "I've been meaning to talk to you about Franny and her acting ambitions."

"Franny's a beautiful girl," Stella said. "I think she'd really have a shot at an acting career."

"She's got some crazy idea that you think she doesn't need

to go to college or even finish high school in order to become an actress," said Mary Jean. "Though I'd hate to think you were really encouraging her to quit school."

"Oh, of course not," Stella said. "Though who ever figures out you don't have a high school diploma unless you tell them?"

That was exactly the kind of thing Mary Jean didn't want Stella saying to Franny, the kind of thing that would drive Pete, with his code books and ethics tomes, insane.

"She really admires you, Stella," Mary Jean said. "We'd really like her to go to college. Or at the very least, finish high school. Please use your influence in a positive way."

"That's exactly what I'm trying to do."

"Then tell her to stay in school," Mary Jean said flatly. "I told her she could keep babysitting for you, but if she comes home again talking about how you think she should just go out to L.A., I'm going to put a stop to it."

Stella opened her mouth and then closed it again. "First you and then Franny," she said finally. "What's next? Are you going to stop Jimmy from playing with Idaho?"

At the thought of how devastating it would be for Jimmy to no longer see Idaho—and, Mary Jean assumed, vice versa—she softened. She never meant for her and Stella, and certainly not their families, to become so polarized.

"Of course not," she said. "Hey, I don't like feeling as if you and I can't be friends. But I'm not the one who's going out with Henry fucking Sladowski."

"And I'm not the one who's insisting on running for mayor against him."

"This isn't some self-indulgent exercise, Stella. I'm sorry, but I really think he's out to ruin this town. All he cares about is power and money."

"That is not true, Mary Jean," Stella said. "Here's something I bet you didn't know. On his Jaguar, his brand-new Jaguar that he loves as much as he loves Homewood, he's got a bumper sticker that reads GREED KILLS. Now why would he do that if all he cared about was power and money?"

Mary Jean stared at Stella, wondering whether she should confess that she'd put the bumper sticker there. But if Sladowski didn't feel he needed to tell Stella the truth, she decided, neither did she.

"You're not going to change my mind, Stella. I don't know, maybe he's a great boyfriend, lover, whatever. He might be great in bed or a lot of fun to be with, as far as I know. I'm only concerned about what he wants to do to the town."

"And I don't care about that at all. I mean, of course I care, but I'm interested in Henry as a man, as someone I can have a relationship with. I'm just trying to have a real life here."

"Well, congratulations," said Mary Jean. "You have one."

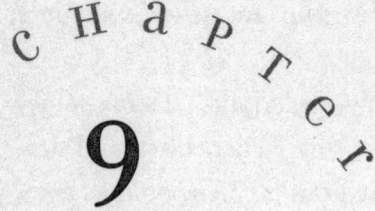

CHAPTER 9

When Pete came to the door to drop off Franny and Jimmy on his way to work, Idaho hurled herself at him, trying to shimmy up his uniformed body as if he were a tree. Jimmy looked on for only a moment before following suit.

"Daddy, Daddy!" Jimmy cried.

"Daddy, Daddy!" Idaho echoed, giggling.

Oh, Lord.

"You kids go upstairs with Franny now," Stella said, peeling her daughter off Pete's lanky frame. "Franny, I have my cell if you need me. You're welcome to sleep in my bed. I mean, my mother's bed."

"Sure," said Franny, following the kids upstairs.

"I hope it's okay that Jimmy is here," Pete said. "Caitlin's away on a Model UN trip, and Mary Jean had some political thing—"

"Are you kidding? Idaho's thrilled."

They both listened to the sounds of Idaho and Jimmy squealing at the top of the stairs.

"As long as it's okay with Franny, it's okay with me," Stella assured him. "I'll bring them home tomorrow when I get back, probably around noon."

Stella called a good-bye and, hoisting her overnight case, left the house with Pete. When they reached the sidewalk and it became apparent that she was planning to walk, Pete hesitated and pinched the brim of his cap.

"Can I give you a lift somewhere? The train?"

Henry didn't want anyone to know she was staying over. She'd decided to walk because he was even paranoid about anyone seeing her car in his driveway overnight. That was okay; she needed the exercise anyway. In the absence of her trainer and the presence of Vesuvio's pizza and Cozy Corner shakes, she found to her horror that she was spilling out of the thongs and bras that had recently arrived from California. Nor, she discovered when the shipment of the clothes that had been in storage arrived, did any of her old size 2s and 4s fit, much less look even vaguely appropriate for suburban New Jersey life.

"Oh, no," she said. "I'm not going into the city."

Pete frowned and looked at her strangely. It hadn't occurred to her to prepare a lie. When she'd asked Franny to babysit, she'd just said she had to be somewhere overnight and would it be possible for Franny to stay over, promising to pay her the regular rate even for the hours she slept.

"I'm just going to visit a friend," she said. "In town. We're going to kind of have a sleepover."

When Pete continued to stare at her with that weird look on his face, she couldn't keep acting anymore.

"I'm going to see Sladowski, okay? My boyfriend. He just thinks people would be scandalized if they knew I was sleeping over."

Pete raised his eyebrows. "He might be right. People here aren't as liberal as they claim to be."

"That's what Henry's always telling me."

"Now that you've told me," said Pete, "why don't you let me drive you up there?"

That made sense, for about a second and a half. "He'd be mad if he saw you," she said. "At both of us. In fact, it would probably be better if you didn't mention to him that you knew."

"You know I hate to lie, Stella."

She rolled her eyes. He was still the four-square boy she'd dumped for being too ethical.

"I'm not asking you to lie, but you don't have to go shout it from the rooftops, do you? Pretend I'm an informer, and I've just passed you a piece of privileged information and it's vital to your investigation to keep it quiet."

Finally, he nodded. "I can be discreet."

"Okay," she said. "Thank you."

Then she had another thought. "Pete," she said. "What do you think? About Henry and me, I mean. Mary Jean just hates him so much, I can't even talk to her about him. But I could use some advice about the relationship."

Pete's mouth dropped open, and he turned bright red and looked up and to the side, everywhere except at Stella. For the first time, she saw how strong the resemblance was between him and little Jimmy.

"Gee, Stella," he said. "I don't know anything about that."

"But you know me," she pressed. "You went out with me for a long time."

"I never knew what you wanted then. You were too wild for me, Stella."

"That's not true." She laughed. "It was only at the end that you straightened up. When we were younger, you were the wild one."

"That was a long time ago. All I can tell you about Henry is, he's a pretty traditional guy."

"So what does that mean? I shouldn't sleep with him at all? Pretend I'm a virgin?"

Again, Pete's face flamed and his eyes darted around. "Please don't ask me this kind of thing, Stella. I have no idea what to say."

"That's okay, Pete. I didn't mean to put you on the spot."

She patted his arm, which felt alarmingly muscled through his dark blue uniform sleeve. Don't go there, she warned herself, drawing back her fingers as if she'd been burned. What felt like an electric shock to her groin told her it was time to hike up to Henry's, where she hoped she'd be able to put these illicit impulses to good use.

Was she oversexed? she wondered as she walked up the hill. From the time she lost her virginity with Pete in high school, she'd always loved sex. The only exception was when she was pregnant through the first few years of her daughter's life, when she began to think maybe she just wasn't a sexual person anymore. It was so ironic: people would see her on the screen, half-naked or maybe even pretending to make love, and think she was this sex goddess. And meanwhile she went home and buttoned up her pajamas and read parenting guides and rarely went on a date.

And then she made a movie with an actor who was married, but very handsome, and very sexy, someone even she had fantasized about. At first she thought it was a joke; he'd probably turn out to be a nerd, or have bad breath, or leave her as cold as she'd been for the past two years.

But in fact, he more than surpassed the dream lover expectations everyone had of him. He pursued her ardently, brushing aside all her protests about his wife, and for the duration of the shoot—in Vancouver, with Idaho and her then-nanny installed in a rented house—she and the actor did it two or three times a day, in his hotel room, in her trailer, between scenes, during lunch break, unable to keep their hands off each other.

And then, when the movie was over, so was their relationship. He kissed her on the cheek and went back to his wife.

The only thing he'd left her with was her jump-started sex drive. It had been all sex with Eddie, and indeed with all the men between the actor and Eddie. But now she felt that being with someone only for the sex was as big a mistake as thinking—the way she had with Idaho's father—that the sex didn't matter.

What would Henry be like in bed? Her experience with the actor—someone who was as exciting in fact as he was in theory—was the exception rather than the rule, she'd long ago discovered. Pete, for instance, cute and sweet, was a much more energetic lover than anyone would ever guess. Her agent husband, driven and focused and emotionally aloof, had been unexpectedly sensitive in bed, the auteur of her first vaginal orgasms, though she'd had her best sex ever with an overweight, mouth-breathing journalist who came to interview her soon after she broke up with the agent. And Eddie, who seemed to sweat sex from every pore, was thrilling on the buildup but suffered from erotic ADD—even before his attention was diverted by the nanny.

Judging from Henry's personality, she'd figured him for the take-charge type—though maybe that meant she should be prepared for the exact opposite, and he'd want her to don a leather cat suit and tie him to the bedposts. Which at this point, she was prepared, if necessary, to do.

She'd been to Henry's house only once, when he stopped on their way to dinner with Cameron and her husband to pick up a special bottle of wine, so she'd gotten only a quick peek. They'd been driving then, so she hadn't divined exactly how far uphill it was, way above both the Tree House and even Cameron's place, the very uppermost house in Homewood, looking down from its cliffside perch over the town and the stretch of New Jersey flatlands to the Hudson River and the towers of Manhattan beyond. Stella stood in Henry's driveway, breathing hard while she looked over the spectacular view and waited for the sweat on her brow to dry.

Finally she was ready. With one more deep breath, she turned toward the house.

He was apparently ready for her too. When he opened the tall heavy cedar door, she saw that the lights were off in the large open living area. Two tall candles gleamed on the glass-and-steel dining room table, and dozens of votives in glass holders glittered on the wooden slab of a mantel, on the coffee table, even on the distant kitchen counter, mirroring the lights of the city twinkling in the distance.

She raised her eyebrows. "Very nice."

"It's all for you, darling," he said, taking her hand and leading her inside.

She had to admit it, she was impressed. All over again, she felt that a man who went to this much trouble for her deserved to be taken seriously. A bottle of wine stood uncorked on the dining room table, and he poured her a glass, inviting her to sit on the caramel leather sofa.

He was nervous, the way a fan or an underling was nervous meeting her for the first time. She could smell this, even when someone was trying to act cool and cover it up. But this had never before been Henry's demeanor, even the first time they met at the Tree House. He'd always been self-assured, cocky, which she found more appealing than the nervousness.

"Relax, Henry," she said, patting his shoulder. "I'll be gentle with you."

He managed a brief smile at that, and she took a deep swallow of her wine, which was delicious. Henry definitely knew how to choose his wines.

"The house looks beautiful," she told him.

She admired its spareness, even though her own style, if she had one, involved more clutter, more antiques, more, well, quirkiness. Henry's place had nothing except candles on any of the surfaces, no rug on the dark wood floor, no pillows or afghans on the leather furniture, no color save for neutral grays and browns and black. There was one large abstract painting, a slash of black across a cream background, and a primitive metal sculpture in the far corner of the dining room, but no photographs or books.

"Oh," he said, looking around as if he were noticing it for the first time. "Thank you."

"Really, Henry. I appreciate your going to all this trouble. It means a lot to me."

"I'm glad to hear that," he said, smiling. "Are you hungry? I got some prepared stuff at Whole Foods, some sushi, portobello mushroom enchiladas—"

"No, Henry," she said gently, taking his hand. "I just want to be with you."

"Oh," he said. "I could put on some music." He stood up.

"What would you like to listen to? Jazz? Or maybe something classical. Mozart?"

"Henry," she said, standing up too and moving in close to him. Finally, he was wearing jeans, which reawakened the attraction she'd felt toward him that first day under the tree, though his shirt was buttoned up nearly to the collar. She didn't even know, she realized, whether or not he had hair on his chest.

She ran her hand over the starched fabric of his shirt. No hair. Wrapping her arms around him, she squeezed. He held his arms slightly away from his body and let her.

"Henry," she said softly. "Let's go into the bedroom."

"Don't you want to finish your wine?"

She looked directly at him. "Don't you want to make love to me?"

"Yes," he stammered. "Of course. Of course I do."

She tilted her face up to him, and finally he met her halfway and kissed her. They'd kissed before, naturally, good-night kisses without much heat in them. But now she let her lips fall open, and he responded, thank God, with an adroit flick of his tongue. She nibbled his lower lip, he licked her upper one. He was, she was excited and relieved to find, an excellent kisser. That was an important harbinger of what was to come, wasn't it? Wasn't it?

"Mmmmmm," she murmured, moving against him, feeling herself get even more turned on, hoping it had the same effect on him.

She tugged his shirt out of his pants, ran her hand up his muscled torso.

"You feel so good," she said, nudging him toward what she guessed was the bedroom.

"The wine," he said.

"Fuck the wine."

He pulled back, surprise in his eyes.

"I mean—" She laughed. "I just want to fuck you."

When he still hesitated, she said, "Come on, Henry. Millions of men would love to be in your position. Let me take off my clothes for you."

She never thought she'd feel this way, but she suddenly missed Eddie Skinner acutely. What she wouldn't give for some of that chemistry, some of that sexual drive, right now.

And then, as her mind drifted into the past, she froze. She flashed on Idaho's father, who was the only other man who'd acted anything like this when she tried to take him to bed. Who'd always been loving, devoted, and sexually remote, because, it turned out, he liked boys.

"Henry," she said. "I have to ask you something."

Now he looked as alarmed as she felt. "What?"

"I know you might not want to tell me this. But I swear, if it's true, I wouldn't say anything to anybody. You could still be seen with me, if that was what was important, until after the election . . ."

"*What,* Stella?"

"Henry, are you gay?"

He stared openmouthed at her for a long moment, and then he burst out laughing.

"Why would you think a thing like that?"

"You don't seem interested in having sex with me, and when I started to think about it, it all seemed to come together—you've never been married, you're really tidy . . ."

He laughed again, and put a finger to her lips. "I have a very good housekeeper." He shushed her. "And I was married once, long ago. I'm not married now because I've been waiting for the right woman to come along."

He kissed her neck.

"But now I've found her," he whispered.

Stella felt herself morph back to the more comfortable role of lovee as Henry took her hand.

"I can't wait to make love to you," he said, still, irrationally, whispering.

Finally, she thought, as he led her to the bedroom. Finally, she thought, as they lay down on the bed, from which he first carefully folded back a real suede bedspread, and began kissing. He *was* a fantastic kisser, and she felt herself get excited all over again. And he seemed more into the whole thing too, which helped *her* relax into it. She let him take the lead in unbuttoning her shirt and unhooking her bra, gasping as he touched her breasts and unzipped her pants and moved his hand beneath her panties.

He was less aggressive about removing his own clothes but she found this a turn-on, being naked when he was dressed, or half-dressed anyway, his shirt unbuttoned to reveal his, yes, hairless but nicely muscled torso, his jeans still firmly buckled and zipped. If his touch was a bit soft (she'd teach him to rough it up), his tongue a bit wet (unlike other women, she wasn't a big fan of oral gymnastics anyway), these were all minor details, correctable over time. What really mattered was the main attraction, and as he undid his fly and lowered himself onto her, she gasped in anticipation.

And then couldn't figure out what was happening. He was on top of her, heavier than she would have guessed, and he was moving up and down, and grunting, but she couldn't feel anything. His jeans were still on, true, but they were definitely open, and that was definitely not denim she was feeling down there, but flesh. But she didn't have any sense of him inside her. Had he just somehow gotten lost down there? Was he rubbing against her belly but had somehow mistaken it for someplace more intimate? It felt all wrong to her, but he was carrying on as if all was normal.

"Henry," she said, confused. "Henry! Where is it?"

"Where's what?" he mumbled.

"It! Your penis! Aren't you going to put it in?"

"It *is* in!" he said. "Oh. Oh, God. Ohhhhhhhh."

He shuddered to a climax and then lay heavily on top of her. As she felt the wetness begin to ooze out between her legs, she finally believed him. He had indeed, from all evidence, been in. Though she hadn't felt a thing.

She lay there trying to stifle her disappointment as he curled heavily on top of her. Finally, the denim of his pants began to chafe between her legs.

"Henry," she whispered, shifting to show him she was uncomfortable.

"Sorry," he said, rolling off her but not taking his arms from around her.

She stole a glance at him to see whether he was about to apologize or explain, but his eyes were firmly shut, on his face a look of perfect contentment. Finally, he sighed.

"I love you," he said.

Her first impulse was to shout, No! and leap from the bed.

But she did care for him. Despite the huge—or rather, minuscule—letdown of the sex, she wasn't ready to write off their relationship. It was unfair to judge everything by the first time.

On the other hand, she certainly didn't love him. Not yet, anyway.

She was trying to form her response, but instead of waiting, he pulled away suddenly, zipping his pants as he got to his feet by the side of the bed—spoiling her chance to get a look at the organ that had left so little impression—and then hurrying to a tall dresser, where he retrieved something from the top drawer. As he walked back to where she lay, the pressed white cotton sheet drawn hastily over her bottom half, he held whatever it was behind his back, smiling slyly.

"Stella," he said.

She had begun to return his smile when he drew the small blue Tiffany box from behind his back. Oh, no. He thrust the box toward her, and she took it, tugging on one end of the white satin ribbon as a queasy feeling rose in her throat. She lifted a smaller velvet box from the blue cardboard one. Very slowly, almost not wanting to press forward but not able to resist either, she opened the lid of the velvet box. And there was the thing she had been afraid would be there: a huge honking square-cut diamond ring.

"Stella," Henry said, taking her hand. "Will you marry me?"

She stared dumbfounded at him, at his utterly serious face. She was waiting, she realized, for him to burst out laughing. But he just kept gazing at her.

"Oh, Henry," she said, silently asking her mother to forgive her for what she was about to say. "That's very nice. But we hardly know each other."

"I know you," he said. "I know enough to know I want to marry you."

"You just think you know me because you've seen me in the movies," she said gently. She'd been through this before, with men, with friends, even with other people in the industry who should have known better. With Eddie Skinner, she'd even believed it herself.

Reluctantly—the diamond really was gorgeous—she set the box with the ring still nestled inside it back in Henry's hand. It was such a soft hand, the hand of a man who went to meetings for a living, not worked on houses.

"You know," she said softly, "you still haven't spent any time with my daughter, and that's important, not just for me and her, but for you. And I've never met your family. I don't even know whether you *have* a family. Where did you grow up, for instance?"

"Scranton. But the important thing is—"

"Scranton, that's interesting," Stella said. "I've never been to Scranton. Do you still have relatives there?"

"My mother, but she has Alzheimer's, she's in a nursing

home," said Henry. "I really think the more important thing is the here and now. I'm ready to get married, Stella. I'm ready to have a family. And I want to do it with you."

"Whoa whoa whoa!" Stella said, holding up her hands. "If it's time to lay our cards on the table, Henry, you should know that I'm really almost forty years old. I don't know whether I even have time to have any more children, much less whether I want to."

"Oh," said Henry. "I think you said you were younger than that."

"And I think you never said how old you were at all. Forty? Forty-five? When's your birthday? Do you have any brothers and sisters? Who's your best friend? Do you even have any friends, other than the people who are involved in your campaign? I don't know anything about you."

He shook his head, looking like he was about to cry. "I love you, Stella," he said. "That's all I need to know."

If she'd thought for even a minute that he was serious, she might have felt sympathetic. But instead she shook her head.

"I'm sorry, Henry," she said. "But I don't really believe that."

"So you're saying you don't want to marry me?"

"I might want to marry you, Henry. I'd like some time to find out."

He snapped the ring box closed, and his face shut down too. "When you've had enough time to think about it, let me know," he said icily.

"I don't just need time to think," she said, reaching for him.

"*We* need time to be together, to do things together, to do things with my daughter . . ."

Without responding, he pulled away and began tidying the perfectly tidy room. Finally she got out of bed and picked up her clothes from where they'd fallen on the floor and began getting dressed. He made the bed, resolutely ignoring her.

"Maybe I should just go home," she said, thinking that at least then he would respond to her, if nothing else offer to drive her home.

But instead, still without looking her way, he said, "Maybe that would be best."

It was as if they'd accidentally watched the last scene in the movie, and now felt completely unmotivated to go back and sit through the middle. Did that mean it was over between them? It can't be over, just because I'm not ready to commit to marriage right this minute, Stella told herself. That would be insane.

"I guess I'll go now," she said.

"Then go."

She turned around and walked out into the night by herself.

At least it was downhill all the way home. Fueled by her agitation at what had happened with Henry and her anxiety about who might be hiding in the copious shrubs of Homewood, Stella walked faster and faster, her thoughts coming with similarly dizzying speed.

Was it over? It was definitely over. Even if Henry wasn't saying it was over, *she* was. There was no way she wanted to stay with him now.

But if she broke up with him, what would happen with her house? Nothing was resolved in California; she had no idea when she'd be in a position to get a mortgage and to close on the house here. But on paper the closing date was just a week away. If Sladowski held her to that date, she could lose everything, not just the house but all her liquid assets.

He wouldn't do that to her, would he? He said he loved her, that he wanted to marry her. Did he really feel that way? If he felt that way an hour ago, did he still feel it now? Maybe she'd been too hasty. Maybe she was just scared because he *was* serious, the way she'd always been. If marrying for great sex had proved such a huge mistake, maybe it was all right to marry someone even if you had *bad* sex.

But that wasn't just bad sex, that was *horrible* sex. And while size wasn't supposed to matter, this wasn't a mere size issue, this was some kind of physical *deformity.*

And then he'd been so cold. So dismissive.

As dismissive as she'd been to Mary Jean, all the times her old friend tried to warn her about Sladowski. Mary Jean had been right, it seemed clear to her now. Why had she moved away from her old friend in favor of a man she hardly knew? She'd been trying to please her mother, but her mother wouldn't really have liked Henry Sladowski, she knew in her heart. And furthermore, her mother was dead.

Her mother was dead. For the first time, it seemed, the full weight of that reality descended on her. Her mother was dead.

She could marry whoever she wanted, make whatever kind of life she wanted, stay in fucking Homewood, New Jersey, until the end of time, and that wasn't going to bring her mother back. That wasn't going to make her mother happy or unhappy or anything at all, because her mother was lying unfeeling in the ground.

When she reached her house, it was after eleven, and she thought at first that all the kids, including Franny, had gone to bed. She'd told Franny that she could sleep in her room, or rather, her mother's room, since she expected to be out all night. When she let herself in the back door and found the downstairs deserted, only one lamp on, she figured she'd tiptoe upstairs and get a blanket and pillow from the hall closet and sleep on the couch.

But when she went up, she saw the light on in her mother's room through the cracked door. Gently pushing the door open, wanting to show the girl it was her and not a stranger in the house, she whispered, "Franny?" And then, seeing that the bed was empty, a little louder, "Franny?"

"Whooop!" the girl screamed, whirling around from where she stood in the door of the closet, her hands clasping Stella's big green purse.

"Franny," Stella said, not wanting to believe any of the things that were going through her mind. "What's going on here?"

"Oh, I'm sorry, Miss Powers," Franny said, blushing wildly. "I just . . . well, I was just getting ready for bed, and I forgot to bring pajamas or anything to sleep in so I was going to borrow something, and then I saw your purse and I just . . . well, I just thought I'd look in that book I saw you writing in."

"What book?" Stella asked, confused.

Franny, her face still as crimson as her hair, reached into the purse and pulled out Stella's bright orange leather Filofax, cards and clippings sticking out every which way.

"You were using it when you were talking to someone on the phone," Franny said. "Someone in L.A., your agent or lawyer or somebody. I thought maybe I could find some phone numbers in there, for when I go to Hollywood."

Stella crossed the room to where Franny stood and took the Filofax and the purse from her hands. It was outrageous, what she'd caught Franny doing. Anybody else, she would have fired her on the spot. But this was a small town, and Franny was the daughter of her oldest friends, the sister of Idaho's best friend. Plus, she was a sweet girl, and her instant willingness to confess what she'd done made it less of a trespass. If she'd been faced with the same opportunity at the same age, Stella reminded herself, she would have grabbed it in a heartbeat.

"Listen, Franny," she said, leading the girl to perch on the edge of her mother's bed. "I already told you, if you want help going out to L.A., I'll give it to you. I'll put you in touch with everybody I know that might help you, and you'll be free to use my name, for what that's worth. You don't have to sneak around copying phone numbers out of my notebook, do you understand?"

The girl nodded, plainly embarrassed.

"Now I talked to your mother about this, and I promised

her I'd tell you I thought it was a good idea for you to graduate from high school, even to spend some time in college, before you try to go out there."

"Jesus, I can't believe my mother said anything to you. That is so out of line."

"That is *not* out of line, Franny. She said it because she's your mother and she cares about you. And I happen to agree with her, do you understand?"

"But you went out there—"

"I never thought I'd say something like this, but don't do as I did, do as I say. All right? I never told anybody this, but I slept on the beach when I first went out there. I'd eat nothing but a hard-boiled egg the entire day."

Stella hesitated. She didn't want to terrify the girl, but she wanted to make her point. "I slept with guys who said they could help me because I was too scared to say no. You get taken advantage of if you're young and naive, Franny."

Franny stuck her chin out. "I know how to take care of myself."

"I'm sure you do."

"Guys in high school can be assholes too. And it worked out for you in the end."

"I'm nearly forty years old, and I don't have any career, Franny. I don't know anything about anything except acting. Please, Franny, take my advice."

Franny nodded, but something in her had hardened against Stella, Stella could tell, as if Stella had crossed the boundary from idol to parent-equivalent.

"Well, I guess I'll go home now," said Franny.

"No, why don't you just stay over as we planned?" Stella said. "I don't want to leave the kids here alone to drive you home, and I don't want to wake them up. I'll pay you for the whole night."

"Are you sure?"

"Sure I'm sure. If you wouldn't mind sleeping downstairs on the sofa, this way you can get up early with the kids. I've got some thinking to do tonight yet, and I have a feeling it's going to take a while."

CHAPTER 10

At 4:10 a.m., Mary Jean was lying in bed wide awake, running over and over everything that had happened at the three town events she'd visited the night before. First she had stopped in, thanks to her brothers, at the main firehouse. Then she'd gone to an opening at the museum, mingling with the art lovers and big museum donors in town. And then she'd visited the Saturday-night pig roast thrown by the first ward neighborhood association, which included most of the African-American residents of Homewood.

Each stop was more or less the same, shaking hands, passing out her computer-generated flyers, trying to explain how she was different from and better than Sladowski. And each encounter ended with people backing away and shaking their heads, saying some variation on "This Sladowski fella sure seems to know what he's doing."

She felt like a mouse to Sladowski's lion, and wished she could think of some way to get her message across more effectively. She'd been studying her material nonstop, researching what the problems were in the town, what the various community groups wanted, and how to address those issues. But no matter what she said, how much she knew, she kept running up against a brick wall with Sladowski's name scrawled all over it.

If only *she,* and not Sladowski, had Stella's help. Besides the money, the power, and the backing of all the most influential people in town, Sladowski had the advantage of parading Stella all over the place to get attention and make himself more glamorous. If anybody should have Stella as their very own celebrity spokesmodel, it should be Mary Jean.

She heard the front door open, Pete's feet pad around downstairs. When he worked nights, she was usually asleep by the time he slipped into bed beside her. They were still barely speaking, sleeping with backs turned to each other, careful not to touch.

Tonight, though, he opened the door to the bedroom and stood there for a moment—she'd clamped her eyes closed; she didn't want to have to talk to him—and then he said, softly, "Mary Jean?"

When she didn't respond, he crossed to the bed and sat down.

"Mary Jean?" he said again.

She turned on her side, moaning a little, feigning a mumbled query. Stella may have been the one who'd gone to Hollywood, she thought, but she'd done some pretty convincing acting in her day too.

She heard Pete take off his shoes, stand and remove his pants, then sit back down on the bed and slip between the covers. And then he scooted right over to her side and took her in his arms. He was, she could feel, completely naked.

"Pete," she said, trying to make her voice sleepy. "What are you doing?"

He kissed her on the neck.

"I still hate you," she muttered.

"I hate you too," he said. "But we're all alone in the house."

Her eyes shot open. "Completely alone?"

His kisses moved down toward the edge of her nightgown. "Caitlin's away on that Model UN trip, and Jimmy and Franny are staying over with Idaho."

She was really losing track these days. "Tell me again, why are they staying over?"

He hesitated, but then she figured it out.

"Oh, I get it. Franny had to lug Jimmy along so by the time Stella got home it wouldn't make sense to wake him up to bring him home so Franny might as well just go to sleep over there."

"Something like that," Pete mumbled, resuming his kissing.

She rolled onto her back, and he began to push her nightgown up over her hips. But if they were really alone, there was no point in making do with that.

"Wait a minute," she said, pulling away and getting out of bed.

She lifted her nightgown over her head and stood there naked in the moonlight.

"Wow," Pete said.

"Do you like it?"

"I love it."

Ironically, it was only when she had clothes on, and they weren't making love, that she worried that Pete was turned off by her body. Now, as she watched him looking at her, she felt completely confident.

He reached up for her, and she leaned into him, pulling the covers back and climbing on top. Sex with the kids gone was a totally different thing from sex with the kids there, and in her view, the only kind really worth having. But that was because it was the only time she felt free enough to move and cry out in a way that was somehow all tied up with coming. Pete, of course, came every time. But when the kids were on the other side of the wall, she found herself too worried about the sound of the bed squeaking, too concerned about breathing hard or making noise, to let go.

Now, though, she rode on top of Pete like a cowgirl in a rodeo, the old bedsprings singing like frenzied crickets. It was nearly miraculous, after twenty-something years, how their sex got better and better, at least for her. Pete was moaning, his eyes shut, but he was more beside the point than he used to be. It wasn't until the girls went off to school that she ever even tried masturbating, that she had her first orgasm. She'd learned to do it with Pete since then, but while he was an exciting addition to the process, he was not strictly necessary.

She felt herself getting close when Pete suddenly pushed her off, nudging her onto her back, looming over her. He lifted her legs up and began to hook them over his shoulders, the way he had always done, the way he liked to come.

But now she stopped him.

"Pete, I don't like that."

He looked concerned. "What's wrong? Are you okay?"

She edged away from him. "I'm fine. The truth is, it's always kind of uncomfortable."

"What do you mean, always?"

She meant that, from the very beginning, and on through the next twenty-five years, when he flipped her onto her back and hoisted her legs up and drove his penis deep inside her, it hadn't really felt good. Not bad, exactly. But just not good.

"It's just not that comfortable. It distracts me, and I can't come."

"Since when?"

"I told you, since always, Pete."

He sat up on his heels. "I'm floored. Why didn't you ever tell me this before?"

Oh, God, there was a question.

I didn't tell you, she thought, because when we first started having sex, when I was a virgin, I was afraid to say anything that might turn you away from me—not "I don't like that," not "You better use a rubber." She was so crazy about Pete, and

PAMELA REDMOND SATRAN

so insecure about his feelings for her, that she didn't want to do anything to risk driving him away.

And then she didn't tell him because she thought maybe there was something wrong with her, something substandard, that made it uncomfortable, and she didn't want to confess that. And then she thought no, maybe this was uncomfortable for Stella too, and she made him stop, and so he was doing it to passive Mary Jean to somehow get back at Stella. Or maybe the fact that she did it with Pete made her *better* than Stella, more desirable in his eyes.

Or maybe she didn't tell him because she was twisted and she liked not liking it—which in fact, sometimes, she did. Until she started having orgasms for real, she even thought that maybe the pressure she felt when his cock swelled inside her *was* an orgasm, it was that intense.

And then of course, once all this was past, she didn't tell him because it had gone on so long, how could she suddenly change the rules?

Except now, it seemed, she had done just that.

"I don't know, Pete. I guess I just think we can do better."

"I don't know what to think." He flopped onto his back and stared up at the ceiling. His penis was completely soft now.

"I could give you a blow job," she offered.

He continued to gaze miserably upward.

"Come on," she said. "I don't like to see you so unhappy."

She moved down and took him in her mouth. Yes, it was a pity blow job—she definitely was not as into being on the giving end of this as Pete was—but at least it didn't hurt. The

194

relief of finally telling him and the wish to salve his hurt feelings fueled her enthusiasm. Of course, this had an element of masochism to it too—one that had always seemed more obvious to her—but she found herself genuinely enjoying it without once having to pretend she was sucking on a popsicle.

And he was responding, despite his best efforts, she could tell, to play it cool. His silence turned to moaning turned to active encouragement, his fingers stroking her hair, his back arching and then cries that began mounting in intensity.

Precipitously, she pulled away. He looked at her as if he couldn't believe she'd betrayed him once again.

"Sssssh," she said, putting a finger to his lips. "I want you."

She lay down next to him and pulled him on top of her. She had to resist the impulse to put her legs back exactly as she had earlier refused to do, the habit was so strong—the habit of pleasing him as well as the habit of moving her legs in that way. But instead, she maneuvered so that he pressed against her more directly, so that she felt her own excitement grow along with his. She wasn't always able to come from just having intercourse, but she was tonight, pulsing against him as she felt him begin to do the same to her.

Finally he rolled to the side, holding her lightly.

"How were your things tonight?" he asked sleepily.

This was the first time he'd asked her anything about her campaign, and she was pleased that he wanted to know.

"Horrible," she admitted, as she might not have done in the daytime. "It was really depressing."

"So quit."

His eyes were still closed; his arms were still around her.

"I'm not quitting," she said, pushing him away, turning over so that her back was to him.

He turned then so that he was facing away from her, leaving the customary gap between them.

"I'm still pissed at you," he mumbled.

"I'm pissed at you, too."

She was nearly asleep when he spoke again.

"I love you," he said.

And she replied the way she always did: "I love you more."

The next morning, Mary Jean left Pete snoring in bed, gathered her leaflets, and headed down to the Cozy Corner. Henry Sladowski might have a million times more money than her. He might have a huge organization and the support of political big shots in both parties.

But he didn't, couldn't, believe in Homewood the way Mary Jean did. And he didn't, couldn't, be as motivated to get out there and make people listen.

"Hi," Mary Jean said, thrusting one of the hot-pink flyers that Caitlin had made her on the computer toward a middle-aged man heading into the Cozy Corner. "I'm Mary Jean Wright, and I'm running—"

He shook his head and his hand, hurrying into the restaurant.

"Hi," Mary Jean said to the next person, who seemed more willing to take a leaflet. "Vote for me, Mary Jean Wright, for mayor."

When someone stopped to listen for a moment, she was buoyed, and when they hurried past or scowled at her, she was stung. And when someone was rude to her, when they said something like, "I think you're ridiculous, and I'd never vote for you," she felt like bursting into tears and running home.

But she wasn't going to give Sladowski that satisfaction. She wasn't going to give *Pete* that satisfaction. Pete might think that by doing this she was taking something away from the kids, but Mary Jean felt that by sticking it out she was showing her daughters—and sons too, for that matter—that it was important to stand up for your beliefs and keep going in spite of adversity.

Now, coming down Broad Street, she saw a mom and several children and stood straighter, readying her spiel. But as they got closer, she saw that it was Stella and Idaho, along with Franny and Jimmy.

Jimmy spotted her first and tore down the street in her direction, grabbing her around the waist so she had to lift her leaflets high to keep them from getting crushed.

"Hi, sweetheart," she said. "Did you have a fun sleepover at Idaho's?"

"Yes, Mommy," Jimmy said, rushing to tell her about all the games they'd played and the videos they'd watched and something she couldn't follow about wanting to have ice cream but Franny saying they had to eat their pizza first and then not letting them have as much ice cream as they wanted.

Mary Jean nodded as her little boy spoke, smiling and raising her eyebrows at appropriate intervals, until the rest of the group arrived.

"Vote for me?" she said wryly to Stella, giving her a tiny smile. She had not seen Stella since their confrontation in the school, and she felt even more awkward with her old friend than she had before.

"I don't know, maybe," Stella said, taking one of Mary Jean's flyers and looking it over.

"Really?" Mary Jean said, stunned.

"I'll think about it," said Stella, looking her in the eye now and grinning. "I think you're doing a great job."

"Well, *I* don't!" cried Franny, grabbing the stack of flyers from Mary Jean's hand and stuffing them in the trashcan. "Really, Mother, this is so embarrassing. I can't believe you're doing this to me."

"I'm not doing it to *you*, Franny," Mary Jean said, horrified. "I'm doing it because I think it's important for the town. Because it's important for *me*."

"That's all you think about, is yourself," Franny said.

Franny turned to Stella.

"Can I go now? Am I finished babysitting? I can take Jimmy if you want."

"No," said Stella, looking nearly as shaken as Mary Jean felt. "It's okay. Just a minute, let me pay you—"

"That's all right," Franny said. "You can catch me next time."

And with that she was gone.

"Well," Stella said finally, as they both gazed after the girl.

"Yeah," said Mary Jean. "I'm sorry you had to see that."

"Quite a performance," said Stella.

"She's a handful, all right."

"I see what you mean."

They both continued to watch Franny until she disappeared from view. For once, Mary Jean felt, she and Stella seemed to be on the same side, even about things she didn't expect, like her running for mayor and her rebellious daughter.

"Were we like that?" Stella said, finally looking at Mary Jean.

Mary Jean couldn't help but grin. "You definitely were."

"Well, you were the one who got knocked up. I wish I'd been around to see your mother's face when you broke that to her."

"It wasn't pretty," Mary Jean said, shaking her head at the memory and watching as Jimmy and Idaho, oblivious, skipped in circles around each other on the sidewalk.

"I don't know, do you think it's inevitable, between mothers and daughters?" Stella said. "I can't imagine Idaho ever being like that, but I guess it's hard to tell when they're little."

"Franny used to push her sister off my lap because she couldn't bear not being close to me."

"I really regret now all the grief I gave to my mother," Stella said, beginning to tear up. "She definitely didn't deserve it."

"My mother deserved it more," Mary Jean said. "But I still can't help feeling that I'm being punished somehow for giving her a hard time."

"Franny's just asserting her independence," Stella said. "She's bent on making her own way."

"Well, it makes me feel better somehow that you see that, too. All I hear from her is how wonderful you are. I figured she showed you only her sweet and charming self, and saved her evil self for me."

"She tries her best to show me only her charming wonderful self, but the more I get to know her, the more I understand why you feel like you've got to keep an eye on her."

Jimmy and Idaho were struggling to open the heavy old door of the Cozy Corner when suddenly, someone on their way out let them scoot inside.

"Uh-oh," said Stella. "I better go in after them."

"Do you want me to take him?" asked Mary Jean.

"No, no, it's easier for me when the two of them are together."

"I remember hearing your mother say that to my mother," said Mary Jean. "About us."

Stella sighed. "They remind me of us."

Mary Jean could see the children through the window scrambling to slide into one of the big round booths. "Funny, though, Idaho doesn't really remind me all that much of you."

Stella laughed. "No, in that pair, I'm Jimmy."

Mary Jean chuckled. "It's true," she said. "You're kind of part Jimmy and part Franny. Genetically, I don't know how you swung that."

"Say," said Stella, "do you want to come in? Have breakfast with us?"

Mary Jean hesitated. "Do you really want to risk consorting with the enemy?"

"You might be surprised."

"Is something up between you and Henry?"

"Not really," said Stella. "Why don't you come inside?"

Down the street, a Sladowski worker began setting up one of their fancy booths in time to catch the after-church crowd from St. Kieran's. If Mary Jean made it to the trashcan before that guy carrying the bag of doggie poop, she just might be able to salvage the flyers Franny had thrown away.

"I better not," said Mary Jean. "Too close to election day."

"Okay," said Stella, opening the door of the restaurant. "Let me know if I can help you in any way."

Mary Jean was surprised. "That would mean so much to me," she said.

But she found she was talking to a closed door; Stella had disappeared into the restaurant, and she was out here all alone. Despite Stella's denials, she was sure something had happened between Stella and Henry. And if Stella was really willing to help on her campaign, she just might have a prayer of winning this race.

CHAPTER 11

Once the high emotions of Saturday night wore off, Stella found herself thinking maybe she and Henry had both overreacted. What happened proved her point exactly: they didn't know each other very well. They needed to talk and figure out where they stood with each other, with the election, with the house. Surely Henry, a pragmatic businessman, would see things the same way. But Stella waited all day Sunday for Henry to call her, and he didn't. Then, first thing Monday, she tried calling him, but she left messages on his home phone and his cell phone and with his office, and he still didn't get back to her.

Finally, late in the morning, she decided to hike up the hill and see if she could find Henry working at the Tree House.

Her excuse would be those paint chips she still wanted to look at against the walls. And if he wasn't there, then he wouldn't be able to stop her from marching into the house. Even if it was a mess, she wanted to see what they were doing in there, and if it was safe enough for the workmen, she didn't see why it wasn't safe enough for her.

Walking up Beech Street, she could hear the familiar whine of construction at the top of the hill, undoubtedly coming from her house. That was reassuring. When it became apparent that Henry was avoiding her, she started to imagine that he would call off work on her house, leaving her completely in the lurch. But at least the renovation was still going forward, even if the future of their relationship was in question.

Which was why she wanted to talk with Henry, and why it seemed so ridiculous that he wouldn't speak to her. Well, maybe she'd misread it, and he was simply too busy campaigning and working to call her. Maybe he wanted to step back, let things cool down for a few days, before they talked. Clearly, his ego had been wounded by her turning down his marriage proposal. She undoubtedly should have dealt with that—that and his declaration of love—more sensitively. Really, the first thing she had to do was apologize, before they even started to try to figure out what happened next.

Now her prize tree came into view, its leaves more properly copper now that fall had arrived. This was one thing she was really loving about being in New Jersey, something she hadn't realized she'd missed so much in California: the beauty of the fall leaves. The golden maples, the smaller Japanese maples, brilliantly scarlet, even the honey-colored oaks, all thrilled her, though her own copper beech, she felt, was most beautiful of all.

The leaves of the beech swayed up ahead, an idyllic sight, the enormous tree stirred by the wind. She couldn't feel any wind at all where she walked, or maybe she was just warm from the uphill hike, or maybe the breeze was stronger at the top of the hill. But that much stronger? Now the tree's limbs were shaking so violently it looked as if it were being buffeted by a hurricane.

There was the loud buzz of something that sounded like a saw and then suddenly a huge piece of Stella's tree dropped to the ground. Where there had been leaves a moment ago there was now a space, and a view to her house beyond.

"Stop!" Stella shrieked, breaking into a run, unable to believe that what she was seeing was real. "Please, stop!"

It was uphill, and she'd lost speed and stamina in the past few months since she hadn't been working out, plus it was a choice between calling out and running at all, and since it was unlikely that anybody could hear her over what she now knew was a chain saw, she had to keep running.

But meanwhile the sound of the chainsaw escalated again, and another chunk of the tree fell away.

It was as if she were watching from a distance as people she loved were gunned down, that horrifying, that beyond her control. She felt as if she were running nightmarishly through water, her mouth open as if to scream though no sound emerged.

Finally, she made it across the street, to the side of the thug with the chain saw, who was even at that moment revving up to make another cut.

"Stop!" she screamed.

And then, when he ignored her, though she was certain he heard, she reached out and shoved him, yelling again, "Stop! Stop!"

It was only then that she realized he was not alone, that he had a partner who was far up in the tree, who was even at that moment slicing a branch off at the top.

"Jesus fucking Christ, stop it!" she screamed up to him. And when he didn't shut off his saw, she screamed, "You're fired effective immediately, you fucking moron!"

That got his attention. He turned off his chain saw, hooked it onto his belt, and began easing down the tree.

Stella looked at the guy on the ground.

"You, too," she told him.

"Who the fuck are you, lady?"

"I'm the person who owns this tree, *and* this house, and I want you off my property."

"This is Mr. Sladowski's property," said the guy on the ground.

"Yeah," said his partner, jumping down from the lowest re-maining branch—now far too high for Idaho or anyone else to sit on—and landing threateningly close to her. "We work for Sladowski."

"Well, Sladowski works for me," she told them. "Where is he?"

"He was here earlier," said the one on the ground.

"Did he know you were doing this?"

"He fucking told us to do it," said the one who'd just climbed down.

"I mean it," she told them. "Get the hell out of here, or I'll have you arrested."

She stalked toward the house, feeling as if she were breathing fire. And to think she'd fucked Henry, *kissed* Henry, just two nights ago! Was it possible that he didn't understand how much she loved that tree? Absolutely no way; she waxed on about it, to him and anyone they talked to, more enthusiastically than she'd ever, come to think about it, rhapsodized about him. Was there any possible excuse for what he'd been doing, any disease in the tree, anything related to the lawn or the house that might have given him a reason to trim it back or reshape it? But no, she'd even, over his objections, called in her own botanist to certify the tree's health and to assure her it posed no threat to the house.

There was machinery going inside, too, the usual windows open, the usual dust pouring out. But there was no Henry to stop her this time, and she pushed the front door open.

She intended to call for Henry immediately, but what she saw stopped her. Even through the fog of dust, even from this limited vantage point, she could tell that nearly everything she loved about the house was gone. The light fixtures, the molding, the mantelpieces, the woodwork, even the old glass doorknobs: all gone. She walked, holding her breath, looking in horror. The five-paneled doors, the parquet floorboards, the oak ceiling beams, the nickel bathroom fixtures: all gone. Work—hammering, sawing—raged on all around her, but she was so overcome she didn't even notice, couldn't even tell the workmen to stop what they were doing. It was too late, anyway. They'd already stripped everything of value—of value to her, anyway—out of the house.

As if sleepwalking, she turned to the workman nearest her.

"Where is Henry?" she asked him.

"I don't know. Reinholt knows. Reinholt?"

A thin man with a handlebar mustache turned, and the workman jerked his thumb toward her.

"Lady wants to know where the boss is."

"I'm Stella Powers," Stella explained. "I'm the person who owns this house."

Without speaking, Reinholt took a cell phone from his overalls and dialed, spoke so that Stella couldn't hear, flipped the phone closed.

"He's on his way," he told her.

She went outside to wait. At least the tree guys had left. At least the tree was still standing, even if its bottom branches were shorn off at least twenty feet up the trunk, its top part lopsided as if it had been given a very bad haircut. But chopping into these trees was traumatic for them, Stella knew. Who knew what kind of cuts they'd made? Whether the tree would even survive?

It wasn't long before Stella saw Henry's golden Jaguar racing up Beech Street, turning into the driveway. She sat where she was, on one of the stone balls flanking the front door, waiting for him.

He didn't smile at her as he got out of the car and approached her.

"I hear you want to see me," he said.

She got up then and dusted off her butt. Walked over to him slowly, trying to contain her temper. She felt like reaching out and strangling him.

"What the hell is going on here, Henry?"

"I don't know what you're talking about."

"The tree! Your guys are cutting down my tree, and they say you ordered it! And what the hell have you done to the house? I thought you told me you were saving all the old detail, and everything's been stripped out!"

He shrugged, as if she were complaining that he'd used the wrong shade of white on a windowsill. "I'm proceeding as I see fit on the property. It is still my property, after all."

"This is *my* house, Henry. We have a contract. Or did you think you could just stake your claim to the house the way you tried to do with me?"

He raised his eyebrows. "This house and this property and even this *tree* are still mine, Ms. Powers, until the closing. When and if there is a closing."

Stella stopped. Stopped moving, stopped blinking, stopped breathing. *"If?"*

"In case you've forgotten, the closing is set for a week from now. I understand you might have some problem coming up with the rest of the down payment and getting a mortgage in that time."

She couldn't believe this. "Our agreement has always been

that the closing date is flexible. You said all along that we'd close when my divorce was final and I had access to my money."

"That was when we had a personal relationship. Things have changed."

"You *pig*. You know I can't close now."

Finally, he stopped moving and looked at her. "As long as we had a personal relationship, I was willing to make certain allowances. But it seems we don't have a personal relationship anymore."

She crossed her arms over her chest. "Right. Because I don't want to marry you, you won't let me have my house."

"It doesn't have to be that way," he said. "We might be able to negotiate a different deal."

Stella squeezed her arms more tightly around herself. She could only imagine what he had in mind. "What?" she said. "If I keep sleeping with you, you'll extend my closing date and let my tree live?"

"I think you know by now that sleeping with you is not at the top of my list," said Henry. "No, in fact, what I want is for you to continue to be involved in my campaign. Go to fundraisers with me, be photographed with me, pretend as if we're still together. Though of course there would be no actual physical or even emotional obligation."

"And then I get the house."

"I'll tear up the old contract and write a new one with a closing date a year from now, two years from now, whatever you want. I'll finish the renovations to your exact specifications. I'll even let you live here rent-free."

The man was serious. She was insulted enough when she thought he was suggesting she sell him her body in exchange for the house. But her soul? She'd discovered, over the past few months, that she'd survived the movie business with her soul intact. She certainly wasn't about to trade it away now.

"You know what?" she said. "I don't want your house. You've wrecked it anyway."

She'd be able to find another great house in Homewood, Stella thought wildly. It wouldn't be as special as this one, but she could put down the cash she had now, and spend money to fix the place up later.

"Just give me back my deposit," she said, "and I'll walk away."

He faced her. "Oh no. You walk away, and I keep the deposit."

She walked slowly until she was very close to him. She could tell he was having trouble holding his ground. She brought her face in until she nearly choked on the scent of his cologne and sweat.

"That money doesn't mean anything to you," she said. "And it's everything I have in the world."

He shrugged, though his nonchalance, it was clear to her, was faked. "That's business."

Fireworks exploded in her head.

"All right," she said. "Fine. Keep the money. Take the house. It's worth it to me."

His eyes widened, and she was gratified to see that she'd managed to shock him.

"What's worth it?" he managed to stammer.

She raised her voice so she was sure it would carry to the workmen who were still loitering around the edges of their converstion.

"It's worth it to get as far away as possible from you and your teeny-tiny pathetic little cock."

By the time Franny dropped off Idaho after school, Stella was already packing. There wasn't much to take: the clothes they'd come with along with the few things they'd bought while they were here: Idaho's toys and books, some of the most precious family pictures and Stella's old diary.

But still, Stella needed to go through the house and try to cordon off those things she wanted kept in storage from everything that could be sold or donated or dumped. She'd hand over that job to Cameron Dunn, or anyone Cameron might find to hire. She'd already called Cameron to put her mother's house on the market; the sign would be up by tonight. She hoped, once she left this evening, never to return to this house or this town again.

As soon as she heard Franny call, "I'm going to run now, Stella, okay?" and the door shut as she left, Stella went downstairs and asked Idaho if she wanted some pasta. Idaho rarely ate anything but the cookies in her lunchbox, and was always starving when she came home from school. Idaho nodded eagerly and sat at the little linoleum table in the kitchen, chattering to her mother about her day. Stella boiled the water and poured in the bow ties and stirred the noodles with one of her mother's scarred wooden spoons, nodding and making sympathetic sounds but really thinking about how she was going to tell her daughter the news.

She waited until she set the steaming buttered pasta down before the little girl and watched her gobble most of it, ignoring her paper napkin and wiping her shiny lips on the back of her hand, before speaking.

"Sweetheart," she said gently. "We're going to leave on a trip tonight."

Idaho looked up at her and blinked slowly. "Where are we going?"

"We're going back to California. Won't you like that?"

Stella had already called her lawyer in L.A., who assured her that Henry was within his rights to call the closing on the house and to keep her deposit. If she really wanted to buy the place, he could get in touch with an attorney he knew out there, try to put something in motion to delay the closing. It wouldn't be easy, and it would cost her a lot more money, but if it were important . . .

Forget it, she told him. She just wanted out.

"Are we going to visit Greta?" Idaho asked.

The nanny who'd slept with Eddie.

"No, sweetheart, we're not really friends with Greta anymore."

"Can I get my silver bike when we're there?" said Idaho. "I want to show Jimmy my silver bike."

"No, Idaho, we're not going back to the old house in California. Tonight, we're going to stay in New York, at a really fancy hotel, just like Eloise, and tomorrow we're going to fly to California and look for a new place to live."

Idaho's smile faltered as her eyes darted around the kitchen.

"But we live here now," she said. "Here and later in the Tree House."

"That's changed," Stella said gently. "We're going to move back to California now."

She'd considered other places—Italy, maybe, or someplace in the Caribbean, with winter coming—but decided that California would at least offer Idaho some stability. She'd probably, with her name, be able to get her into a school where she'd know some of the children from nursery school. Even if they were in a different house, Idaho was familiar with Los Angeles and had some favorite spots there. And Stella had some connections, might go back to work, or not. In any case, it seemed the best place to alight for now, and if down the road they changed their minds, they could always go somewhere else.

But Idaho was already shaking her head. "I don't want to move back to California. I likeded it here."

"I know you like it here," said Stella, "but this isn't a good place for us anymore."

She hesitated. How much to tell Idaho, and how?

"Mommy isn't going out with Mr. Sladowski anymore, and he did some not very nice things when he was fixing up our house."

Idaho frowned, sticking out that lip. "He *is* a bad man."

Stella nodded. "Yes, sweetheart, maybe he is. But the point

is, it's better for us now to go back to the place where we have some friends instead of staying here."

"But we have friends here."

"I know you have Jimmy, but we have lots of friends in California."

"We have lots of friends here," Idaho insisted. "We have Jimmy, and Franny, and Jimmy's other sister, and Jimmy's mommy, and Jimmy's daddy." Idaho thought for a minute. "We have my teacher Mrs. West."

"Yes, of course," said Stella, feeling her patience begin to wear thin. "But we have lots of friends in California, too. And you'll have a nice teacher there. And you can write to Jimmy, and maybe he'll come visit us."

That might be nice, actually. Stella figured Franny would definitely land on their L.A. doorstep at some point, and if Idaho and Jimmy actually remembered each other long enough to keep in touch, Jimmy could visit too, along with Mary Jean and Pete. When Stella had left before, she'd cut off all contact with her old friends so completely, feeling as if they could never reconnect, that she'd never want to. But now she could imagine wanting to see the Wrights out there, spending a day together at Disneyland or something, showing Mary Jean where she'd worked when she first went to California, filling in some of the blanks of the two decades they'd missed in each other's life.

Idaho was on her feet now, stamping the patent leather shoes she insisted on wearing every day on the kitchen's tile floor, waving her hands and yelling, exploding in a way that Stella had never experienced.

"I don't wanna move away!" Idaho screamed. "I don't wanna go to California! I like it here! I wanna stay here!"

Stella, alarmed, moved to encircle her, but Idaho immediately pulled away. "I don't want to leave here! You can't make me!"

"Idaho, please," Stella said, trying again to put her arms around her daughter. "Please, honey, you have to calm down."

"I don't want to, Mommy! I don't want to!"

She tore away from Stella and started running around the living room, around and around in circles. Stella had never dealt with anything like this. Idaho was always so sensitive, so quick to dissolve into tears, never rebellious the way Stella herself had been. Stella tried to cast her mind back to tricks her mother had used on her when she was small, to bring her into line. In general, her mother had tended to be more indulgent than the other moms; Stella had always been well aware, for instance, that Mary Jean's mom considered Stella spoiled. But when pushed to the wall, Stella's mother had taken on a commanding tone that let Stella know she meant business. Then, Stella would let go of whatever theatrics she'd been pulling and do what her mother wanted.

"Idaho Powers," Stella said sternly, trying to channel her mother's voice. "I want you to stop this nonsense immediately and listen to me."

At the unaccustomed sound of her mother's anger, Idaho stopped running and stood with her arms rigid at her sides like an army recruit. Stella felt a small wave of satisfaction pass over her. She was obviously on the right track.

"We are packing our things," Stella said, maintaining the strict edge to her voice. "If you want to take your toys and books, I suggest you go up to your room immediately and get them together."

Idaho continued to stand there stiffly.

"Now!" Stella said.

Idaho ran upstairs, looking terrified, and Stella could hear her moving around in her room, hear the thump of objects being tossed onto the floor.

Finally, Stella released her own breath, climbing the stairs more slowly. The door to Idaho's room, her old room, was shut tight.

"I'm going up to the attic, but when I come down, I expect you to have everything packed up in there," she said as she passed the room.

From within, there was only silence.

"Do you hear me?" Stella asked.

"Yes," came Idaho's muffled voice.

"Okay, then. If you need me, I'll be upstairs."

CHAPTER

12

The phone rang, as it always seemed to do, right after they sat down for dinner.

Franny made a move to answer it, but Pete said, "You know the rule."

The rule was that if the phone rang during dinner, they didn't answer it. The girls found this hugely unfair, especially as they didn't have voice mail. But Franny only rolled her eyes and lifted her fork.

"It's probably for your mother anyway," said Pete.

Mary Jean was already on the edge of her seat, running through the possibilities. The Mothers' Action Committee, in response to her request to speak to their group. Jimmy's old nursery school teacher, who said she might be able to help on the campaign. Or a return of one of the other eighty-five calls she'd made today. The way things were going, she was in no position to miss a message.

She bolted for the phone, trying to ignore Franny's outraged cry of unfairness.

But it wasn't anyone calling her back about anything relating to politics. It was Stella, wanting to know whether they'd seen Idaho.

"No," Mary Jean said, confused. "Wasn't Franny supposed to drop her off after school today? What? Okay."

She held the phone to her chest. "Franny, did you see Idaho after you brought her home? Stella says she seems to have disappeared."

"No," said Franny, looking equally baffled. "We didn't stay at all. I brought Jimmy right home because I have to study for my class."

Completely of her own volition, Franny had signed up for an SAT prep class at the high school, which made Mary Jean believe that Franny was coming to her senses after all. That jacket was turning out to be the best $300 she'd ever spent.

"Uh-oh," Caitlin said. "Franny lost one of her charges."

"Fuck off, Caitlin."

"Quit it, both of you. Jimmy?" said Mary Jean, trying to catch the eye of her son, who sat staring at his plate. "Did you see Idaho after you dropped her off at home?"

Jimmy furiously shook his head no.

"Jimmy?" said Mary Jean. "Are you sure that Idaho hasn't maybe called you on the phone or anything?"

Again, Jimmy shook his head no, and Mary Jean thought that idea probably was pretty ridiculous, since Jimmy had never received a phone call in his entire life and probably would have no idea what to do if he did.

"I'm sorry, Stella," she said, returning to the phone. Then she had another idea. "Do you want to talk to Pete? Have him maybe put out an informal call for the squad cars to watch out for her?"

But Stella said no, she wasn't ready to do that. Idaho had developed a habit of hiding in the house, holding herself very still and quiet, sometimes doing it for hours at a time. Stella was going to make one more thorough search, and if she still couldn't find her, she'd call back.

When Mary Jean sat back down at the dinner table, she told them all what had happened. Franny laughed and said, yes, Idaho had done this once or twice to her, scaring her to death. It was spooky how clever she was about finding inventive hiding places, about never giggling or otherwise giving herself away no matter what you said or how close you came to where she'd hid. Franny said she was sure Idaho was there somewhere, in the house or in the yard, and that eventually Stella would find her.

Mary Jean relaxed after that, asking Franny about her test, listening to Pete's tale of a lost dog who had wandered into the police station, barely noticing when Jimmy hopped up before the rest of them were finished eating, grabbing a handful of cookies from the plate on the stove.

"Hey, mister," Mary Jean said, catching him just in time. "Where are you going with all those cookies?"

Jimmy shrugged. "My room."

"What are you going to do in your room?"

Again, the quick bob of the shoulders. "Eat cookies."

Mary Jean laughed. "All right," she said. "Go on."

It wasn't until they were clearing the table and she stood at the sink that she noticed a red wagon in the backyard, abandoned among the rest of the bikes and scooters and balls. What she noticed first was not so much the wagon itself but the feeling it evoked, a kind of warm misty nostalgic fondness. Had she had a wagon like that herself growing up? Was this a Rosebud moment?

But no, now it was coming back to her, fuzzily, through the cloud of steam rising from the hot water cascading onto the dishes. It wasn't she who had a wagon like that, it was someone she knew, it was . . . Stella. Yes, she thought, peering closer. In fact, not only did that look like Stella's old wagon from childhood, that *was* Stella's wagon. Yes, she was absolutely sure of it. She knew that white writing, knew the butterfly-shaped rust spot on the rear flank, the tires that Stella, in a fit of creativity, had edged in bright blue.

The one thing that was odd, in the darkening yard, was the hulking shapes within the wagon. Snapping off the water, ignoring the questions of her family, Mary Jean stepped outside into the chill autumn evening. There were two paper grocery bags, she could tell now, sitting in the wagon. When she got closer, she saw that one of them was filled with toys. And the other one was filled with pink and purple clothes.

Lifting the sacks, she strode into the house, thrusting them at Pete.

"What's this?" he said.

"What's this? It's Idaho's stuff, Sherlock. I'll bet that little girl is hiding, all right. Except I've got a feeling she's not hiding at Stella's, but right here under our very own noses."

Ten minutes later, Mary Jean pulled up in front of Stella's house, where every window blazed with light. Stella had obviously been through every room in the house, turning on every overhead light, every lamp, probably even using a flashlight to try to flush out her little daughter. Even in Jimmy's teeny room in Mary Jean's small house, Idaho had flattened herself between layers of dirty clothes in the bottom of the closet, and it was only Jimmy's hysterical protests, which grew louder the closer Mary Jean got, that gave the child away.

Mary Jean had left Idaho in Pete and the girls' care back at her house. Idaho insisted that if Mary Jean brought her back to her mother's, she would only run away again. And Mary Jean decided it might be better for her to reassure Stella that Idaho was safe and talk to her about what was going on if they didn't have to worry every second that the little girl might dart out the door or dive under the laundry.

Oh, my God, there was a For Sale sign in front of the house. So maybe the whole story that Idaho had choked out was true, not 90 percent fantasy, the way it would undoubtedly have been had it been coming out of Jimmy's mouth. Maybe

Stella really was planning to take her back to California, maybe she really was intending to leave very soon. "Please don't make me leave Homewood," the little girl had begged Mary Jean. "Please let me come and live with you."

Mary Jean lifted her fist to knock, but then just pushed the door open and called Stella's name.

A minute later, Stella appeared on the stairs, looking as if she'd been locked in the attic for a dozen years. Her hair was tangled, with dust and leaves caught in it. Her luminous face was smudged with dirt. Her eyes were wild, her clothes askew.

Mary Jean held up her hand. "She's at our house," she said.

"Oh," Stella said, all the air visibly leaving her body as she sank onto the stairs. "Thank God."

"She's fine," said Mary Jean. "She took your old wagon and somehow found her way over there. I discovered her hiding on the floor of Jimmy's closet."

"But I don't understand," Stella said. "Why didn't you bring her with you?"

Mary Jean considered how to put this most diplomatically, especially considering Stella's understandably fragile state.

"She's really freaked out, Stella," Mary Jean said. "She's still threatening to run away if you try to take her to California."

"She doesn't have a choice," Stella said, her mouth tightening. "I'm leaving tonight, and she's coming with me."

Mary Jean shook her head. "What's going on?"

"It was a mistake, thinking I could stay here," Stella said.

"Now it's time to get out, before I dig myself in any deeper."

"What are you talking about?" said Mary Jean. "You bought yourself this beautiful house. You were in this relationship. Did something happen with you and Henry?"

"He's a total nightmare," said Stella. "You were right about him."

"Okay, so, I can't pretend to be unhappy that you finally came to your senses about that. But why does that mean you have to leave?"

"Don't you see?" said Stella. "He was the reason I was staying in Homewood in the first place. He made it possible for me to buy that house, he introduced me to everyone in town, he gave me a life here."

"*He* gave you a life?" Mary Jean said incredulously. "You had a life here long before Henry fucking Sladowski set foot in New Jersey."

"When I was a kid, Mary Jean. If I stay here now, I'm going to be totally alone, stuck in this little house, with no money and no way of earning any. And every week I'll open the *Homewood Herald* to see my new mayor's asshole face taunting me. I don't think so, Mary Jean. It's better if I pack up what's left of my dignity and go back to L.A."

"Better for whom?" Mary Jean pressed her. "Definitely not better for Idaho, Stella. She's not doing this to make trouble for you; she genuinely wants to stay here. And not better for me, I'll tell you that. I need you, Stella. I've been missing you for a long time. And I was just beginning to think I might get you back again."

That seemed to give Stella pause. But only a brief one.

"It's better for me," Stella said. "I'm a selfish bitch, okay? But I'm leaving because it's better for me."

"But better for you *how?*" Mary Jean said. "Is there really something out there that you think is going to improve your life? Or are you just running away from what's here?"

Mary Jean hesitated. She could pull back now and say nothing more, making things easier for both Stella and herself. Or she could finally tell the truth, no matter how messy it was, knowing it might not even have any effect.

"Do you have anything to drink?" she asked.

"Of course," said Stella, crossing to the hutch. "I have Grey Goose, Glenfiddich, Bombay Sapphire, Martel—the finest bottles of everything. All full. My mother was saving them for some occasion that never arrived."

"Well, it's arrived now," said Mary Jean. "Pick one. Any one. I'll get the glasses and the ice."

It felt as if she were deciding to descend into something from which there would be no return—no return for their friendship, a confrontation that could drive Stella away forever. But it doesn't matter, she told herself, because if I let Stella leave now without telling her these things, she's never going to come back anyway.

Returning to the living room with two crystal glasses filled with ice, she set them down on the coffee table and waited while Stella filled each of them with the brandy she'd un-corked. Mary Jean took a long swallow before speaking.

"It seems to me you're always running away, Stella," she

said, keeping her voice steady, "instead of hanging in there and working out a real life for yourself."

"So what do you think I should have done instead?" Stella shot back. "Stayed here in Homewood and rented a little cottage and had four kids, like you?"

Mary Jean felt her hand tighten around her glass. "At least when I make a commitment, I stick to it. When I'm friends with someone, I don't just decide to leave them in the middle of the night and never come back and never even tell them why."

"Okay, you want to know why I left? I left because I wanted more for myself than I could get in Homewood fucking New Jersey. There was nothing keeping me here. I knew my mother would be behind me no matter what I did. Pete and I had broken up. And you—well, you had Pete. You didn't need me anymore."

"Of *course* I needed you! All the things I went through in my life, marrying Pete, having the kids, losing my mother, I always wished I could talk about them with you, lean on you. But you were never there for me."

"Well, you were never there for me either. I went through two divorces, had a kid on my own. Don't you think that I was lonely too?"

"In case this never occurred to you, you can't just pick up the phone and call a movie star. Hello, information? I'd like a number for Stella Powers, please. Yes, *that* Stella Powers."

"You could have gotten my number from my mother. Or told her you wanted to see me when I came to visit."

That was true. "But you were the one who left. You were the one who got famous. It was up to you to call me."

"Okay," said Stella. "Okay, since we're being so fucking honest, you want to know why I never called you, Mary Jean? I figured you'd become this boring housewife in the suburbs who'd have nothing to talk about."

"And I figured you'd become this snotty self-centered movie star who'd make me feel like shit about myself."

"Let's face it, Mary Jean. We were friends a long time ago, and a lot has changed, and we don't even like each other anymore."

"You're right," Mary Jean said, standing up and draining her glass. "I don't know why I even tried to connect with you again. You obviously don't care anything about me."

She felt as if she were going to burst into tears, but she wouldn't do that, refused to let herself break down in front of Stella, so instead she slammed her glass down on the coffee table hard enough to underscore her feelings. But the crystal shattered beneath her hand, slicing into the tender flesh between her forefinger and her thumb, a bright red bloom of blood spilling across the wood along with the golden brandy.

"Oh, my God! Here, I'll get something," Stella said, rushing toward the kitchen.

"Don't bother," Mary Jean said, holding her hand up, pressing her thumb across her palm in an effort to stop the bleeding. The blood kept pumping out at an alarming rate, faster as she walked toward the door.

"Don't be ridiculous," Stella snapped. "You can't drive like that."

"Then I'll wait in the car until it stops."

"You moron. Sit down here and let me get a towel, will you? We might have to go to the emergency room."

Mary Jean sank into the chair nearest the front door, her elbow propped on her knee, her hand still held aloft. Her arm was now covered with blood, and it was draining onto her pants. It didn't hurt, but she looked like a victim in a horror film. She felt as if she might faint.

Stella came scurrying out of the kitchen with a sheaf of wet paper towels and an ice cube tray.

"What's the ice for?" Mary Jean asked.

"Never mind. Just let me take care of you."

Mary Jean clamped her mouth closed while Stella tended to her, pressing a wad of paper towels into her palm and instructing her to hold them tight, then cleaning the dripping blood off her arm. After a few moments, she inspected Mary Jean's wound and replaced the plain towel with one wrapped around an ice cube.

"I think you're going to be okay," Stella said, hurrying into the kitchen to dispose of the bloody towels, coming out and pouring Mary Jean a fresh glass of brandy.

Mary Jean sat there, only now feeling the sting in her hand. She lifted the towel to check the cut, and as soon as she did, it started bleeding again.

"Maybe I should call Pete," she said to Stella.

"If you need to go to the emergency room, I can take

you. Why don't you sit back now and take it easy for a minute?"

Finally, Mary Jean slumped in the chair, lifting her foot onto a nearby needlepoint stool and closing her eyes.

After a long silence that felt more peaceful than awkward, Stella said, "I'm sorry, Mary Jean."

"You don't have to be sorry." Mary Jean didn't even want to look at her.

"No," Stella said. "I didn't mean it, when I said we didn't like each other. At least, I didn't mean it about myself. I love you, Mary Jean. I was so happy to see you again. I really liked it that we were becoming friends, that Idaho and Jimmy liked each other so much, that I was getting to know your family."

Mary Jean drew in a shuddering breath, and she finally opened her eyes to look at Stella, feeling the tears immediately well up.

"You're not just saying that?" she asked.

"I swear. I thought you were the one who was pulling away, with your big Sladowski vendetta and your political campaign and your issues with all those—you know, those blond moms."

Mary Jean managed a small smile. "It's not their blondness that bothers me," she said. "Or the fact that they're moms. It's that all they ever want to talk about is . . . curtains."

"That's not true," said Stella. "Sometimes they want to talk about kitchen renovation."

"And teachers," said Mary Jean. "And of course, property values."

"But I'm not like them," Stella said. "Am I?"

"No," Mary Jean admitted. Stella may have tried to fit in with that group, but she always had more spark, more individuality than that.

"See," said Stella. "I can't do that. I can't be a suburban mom, and I can't spend my life going to lunch with those women and pretending that the most important thing in the world is the color of my sofa."

"So why did you?" Mary Jean asked. "Why did you go out with Sladowski and hang out with his friends instead of with me?"

"I was jealous of you, Mary Jean. I've always been jealous of you. That's a big part of why I went to L.A. in the first place."

"*You* were jealous of *me*? But why?"

"Because you had Pete," Stella said simply, as if that explained everything.

"But you *dumped* Pete, Stella," Mary Jean said, not understanding. "You *told* me to go out with him. When I told you how much I loved him, you said you were *happy* for me."

"I was happy for you. But I was also jealous. I couldn't stand to see you with something so great in your life without trying to get something even greater for myself."

"So you went to L.A. to become a movie star," Mary Jean said, half under her breath. "But I'm confused. I didn't feel like I was in a competition with you."

"Maybe that's because you weren't. I was the one who always had to be the star, who always had to be the best. You were the supporting player."

It was true, Mary Jean saw now. She'd always been happy to

stand back, admire, defer, bask in Stella's reflected light—and sometimes, in the years since, even in Pete's, or now in Franny's. Stella was the one who'd always blazed the brightest, and Mary Jean had been drawn to that flame, relishing her role as the moth. *Preferring* to be the moth, her only responsibility to adore, without any pressure to shine.

"I don't want to be that anymore," she blurted.

Mary Jean got to her feet and started pacing. She could feel her pulse in her hand, but when she paused to look beneath the paper towel, there was no more blood.

"I'm sick of being good," she said. "Compliant. Sweet. Loving. Whatever anybody wanted—Pete, the kids, and yeah, I guess even you—I always said okay."

"And what about what you wanted?"

"I never wanted anything, until now," Mary Jean said, realizing as she said it that it was the truth. "For myself, I mean."

"But now . . . ," said Stella.

"Oh, yes, now. Now I want to be mayor. Or I don't know, maybe I just want to beat Sladowski. Maybe it's like you just wanting to beat me."

"I certainly understand that," Stella mumbled.

Mary Jean drank down her brandy and refilled the glass yet again. She had not had this much to drink since before Jimmy was born, had not really let herself get drunk since she was a teenager, before she had any children.

"I'm ready to win," said Mary Jean, realizing, even as she said it, that it was true.

"You go, girl," said Stella, grinning.

"And I want you to help me," said Mary Jean.

Now Stella's face clouded over. She knit her brows. "I can't," she said. "I told you. I'm leaving."

"There are people who love you here, Stella. *I* love you. And I need you. And you're not going to solve all your problems just by leaving them behind."

Stella considered that. "I'm going to solve some of them," she said.

"Yeah, but you're going to create some, too, with your daughter. Maybe much bigger ones."

"That dickhead Sladowski ruined my house. The Tree House. He pulled out every piece of detail in the place. And now he's forcing the closing when all my assets are tied up, and he's keeping my deposit. I need to go back to L.A. so I can earn some money."

"So we can use that," Mary Jean said, growing even more excited. "We'll blast the story all over the newspapers and shame Sladowski into selling you the house or make him look so bad he'll lose the mayoral race." She grinned. "Or both."

"That might be a way to pressure him to cut a deal with me," Stella admitted. "But I can't take on that house in the shape it's in now. It's much worse than it was before he started. I wouldn't have the first idea how to fix it, who to hire, what to do to make it look all right."

"So I'll help you," said Mary Jean. "All these years of reading *House & Garden* has prepared me perfectly for this moment. And in return, you can help me with my campaign."

"I don't know anything about politics, Mary Jean. It seems to

me that people whisper about Sladowski's shady real estate deal-
ings all the time, but they still like him because he seems important, he seems confident, he seems like—well, like a winner."

"And I seem—"

"You need to pull yourself together, Mary Jean. It's not
really the weight. It's the baggy clothes, the wild hair, the distracted look—"

"I've got four kids and a husband who's doing everything he
can to undermine me."

"Yeah, but if you really want to win this election, you can't
walk around advertising that. Nobody gives a shit about your
troubles, Mary Jean. They want to look at you and see somebody better than them, somebody more together and more en-
lightened and braver and stronger and smarter. Even if you
don't believe it, you've got to act like you believe it. That's what
making it in Hollywood was all about, and it's really not so different from making it here."

"You're the only one who can help me with that, Stella,"
said Mary Jean, feeling in her gut how desperately true that
was. "Please say you'll stay. You can help me, get back at that
fucking Sladowski, fix up your house the way you want it, and
make your little girl happy all at the same time."

"I don't know if I can handle it," said Stella.

"Don't think of it as politics. Think of it like a theatrical
production, and election day is opening night."

"I've always fantasized about doing theater."

"Well, now's your chance. Please, Stella. I love you and I
want you. Please say you'll stay."

"Okay," said Stella. "I'll stay until the election."

"And then?"

"And then we'll see."

"If November comes and you still want to leave, I'll help you pack and I'll do what I can to make Idaho feel better about moving and I won't make you feel the slightest bit guilty. As long as you promise to say good-bye."

"I promise," said Stella, putting her slender arms around Mary Jean and pulling her into a tight hug.

Now she really had her friend back, Mary Jean felt. And she was going to do whatever she needed to do to make sure it was forever.

CHAPTER

13

"**H**ey, lady!"

The voice of the off-duty fireman, one of the friends of Mary Jean's brothers who had taken over work on the house, seemed to be coming from the bathroom. Stella set down the brush she'd been using to paint—very badly—the window frame in the bedroom that would be Idaho's. She'd always thought painting had looked like fun; it had always seemed like such a quick and near-effortless way to transform a room, the only hard work putting up with the smell. After not even two hours spent sanding the frame and taping the panes and working with the brush, she knew better.

Stella pushed gently on the bathroom door in time to see

the fireman who was working in there rip a huge hunk of new drywall off the wall behind the shower. All the beautiful old subway tiles she'd been trying to match had been torn out and smashed into unusable bits by Sladowski's men, who had covered the plaster walls of the bathroom—all the plaster walls of the house, it turned out—with drywall. And now this new workman was tearing *that* off.

"What are you doing?" Stella cried.

"They didn't use waterproof wallboard back here," the fireman said. "This has all got to come out."

"All of it?" Stella said, her heart sinking.

"All of it that's going to get tile on top of it," said the fireman, "but that's not the problem. Come here."

"What?" said Stella, edging closer.

"On second thought, are you sure you wanna see this?"

In fact, that question was enough to make her sure she *didn't* want to see whatever it was he was thinking of showing her. But it also let her know that she had no choice.

"What?" she said again, going to stand next to him.

He jutted his chin toward the wall, peeling off another chunk of wallboard.

"Bugs," he said.

She saw them then, hundreds, thousands of them, antlike creatures scurrying away from the new light, along the old beams.

She did the only sensible thing. She screamed.

"Carpenter ants," explained the fireman, once she'd calmed down. "At some point it got wet back here, and that drew them up. You need to get an exterminator in here pronto, starting in the basement."

"Oh, God," she said, feeling as if she might faint. "Okay."

"We're lucky they didn't tile this over before we opened it up, or it was going to get wet back there forever," the workman said. "Then one of these days you'd crash right down to the floor below."

This constituted a new definition of luck as far as Stella was concerned. Luck, in her past, had involved landing the lead in a movie with a good director. Or finding out your prenup was going to hold when you got divorced. Not apprehending the bugs before they ate a hole in your house so big you'd fall through your own floor.

"Am I going to be able to reach an exterminator on Saturday?" Stella asked.

"Why not?" said the workman. "Bugs don't take weekends off."

She'd been surprised at how easy it had been to get the house from Sladowski. After she decided to stay in town, she called her lawyer in L.A., who made Sladowski an offer, which Sladowski refused until Stella talked to the *Homewood Herald*. The day the *Herald* hit the stands, with her tear-stained face occupying the entire top half of the front page, Sladowski called her lawyer and made a deal. The closing had been effective immediately, with Sladowski holding the mortgage on the house. Stella hated the idea of owing the man anything, much less a couple of million dollars, but her lawyer assured her it was the only solution. Once her divorce was settled, she could get another mortgage and pay off Slad-owski. Until then, if she wanted the house, she'd have to live with this arrangement.

Sladowski even agreed to refund the cash from her original down payment, on the condition that she wouldn't hold him liable for the condition of any of the work he had already done on the house. As with most things having to do with Henry Sladowski, she now saw this offer was far less generous than it originally appeared.

Stella wandered downstairs, calling for Mary Jean to find out what exterminator to hire. She kept coming upon guys painting walls that were ready to be finished, and others tear-ing out things that had been done wrong, but didn't find Mary Jean until she opened the door to the basement and called down.

Stella had never actually been down here before, not even after she'd seized control of the house back from Sladowski. This was Boy Stuff Central, and she had no desire to examine concrete walls and exposed wiring and the mystery of where her heat came from. But then Mary Jean's voice called merrily up to her, beckoning her down.

It was worse than she thought, the furnace resembling a prehistoric octopus, the cement floors cracked to expose the dirt beneath, the ancient drainpipes and wiring that might have been installed by Thomas Edison himself nearly scaring her right back upstairs.

Mary Jean didn't sound frightened, however.

"Stella," she said excitedly. "Look at this."

Stella followed her friend's voice until she found her standing at the far end of the basement.

"It's all the original doors," Mary Jean said, running her hand over the tall wooden planks, each with five panels. "I think these were taken out before Sladowski got his hands on the place."

"Wow," Stella said, coming closer. "These are amazing."

"And there are leaded-glass windows back here, too. Plus some cool old toilets and a cast iron sink and a seriously antique stove."

"This is great," said Stella. "But I have no idea what to do with all these things."

"It could look really terrific, since Sladowski stripped the whole place down, to add these old elements back in. You know: the modern minimalist thing mixed with the truly antique."

Stella was impressed. "How do you know this stuff?"

Mary Jean blushed. "I've been fantasizing about having a place of my own to fix up for years. I even thought I might be an architect or a decorator at one point."

"So what happened?"

Mary Jean waved her hand dismissively. "The same thing that always happened. I got pregnant or the kids needed me and I quit. But listen, you should get in touch with this woman I know, Kennedy, whose daughter is in Jimmy and Idaho's class. She fixed up this old house after she split with her husband and got good enough at it that she turned it into a business. You could hire her to take charge of this place."

"I'd love to," said Stella, "but isn't this something I should be doing by myself? I thought this was part of learning to have a real life."

"That doesn't mean you can't have help. You couldn't do it without those guys upstairs, could you? I'd be glad to give you advice on the design part, after the election."

"You think you're going to have more time then?" said Stella, smiling slyly. "You're going to be mayor! See, this is evidence that deep down you still don't believe in yourself."

"You're right," admitted Mary Jean.

"Don't tell me I'm right. Tell me you don't have time to hang around in this basement talking to me because you've got to get out there and beat that son of a bitch."

"I have to do that," Mary Jean said. "Just what you said. Right now."

"Fuck the house," Stella said. "We'll get this friend of yours to figure out the house. I've got to devote my energy to fixing up you."

So much of what was involved in the campaign was the same as so much of what was involved in the house: painstaking, minute, exhausting work with little visible payoff. How did anybody ever get anything done? Stella wondered. Oh, right. They had a staff.

Mary Jean's staff so far was Stella, a handful of Mary Jean's siblings, and a few moms who were able to give an hour here or there. For Stella, calling random citizens to ask them to vote for Mary Jean, stuffing envelopes, or handing out leaflets got discouraging fast.

On Saturday afternoon, after writing the exterminator a massive check, she went to take up what had begun to feel like Mary Jean's campaign headquarters: the post outside the front door of the Cozy Corner. If things got too grim, she figured, she could always duck inside and drink a milkshake. Jimmy and Idaho were both invited to a birthday party, so the afternoon was clear.

But when she got to the Cozy Corner, she stopped and stared, stupefied. The restaurant was closed down. The windows were papered over. Even the sign was gone. Instead, there was a huge orange and blue plastic banner flapping above the doorway. "Coming Soon," it read. "TGI Friday's."

She turned around and marched down Broad Street, fuming. A few people called out hellos, but the best she could manage in response was a wave. She was heading, blinders on, for Mary Jean's house. Once she reached it, instead of knocking on the door, she walked straight inside.

She was always stunned anew to see how small the house was, the front door opening directly into the tiny living room, the kitchen fully occupied by its round table to the right, one of the crowded bedrooms visible through an open door to the left. How did all the Wrights manage to function in this tiny space? Stella had had hotel rooms bigger than this, private *dressing* rooms with more space to spread out. Her mother's house, which had never stopped feeling cramped to her, suddenly seemed like a palace.

Mary Jean sat in front of a computer on a rickety red table in a corner of the living room next to the TV.

"What's up?" she said.

"Oh God," said Stella, finally remembering her earlier shock, the one that had driven her here. "I went to hand out leaflets, and you'll never believe what happened. The Cozy Corner is shut down."

"The prick," said Mary Jean. "That's been coming for months."

"Yeah, but he knew I loved that restaurant. He even told me he was considering letting them stay on. I bet he did this to get back at me."

"I wouldn't put it past him."

"All right," Stella said. "This is war."

Mary Jean laughed uncomfortably. "I thought it was war already."

Stella blew out a dismissive gust of air. "I haven't even fired my first shot."

Stella plopped herself down on the sofa, grabbing a handful of papers from Mary Jean's stack of campaign literature, trying to think of a plan. Finally she came up with something: they'd surprise Sladowski tonight during a speech he was giving at the Homewood Women's Club. These were mostly older ladies, not plugged into Mary Jean's mom network or part of her townie circle. Stella guessed that many of them had not even heard of Mary Jean. But they would tonight.

At home that evening, after she and Idaho ate dinner and Caitlin—Caitlin had been filling in for Franny more and more lately—showed up to babysit, Stella retreated to her room to get ready for their surprise appearance at the women's club.

This was like getting dressed for the Oscars, she reasoned, or for a first date with someone important: she had to look fantastic. She even unearthed for the occasion one of her L.A. outfits that was still lying in the bottom of a storage box, a Chanel suit that looked gorgeous, powerful . . . as well as drop-dead sexy.

She was shocked when she picked up Mary Jean that evening to find her friend wearing a saggy green skirt and a pilled brown sweater, with what looked like a fresh ketchup stain on the cuff.

"I thought we were going to dress up," said Stella.

Mary Jean frowned down at her outfit. "I did dress up."

Stella sighed. "Remember," she said, "we have to take him by storm. We've got to do better than this."

It was too late to get to the stores in time to buy anything new. Stella first tried hunting through Mary Jean's closet, where she discovered that in fact everything there was in worse shape than what Mary Jean was already wearing. In the twins' room, though, she found a bright red scarf that drew the eye away from the outfit's worst aspects, plus a nearly new suede jacket that was tight but, worn open, made the whole thing look chic and polished.

"You can't wear that!" Franny protested, trying to tug it off her mother's shoulders.

"It is her new jacket," Mary Jean said, starting to take it off.

"You're wearing this," Stella said, pulling it firmly into place. "Franny, really. You need to be more generous to your mother. Come on, Mary Jean. You look terrific."

They were early to the women's club meeting, guessing correctly that this would be a punctual crowd—and moreover that Sladowski wouldn't arrive until it was time to give his speech. The event was open to the public, so they didn't have to declare their intentions at the door, but once they were inside, Stella and Mary Jean began shaking hands and introducing Mary Jean as Sladowski's challenger in the mayoral race.

Stella found herself diverted almost immediately by a group of women who couldn't have cared less about Mary Jean—or Henry Sladowski, for that matter—but knew very well who Stella was and wanted to hear all about Hollywood. Had she ever met Clint Eastwood, and was he as sexy as he looked on-screen? Did she know John Travolta and Kelly Preston? They seemed like such a *happy* couple. And what about that Demi Moore? What did she see in that young boy?

The women were so determined to occupy Stella that she wasn't able to see what was going on until the chairwoman of the club began her introduction of Henry Sladowski. Then the women scurried to take their seats and Stella moved to stand against the back wall, from where she could see Mary Jean still in the foyer, huddled in a whispered conversation with a wheelchair-bound member of the group.

Stella tried motioning for Mary Jean to move into the main room, but Mary Jean didn't respond. Stella started to feel panicky. She had to come up with some way to get Mary Jean to stand up and speak before all these people, or her big plan of crashing Sladowski's event would be pointless.

"And so we are proud to welcome tonight," said the

women's club chairwoman, "Homewood's next mayor, Henry Sladowski."

Henry rushed to the podium—How had he gotten into the room, anyway? Had he been smuggled in through the back door, like the president?—all self-satisfied smiles and fake humility. Stella was so ashamed that she had ever been involved with him. How had she let herself be taken over so quickly and completely? Why had she not been able to see who he really was?

Because I'm just beginning to see who I really am, she thought, with the force of truth. Eddie Skinner, Idaho's father, my agent Marty—all those men were a mystery to me because I was such a mystery to myself.

"When I am your mayor," Henry Sladowski was saying, "I promise that you will live in a more prosperous Homewood, a more beautiful Homewood . . ."

Stella darted a glance at Mary Jean. This was a perfect opportunity for Mary Jean to jump in, to introduce herself and change the tenor of the meeting. But Mary Jean was still locked in whispered discussion with the woman in the wheelchair, utterly oblivious to what was going on in the main room.

"Mr. Sladowski," Stella called, waving her hand and stepping forward. "How can you be so sure you're going to be our next mayor, when Mary Jean Wright is running against you?"

Henry brought his hand up to shield his eyes, finally recognizing her among the crowd.

"Mrs. Wright is not a serious contender for the office," Henry Sladowski said. "There are often these fringe candidates, from the Socialist Party or some such . . ."

"Mary Jean Wright is not a Socialist," said Stella angrily, moving toward the front of the room. "Mrs. Wright is a life-long member of this community, as were her parents before her. She's a mother, the wife of a Homewood policeman, the sister of firefighters, an advocate for all the residents of this town. How long have you lived here, Mr. Sladowski?"

"Longer than you, Ms. Powers. As I understand it, you're not even registered to vote in this town or this state. You're a resident of California, are you not? Where you're embroiled in a lawsuit with your estranged husband?"

Shit, score one for Sladowski, but Stella had not played crusading attorneys in three feature-length films for nothing. She drew herself up as tall as possible and strode with what she hoped was a commanding air toward the front of the room.

"You're correct, Mr. Sladowski, though I'm in the process of changing my permanent residence from California to New Jersey, where I was born. In fact, many of the women in this room knew my late mother, Josephine Powers, who founded the soup kitchen in Homewood and worked at the local chapter of Planned Parenthood."

There were nods and murmurs around the room.

"And of course, I'm sure many of you know me, if only from my movies."

A few of the women who'd crowded around Stella began clapping, and soon the whole room broke out in applause. Stella noticed that even Mary Jean had interrupted her hallway conversation and, though still sitting beside the lady in the wheelchair, was at least clapping along with everyone else.

"Thank you," said Stella. "But the real star here is Mary Jean Wright. Mary Jean, stand up and allow me to introduce you."

Mary Jean stood in the back of the room to scattered applause, holding up her hands, nodding in gratitude, and then, to Stella's consternation, sitting back down.

"Well," said Stella, trying to improvise. "Remember, ladies, you do have a choice at the polls this November, so make the correct one and vote for Mary Jean Wright."

"You were great," Mary Jean said happily.

Stella yanked the wheel of the car and pulled over to the curb with a satisfying squeal of her tires.

"I wasn't supposed to be great," she said. "*You* were supposed to be great."

"But," Mary Jean said, confused, "you're so much better at getting up in front of a crowd. And I was talking to that poor woman, who's having her medical benefits cut off—"

"Listen to me," said Stella. "I think it's incredibly admirable that you're willing to spend so much time with someone like that, I really do. That sense of empathy is what's going to make you a fantastic mayor. But you're never going to *be* mayor if you don't learn to kill more birds with each stone."

"B-b-b-birds," Mary Jean began.

"Voters!" cried Stella. "I don't know shit about politics, but I know that when you're promoting a movie, you can't do it by having a long talk with one fan at a time. You've got to get your point across to the maximum number of people at once."

"But it's hard standing up there," said Mary Jean. "I don't feel as confident, I can't be as commanding, as you are."

"Then quit," Stella said.

Now Mary Jean looked scared. But Stella wasn't saying it to scare her. She was perfectly serious.

"Do what I've always done and run away. Because unless you're willing to put yourself out there, to get up onstage and have your picture taken and even go on TV, you don't have a chance in hell of getting elected. You might as well pack it in right now."

"Maybe if I looked like you." Mary Jean faltered. "If I had your hair, your clothes . . ."

Stella took out her phone and started dialing.

"What are you doing?" asked Mary Jean.

"Do you want to feel better about how you look? Have more energy, more confidence? Are you willing to do what it takes to get up there in front of a crowd and win this goddamn election? Because I don't care if you do, Mary Jean, I really don't. I'd be just as happy, now that I have you back again, to keep you all to myself."

"No, I want to," said Mary Jean.

"Sure?"

"Sure," she said more firmly.

"Okay," said Stella, starting to dial again. "We're going to the spa."

Stella secretly offered to pay Franny $200 to stay overnight with Idaho and Jimmy and take them to school on Monday morning. She knew if Mary Jean guessed how much the child care alone cost, not to mention the price of the spa itself, she'd never agree to do it. But Mary Jean needed the equivalent of fitness-and-beauty shock treatment, Stella figured. Some people might think the whole thing was shallow, but without it Mary Jean was never going to break through and become a star.

As soon as they arrived at the pretty old hotel in the country that had been converted to the spa, Stella knew that Mary Jean wasn't the only one who needed it. The prospect of an overnight away from her child, away from the new routines of cooking and cleaning and housework—a few of the elements of real life she could have lived without—made her melt even before anyone laid a finger on her.

"I've never had a massage," Mary Jean said, when they'd settled into their room and changed into their big fluffy robes and were checking off which services they'd like to have.

"Never?" squealed Stella. "I used to have a massage therapist on staff."

"How often did you have massages?"

"In the morning. At night. And sometimes at lunch, if I didn't have a scene right away."

"You know, I never have really asked you about it, your time in Hollywood," Mary Jean said. "Was it fabulous, being a movie star?"

Was it fabulous? It was easier to think so, the longer she lived here, the further away it seemed. But when she'd been back in Hollywood, she'd gotten used to thinking that the hours were too long and the pressure too intense, the constant scrutiny and rejection too much for anyone to bear.

"I think it was fabulous," she said, running her mind over all the years she'd done it, "for about a week and a half, when I was twenty-eight. I had just married my agent, and I thought I was in love, and he was working hard on my behalf, so I got offered all these great parts. It just felt like, for one single minute, that I was really at the top and I was going to stay there forever."

"In my mind, you did stay there forever," said Mary Jean. "Just the fact that you were out there, in the movies, that your picture was in every magazine and everyone knew your name—I figured it was wonderful, and you were happy all the time."

"I figured you were happy all the time," said Stella.

Mary Jean made a face. "How did you figure that?"

"You had Pete, who I knew, don't forget, was truly the love of your life. You had all these babies. You stayed married. You were surrounded by this family and this security that seemed like a dream to me, when I spent every day wavering between believing I was a goddess and wanting to kill myself."

"Oh, Stella, I can't even bear to hear you say that."

Stella couldn't bear to say it either, couldn't believe she'd ever felt it, but she had, she knew she had, remembered feeling so low she'd imagine how she would do it, and the worse she felt, the more often she visited the shrink, the more drugs she took for depression and anxiety, and then the more she felt that life wasn't worth living.

It was Idaho's father, ironically enough, who helped lift her out of that: terrible husband, wonderful friend, and look what a gift he'd given her.

"It's all better now," she said. "I never feel that way anymore; I haven't felt it for a really long time. Come on, let's indulge."

Over the next several hours, they each had a massage and a facial, a hydrotherapy treatment, a haircut, and a makeup application. They ate a 500-calorie dinner that tasted like 5,000 and consumed an entire bottle—surely that made up for the calories they'd saved on the meal—of champagne. Tomorrow, Stella decided, she'd indoctrinate Mary Jean into the diet and exercise program the trainer had put her on when she'd had to wear a bikini through the entire 121 minutes of the deep-sea thriller *Undertow*. But for now, all she could manage was to crawl into bed.

Stella was just about to drift off to sleep when she heard Mary Jean's voice from the other bed.

"Stella?" she said. "Do you think that was better than sex?"

Stella smiled in the dark against her crisp cotton pillow. "Depends on what sex."

"Any sex," said Mary Jean.

"Let's see," said Stella. "It was definitely better than sex with Ben Affleck, but not quite as good as sex with George Clooney."

Mary Jean was quiet for so long, Stella began to think she'd fallen asleep, but then she burst out, "You're *kidding*!"

"I am kidding," Stella said, laughing.

"Come on, Stella, have you ever had sex with anybody famous?"

Stella considered. There was her hot affair with the married actor, but she'd sworn to him that she would never tell anyone, and she never would—not even Mary Jean. She'd slept with plenty of directors and producers and writers and musicians and actors who worked regularly, but whose names nobody knew, so they didn't count.

"Is Eddie Skinner famous?" she asked.

His band was certainly famous, or at least it had been in the era of their few big hits, when Eddie's name had been well known.

"Sort of," said Mary Jean.

"Well, as much as I hate him, I have to admit that he was great in bed. My only mistake was thinking that meant I should marry him."

"What about Idaho's father?"

"Disastrous. Gay, but in the closet. I should have guessed what was going on, but he was so sweet, I really loved him, so I didn't want to see it."

"Oh, that's so tragic," said Mary Jean. "Is he still in touch with Idaho?"

"Sadly, no. He moved back to England and came out, and given his lifestyle choice, we both agreed it was better if he stayed out of the picture."

Stella thought about this, about her own invisible father

whose identity only became compelling to her once she was grown up. Then, when she finally went looking for him, she'd discovered he was long dead.

"But maybe I should reconsider that," Stella said. "He was a nice man, and maybe when Idaho's a little older it might be a good idea for him to come back into her life."

"That's hard," said Mary Jean. "Plus, it sucks that the man who fathered your child was the one who was worst in bed."

"Oh, he wasn't the worst," said Stella, feeling herself begin to smile again. "That honor would definitely go to Henry Sladowski."

Mary Jean half rose in her bed. "Tell me."

"Well, I only had sex with him once. Though it was so pathetic, I wasn't even sure it was happening *when* it was happening."

"Ugh, gag me with a spoon," Mary Jean said, one of her favorite expressions from junior high.

"Yeah," giggled Stella. "Gross me out."

"Do you remember when we were little," said Mary Jean, "and we used to try and figure out what was the big secret the grown-ups were hiding from us?"

"Yeah, and you told me about penises, which you knew about because you had brothers, and I didn't believe you."

"Neither of us even knew we had a vagina until the first time we tried to put in tampons."

"All those movies they showed us at school about getting your period," said Stella, sitting up herself now, hugging her knees and shaking her head. "They acted like they were answering all our questions, and they just created all kinds of new ones."

"And then we'd ask each other. Talk about the blind leading the blind."

"Yeah. 'But where does the boy put his thing, Mary Jean—in your *behind*?'"

"Right, and I remember: 'I hear if you do it right in the middle between your period, you won't get pregnant.'"

"Apparently you believed that one."

"No, actually, I got pregnant with Peter right after my period ended. Pete talked me into doing it without a rubber, and according to the pamphlet on the rhythm method I found in my mother's underwear drawer, it was supposed to be safe."

"You had only to look at your mother to realize the fallacy of that one." Stella laughed. "Though I remember, Pete never did like wearing those rubbers."

Suddenly, the presence of Pete, their shared history with him, hung heavy between them.

"What about you?" Stella asked, trying to nudge the conversation in another direction. "Who was your best and worst?"

"They were both Pete," Mary Jean said, sounding surprised. "Obviously, it's been only Pete."

It was obvious, once Stella stopped to think about. But it was so hard to imagine any woman her age having had only one lover in all those years.

"So how is that?" asked Stella. "Do you get bored? Do you

know each other so well, it's fantastic? Do you ever feel like if you have to do it with him one more time, you'll die?"

"Yes, yes, and yes," said Mary Jean. "It doesn't feel like I've had just one man in my life. He's been all different men: rough and gentle, really routine and really hot. There's one kind of sex when it's Saturday night and we've been out and we haven't done it in a couple of weeks so we just do, and that's okay. And then there's the kind when we're alone in the house and we can really let go and it's amazing."

"Amazing?" Stella asked, feeling amazed herself. "Truly? After, what is it, four kids and twenty-two or twenty-three years?"

"Yes, amazing," said Mary Jean. "I can't even believe it myself, sitting here talking about it. But then it happens, and I'm amazed all over again."

Stella settled back down into bed, pulling her covers up to her ears and feeling as if now she could sleep. By any objective measure, she thought, most people would guess that Mary Jean should be the one who was envious of Stella. But tonight, there was envy in only one heart, and that was Stella's own.

CHAPTER 14

Mary Jean was still floating when she walked into her house the next evening, but her euphoria was cut short by the sight of her family draped across the living room furniture. In a mere thirty-six hours, they'd turned the place into a shambles, dirty plates and empty soda cans and discarded toys and crusty socks littering every surface. What's more, none of them seemed the least bit motivated to do anything about it. The TV was blaring a *Simpsons* video, Franny was thumbing through *Us Weekly,* Caitlin was glued to the computer, Pete was making marks in his beloved Homewood ordinance book. Only Idaho said hello to her.

"Idaho, your mom's waiting outside," said Mary Jean. "I'll walk you out, and you'll see Jimmy in school tomorrow."

Once the little girl had gone, Pete looked at her and said, "What's for dinner?"

"What's for dinner? What's for dinner!? I was going to ask you the same thing!"

"We were waiting for you to get home."

"Obviously!" she cried, alarmed at the edge in her voice. It was hard to believe she'd been in a state of complete bliss only moments before.

Did her family always make her this angry? Or was she usually just operating with so much stress that she wasn't as aware of her emotional needle hopping up into the red zone? She tried to summon the voice of the spa's yoga instructor, telling her to concentrate on her breath, tried to remember the soothing feel of the massage therapist's hands easing the tension in her neck.

"I've been away," she said, attempting to exude calm. "I thought you would have dinner waiting."

"You were at a fucking spa!" cried Franny, leaping to her feet. "Jesus!"

"Don't you dare talk to me like that," Mary Jean said, whirling on Franny. "Everybody else in this family does things for themselves, because it's fun, because they want to. For once, I'm entitled to do that too without feeling like I have to pay for it by coming home and picking up after everybody from the whole time I was gone."

"Oh, Jesus," Franny said, rolling her eyes and looking toward her twin sister, who leaned so close to the computer that her nose bumped the screen.

Mary Jean focused on Pete. "You go to the Y and lift weights," she said. "You have your town meetings and your political events. I don't expect you to come home and pick up my socks and do my dishes and cook my fucking dinner then."

"I've been on my own with the kids for two days," Pete said. "I'm not also going to be cleaning up and cooking dinner."

Mary Jean crossed her arms over her chest. "Well, I'm not cooking dinner."

"I have to study for my SATs," said Franny. "I'm definitely not cooking dinner."

"I have to help her study for the SATs," said Caitlin, who'd scored close to 2400 on the test in junior year and so wasn't bothering to take it again.

Jimmy, who hadn't seemed to be paying attention, suddenly launched himself off the couch, hurtling across the living room to crash full-speed into Mary Jean.

"I'll cook dinner for you, Mommy," he said, smiling up at her to reveal the Oreo crumbs lodged in his teeth.

"That's okay, sweetheart," Mary Jean said, stroking his hair and glaring over his head at Pete. "We'll order pizza from Vesuvio's."

Pete finally looked alarmed. "Vesuvio's? That's too expensive."

"Tough," said Mary Jean.

Even after the Vesuvio's indulgence, Mary Jean discovered the next morning that she'd lost four pounds. Buoyed, she dropped off Jimmy for school and met Stella to begin her new daily regimen. They ran together to the Y, did an hour side-by-side on the elliptical trainer and the stationary bike followed by weight training, then ran back and retrieved their cars and went their separate ways. The next day, Mary Jean was daunted to discover, they did the same thing. And the day after that and the day after that.

Even when Stella wasn't there, she dictated Mary Jean's new routine. Once she got home from exercising, Mary Jean spent another hour getting ready for the day—which was approximately fifty-eight minutes more than she used to spend.

At the spa she'd had her first-ever eyebrow waxing, manicure, and pedicure, and though no one was even going to see her toenails until next summer, now she had to maintain them along with all the other body parts she'd grown comfortable ignoring. Instead of her old supermarket all-in-one shampoo and conditioner, she now used a special shampoo to counteract dryness and a rinse-out conditioner and a leave-in conditioner plus a grooming cream. Mary Jean had made the mistake of leaving these products, which had been purchased by Stella, congregated on the back of the toilet, only to discover that the girls used half of everything the first day, so now she hid the hair care products in the washing machine, along with the skin cleansers and moisturizer and makeup that Stella had bought for her.

Stella had also taken her to a hair salon in Homewood, where she'd had her long hair professionally trimmed for the first time since high school. Pete complained that it was too short—ridiculous, since it still reached the middle of her back—but Mary Jean was amused to discover he didn't even notice that she'd colored her hair. She'd always sworn she'd never do this, but Stella had insisted, so the stylist had covered the gray with Mary Jean's natural brown and then thrown in a few blond highlights. It had looked so radical in the salon, but the only one in her family who noticed was Franny, and she told Mary Jean she thought it looked awesome.

Franny also approved of the clothes Stella had bought Mary Jean, so expensive that Mary Jean had limited the purchases to two pairs of pants and two sweaters that could all be worn again and again. It made her uncomfortable to have Stella spending so much money on her—it was generous, but it also pointed up her own comparative poverty—but Stella had argued that she was charging everything and wouldn't have to pay for it until after the divorce was final, when money would be no object. Stella had insisted on adding a pair of shoes, which cost more than all the shoes Mary Jean had bought in her entire life put together.

"Prada," Franny breathed, reverently lifting the black patent leather pumps. "Can I borrow these?"

Mary Jean was about to say sure, but Stella, who was there helping her prepare for a speech to the Nokomis PTA, cut in. "No, you may not. I happen to know you can afford to buy your own designer shoes. What do you do with all that money you make babysitting, anyway?"

Franny shrugged. "My parents make me save it."

Franny, in fact, was being so obedient about studying and saving her money that Mary Jean felt at least that was one worry she could cross off her list, though there were seemingly dozens of new concerns to take its place. If only she could have Stella's easy command, with her kids, with strangers, with the world. When she heard Stella say something simple yet powerful like the "No, you may not" she'd said to Franny, Mary Jean would whisper it to herself, trying for the same rhythm and tone. It wasn't Stella's words so much as the way she pronounced them that made people listen, Mary Jean felt, thinking that maybe if she could imitate Stella's voice, she might summon the confidence behind it.

There was more to the outside-in approach than she would have thought. After a lifetime of dismissing the importance of such surface qualities as well-shaped nails and good shoes, after an adulthood devoted to believing in the power of compassion and devotion and, yes, love over an easy laugh or a trim waistline, Mary Jean was amazed to find that polishing up her outer self was making people pay more serious attention to what was underneath. Not only other people; it was making *her* take herself more seriously.

It wasn't easy. If Stella hadn't been there waiting for her every morning, she would have fallen off the exercising horse around about day four. And she found it even more difficult to keep eating right, sticking to grilled chicken or fish and salad when her family was chowing down on pasta or hamburgers with ice cream sundaes for dessert. She would have rather died than confess this to Stella, but sometimes on her way home from the gym she stopped and bought herself a jelly doughnut.

"Pretend you're a movie star getting in shape for a role," Stella told her. "Pretend that in a few days, you're going to have to be photographed in a bathing suit and that millions of people are going to see that picture."

Mary Jean's powers of imagination were less vivid than Stella's, and besides, she'd have to eat lettuce and lift weights for months before she could imagine appearing in a bathing suit at the Homewood public pool, never mind on the big screen. So instead, as she ran, she cultivated the fantasy that she was in training for a boxing match, with Sladowski as her opponent. She had to get in shape, physically and mentally, to not only climb in the ring with him but win, and she had to do it in time for their debate next Tuesday night.

"Breathe," said Stella.

"I am breathing."

"Breathe deeply. Remember how Carlos taught us at the spa."

Mary Jean tried drawing the air in through her nostrils, sucking it deep into her abdomen even though the seat belt was cutting into her stomach. But then she thought of Sladowski and it all came rushing out and she started hyperventilating again.

"What if he starts attacking me?" she asked Stella.

"We've been over this," Stella said. "No matter what he says, come back with your own agenda. Just pretend you're George Bush."

"Pretending I'm Bush is going to make me even more nervous," Mary Jean said.

"Well, then pretend you're Clinton, one of those expert politicians who just knows how to deflect whatever's coming in from the outside and maintain their own vision. You better believe Sladowski knows how to do it."

Mary Jean breathed in again and managed to get the air down deep this time. It really did help her feel less panicky, more in control.

"At least I've got my opening line," she said to Stella.

She'd been practicing with the kids before she left the house, trying out her handshake on them as well as different forms of introduction, as a "How to Be More Confident" web site had advised her.

"Let's hear it," said Stella.

Mary Jean squared her shoulders and adopted her people-meeting voice: "I'm Mary Jean Wright, and I hope you'll vote Wright on election day."

"That's good!" Stella said happily.

"Franny came up with it."

"Very good. Remember, we're going to work that room, meeting as many people as we can, getting their names so the crowd will seem friendlier when you're up there. You'll look out in the audience, and instead of seeing a sea of strangers you'll see Linda and Mike and Susan."

"What if someone tries to keep talking?" asked Mary Jean.

"Smile and nod and keep moving."

"I always get stuck at parties," Mary Jean said, remembering all the nights she'd gotten marooned, willingly or more often not, in the corner with someone who wanted to tell her all about their divorce or their mother's recent battle with cancer. "I never know what to say to get away."

"Don't say anything. Or just say 'Excuse me.' Nobody can argue with that."

"Excuse me," Mary Jean whispered, practicing.

"Now, let's try out some questions. Mrs. Wright, how would you handle the school budget and still keep property taxes in line?"

This was one of Mary Jean's pet issues. "We have one of the best school systems in the metropolitan area. People move here specifically for the schools, and to maintain the quality we're going to have to keep property taxes where they are."

"No, no, no," said Stella.

"But that's what I believe."

"But you have to put it in prettier terms. Maybe you should tell them the story of Jimmy. How Jimmy is really blossoming with the arts program and the more creative forms of teaching. How Homewood's diverse and innovative education system has led the way for schools across the country. How our kids, everyone's kids, are the community's most valuable resource. Turn it into one of those sappy television commercials, and by the time you're done, people will be asking you to *raise* their taxes."

"If I say something like that," said Mary Jean, "I'd want it to be from the heart."

"But you have to remember," said Stella, "that you're running against somebody who doesn't have a heart."

When Mary Jean thought about that, the fear was near overwhelming.

"Sometimes I think," she told Stella, "I don't even really want to be mayor. The more I find out about how this town works, the more I see that a lot of the real decisions aren't even made by the mayor—they're made by the town manager or the council. Maybe I'd be better in one of those backseat roles."

"If Sladowski is mayor, you won't get a shot at any role. You won't even live in this town," Stella reminded her. "You're just scared. But you've come so far, you can't quit now."

Mary Jean plastered on her smile as instructed by Stella and waded into the sea of people, Stella directly behind her.

"Hi, I'm Mary Jean Wright, and I hope you'll vote Wright in the mayoral election," she said, feeling as if she were reading from a script as she shook hands with the first person she encountered.

"I want to know what you plan to do about the parking at Broad Street. I was trying to go to the Gap the other day, and I had to circle the block three times and ended up having to park way down by the Food Giant."

"Oh, I know," said Mary Jean. "It's terrible. And then if you're going to buy groceries, there's nowhere to park in the lot. I really have no idea what can be done about the parking—"

She felt Stella's knuckles in her back.

"I'm going to look into it, though. Can I give you a call tomorrow?"

Now Stella leaned in hard, pushing her forward.

"Excuse me," Mary Jean said as she lurched toward the next outstretched hand.

With Stella driving her forward, she had no choice but to find the rhythm of what she hoped was the quick and memorable introduction she'd practiced with the kids.

"I'm Mary Jean Wright. Vote Wright on election day."

"Hi. Vote Wright for mayor."

"Yes, ha ha, it is a handy name for a politician."

When she finally reached the front of the room, she felt a rush of accomplishment: she must have shaken nearly a hundred hands, and collected the names and memorized the friendly faces of several well-wishers—Rita and Kathy, Glenn and Steve, Celia and Larry and Deborah and Ethel—she could search out from the stage.

But then she looked up and there, seated behind the podium, was Pete, in full uniform. He caught her eye and looked quickly away. He hadn't told her he was going to be here, backing up Sladowski, but this was obviously well planned. It wasn't that she minded him being there—she'd known from the beginning, of course, that he was in the other camp—but she hated the fact that he'd hidden it from her.

"You've got to come up onstage with me," she whispered to Stella.

"What? No!"

"Sladowski's got his army up there. I need one, too."

She saw Stella take in the scene, begin to soften.

"But I thought we agreed," Stella said, "that you were going to be the star. I'm afraid if I'm up there, I'll just be distracting."

"I need you," Mary Jean said, grabbing her hand. "I'm willing to be the star, but it can only help having another star on my side."

So Stella mounted the stage with Mary Jean, filling at least one of the folding chairs behind the podium with the placard reading WRIGHT, though Sladowski had six people, including Pete, lined up behind him. Mary Jean looked out into the audience and spotted her brother Bill, the fireman who was leading the renovation of Stella's house. Mary Jean wiggled her eyebrows at him, and a minute later he came up onstage too, followed by her sister-in-law Teresa. Then, without Mary Jean even having to signal, Jimmy's teacher, Mrs. West, joined them. And Celia, the landscape architect she'd just met, filled the last chair.

Just don't look at Sladowski, Mary Jean instructed herself. She drew in one last deep breath, deep as any inspired by Carlos, and looked down at her gorgeous patent leather shoes. Softly, she clicked the heels together, like Dorothy in *The Wizard of Oz*. What had Dorothy always said? There's no place like home. But now Mary Jean wished to be catapulted out into the world.

The auditorium lights dimmed, the spotlights went up, and she felt Henry Sladowski step forward beside her. *Smelled* him, his rich cologne competing with hers. She stood up straighter, pulling in her stomach, feeling strong from all the exercise she'd been doing, slim from the dieting, her hair sleek, her makeup in place.

What did Pete think, looking at her from behind? Did she

even look like the same old wife to him? She hoped not. She hoped he was sitting back there, thinking she looked beautiful. Wishing he were sitting on her side of the stage.

As the introductions went on, as her eyes adjusted and she could pick out people's faces in the crowd, she was amazed to find she wasn't even nervous. Not that nervous, anyway.

There was a panel of community representatives who were charged with asking impartial questions of both candidates. She recognized the principal of the high school, along with Cameron Dunn, the president of the women's club, a representative from the Homewood African American Citizens Union, and someone from the arts council.

Don't get too involved, she remembered Stella counseling her. No matter what they ask you, stick to your own agenda.

And she found, by repeating that mantra over and over in her head, she was able to do that.

They asked about snow removal; she talked about wanting Homewood to be a place where the people who cleaned its streets and picked up its garbage and fought its fires and taught its children could afford to live.

They asked about parking; she turned the focus to downtown development, maintaining locally owned businesses, and not allowing Homewood to be turned into another suburban mall.

Cameron Dunn asked about taxes, how the candidates planned to keep property taxes reasonable while still maintaining quality in the schools.

Mary Jean started to speak, but Cameron interrupted her.

"I'd really like to hear from Mr. Sladowski on this one," she said.

"Well, Cameron." He chuckled. "I know that every single person who buys a house from you is concerned about property taxes. My plan would cut those taxes, which would help raise property values even higher, while making our schools more attractive by going to the neighborhood plan where our children can walk to school instead of being bused all over town. Now, in terms of the environmental benefits of cutting back on all those buses—"

"Mr. Sladowski," Cameron Dunn interrupted, "isn't it true that busing was instituted in Homewood as a result of a state desegregation order, which is one of the foundations of protecting equal rights in this community?"

Mary Jean was gratified to see Sladowski's ears turn bright red. "I haven't seen such an order," he said, "if it indeed exists. But the fact is that the Homewood of today is very different from the Homewood of the 1950s and 1960s. Today, I'm happy to say, all of our citizens have equal rights."

Another panel member jumped in with a question about crime rates, which Sladowski seized as an opportunity to introduce Pete.

"Pete Wright, ladies and gentlemen," said Sladowski, "who will be our new chief of police once I'm elected. He's the husband of my opponent here, but he's chosen to support me, curiously enough."

Sladowski chuckled, and the audience joined in uncertainly.

"The fact is, Pete Wright is supporting my candidacy rather

than that of his own wife because he believes I'll make a better leader for Homewood," Sladowski said. "He believes I'll make the streets safer, for one thing. I want to make this a town where people can leave their doors unlocked again. A town where little children can walk hand in hand to the school around the corner. A town where everyone, black and white, young and old, can join in the prosperity afforded by rising housing prices and beautiful stores."

There was a cheer and a swell of applause at that, but Mary Jean was still stuck on that part about Pete thinking Sladowski would be a better leader than she would. Was that true? Or was it just the thing about Sladowski making him chief, something town code prohibited her from doing for him? Was it too humiliating for him to imagine her being his figurative boss, as he'd implied that night when she first announced her candidacy? Or was it that he wanted her home, figuratively pinned down, where he could be sure of her?

"Mrs. Wright? Do you have a response to that, Mrs. Wright?"

She stared at Cameron Dunn, having completely lost track of the question.

"I think Pete really deep down believes in me," she said.

There was a groan from behind her. She didn't have to turn around to recognize that it had come from Stella.

"Some people don't think a politician should speak from the heart," she said, "but I don't know any other way."

She took a deep breath, another Carlos breath, and felt for the first time this evening as if there truly were no other way for her. She wouldn't have been able to think of a personal agenda or a politically expedient rejoinder or a winning comeback if she tried. All she knew was what she didn't have to think about, what came from deep inside.

"My husband and I both grew up in this town," she said. "Our parents grew up in this town. We went to school here, we got married here, we're raising four children here. I always thought we'd live here until we died. But I don't know if that's true anymore."

She turned to consider Henry Sladowski. "I don't blame all of Homewood's problems on you," she said. "I'm sure prosperity is in many ways good for this town. My daughter loves shopping at the Gap."

Here there was a ripple of laughter.

"But I can't help but wonder what price we're paying for all our cool new restaurants and our perfectly renovated houses. How much character we're losing when we sand every speck of old paint off our shingles, when we get rid of our poky businesses and tax our marginal citizens out of existence.

"We want to raise our students' test scores, to help them get into better colleges, but what about the kid who doesn't want to go to college? I have a daughter who wants to be an actress, a son who's wildly imaginative but can't add two and two. Aren't those kids, those talents, important too? I know that my childhood friend Stella Powers, who's working with me on my campaign, is probably one of the richest, most successful people in town, and she viewed standardized testing as an excuse to cut school."

Now there was warmer laughter, plus a flutter of applause for Stella.

"And what about the kids whose parents didn't go to college, who live in what still counts as the poor side of Homewood? I was one of those kids, and I know when your parents don't go to college, it's that much harder to get there yourself. And then you never have a chance of moving up the hill like Mr. Sladowski. That kid deserves the same education in the same schools as the kids who have so many more advantages at home.

"Henry Sladowski promises to turn this town into a utopia," said Mary Jean, "but I don't believe in utopia. In fact, I think the more a place comes to resemble utopia, the less good a place it is for real people to live. The more power we give a place to embody our dreams and our souls, the less we look to ourselves, to our neighbors and the people we love, to make our lives happy and satisfying.

"It's not the buildings of Homewood, the shops or the houses or how much they cost, that makes this town a great place to live. It's the people, it's our own drive for community and satisfaction that makes this place great. And that's what I want to preserve."

She heard the clapping from her own supporters first, from Stella and the others lined up behind her.

But then it began coming from the audience as well, starting slowly and then picking up until it began to thunder in her ears.

"Bravo!" someone shouted, and then a woman in the second row, someone she recognized from the Y, got to her feet, followed by a person a few seats down, and then there was a wave of people standing, stomping their feet and cheering.

"Wright Wright Wright Wright," someone started chanting.

Mary Jean stood there grinning, taking it all in, nodding and mouthing her thanks, amazed at the response, feeling so overwhelmed she could burst into tears but knowing Stella would never forgive her if she lost it like that. Sladowski, she saw, had shrunk back until he was nearly behind the curtain.

That's when she remembered Pete, remembered to turn around and catch his eye, to make sure he was okay with what she'd said about him and their family, with her dragging them and their life into her campaign.

She was sure that nobody else, not even Stella, could tell that Pete was trying hard not to smile. Or could see that he was sitting with his hands hanging down between his knees, secretly clapping for her.

Chapter 15

WRIGHT FROM THE HEART read the headline in the *Homewood Herald*; MOM AND STAR TEAM FOR MAYORAL RACE.

Mary Jean thought the headline was really dumb, but Stella told her that there was no such thing as bad publicity. "You entered the race late," Stella said. "You don't have the money for ads and posters that Sladowski does. If the *Homewood Herald* wants to run a front-page story on you, ignore the headline and celebrate."

Stella was pleased to find she was right. After that story ran in the local newspaper, a lot of people in town stepped forward to offer their support. People who'd been at the debate, and people who'd only heard about it. People who were willing to offer time, and people who wanted to give her money. Mary

Jean's "speech from the heart," as the *Homewood Herald* dubbed it, apparently connected with a lot of people in town. People said it was refreshing to find a politician who said what she really felt and meant, not just what she thought people wanted to hear. They said they too wanted to live in a town with the best quality of life, that their homes were the center of their happiness, not just an investment whose worth could be measured by dollar value alone.

Stella was surprised and delighted at this outpouring of confidence in Mary Jean. This is another example, she thought, of how I lived my Hollywood life all on the surface, and never dug down to the real thing. Sure, in Hollywood, she'd gotten involved in politics the way other stars did, writing a check or attending an over-the-top gala for some fashionable cause: AIDS or the Amazon or homeless children, whatever her manager told her was professionally expedient. But Homewood was not a cynical place, and people believed in Mary Jean because she not only spoke from her heart, she spoke *to* theirs.

And then the pro–Mary Jean movement really snowballed when first the Style section of the *New York Times* and then the celebrity-oriented weeklies—*People, Us Weekly,* the *Star*—picked up on the story of Stella's involvement in Mary Jean's campaign. They wrote about how the two were childhood friends, how Stella had walked away from her hot Hollywood career (ha!) to devote herself to Mary Jean's mom-and-apple-pie from-the-heart campaign.

At first Stella tried to downplay her involvement, emphasizing that the real star of this production was Mary Jean, but

Mary Jean countered that she never could have gotten this far without Stella. And wasn't Stella the one who told her there was no such thing as bad publicity? Here they were running a sleepy little mayoral race, and they were getting national press!

The tables had completely turned, and it was almost as if Sladowski had ceased to exist. Mary Jean was swamped at every event, was constantly in the newspaper, and now Sladowski was the one Stella would occasionally spot outside the Gap, standing all alone, trying to foist his brochures on people. Stella heard people mumbling that his only interest in Homewood was as a money machine, that he didn't care about the schools or anyone in the town besides the other high-budget newcomers. When Cameron Dunn and her country club friends switched their support to Mary Jean, Stella felt the race was all but decided.

"You know what we should do," Stella said to Mary Jean. "We should have a huge party for you, to raise money and also ride the crest of this wave of support."

"A party," said Mary Jean. "You mean, like at . . . the Fire Hall?"

"No," said Stella, the idea just now catching fire in her brain. "I mean like at my house. The Tree House."

"But the Tree House isn't finished."

"It's finished enough for a party. In fact, the more I think about it, this is the perfect time to have a party there. The floors haven't been refinished yet. The walls haven't gotten their final coat of paint. The kitchen and the bathrooms are functional, but there's nothing anybody can wreck. You don't need furniture for a party; all you need is booze and food and music and something to celebrate."

"Who will we invite?" asked Mary Jean.

"We'll invite everybody," said Stella.

On Friday, the day before the party, everything went wrong.

It was raining, first of all, and cold, and promising to keep raining through the weekend. Stella had been keeping a tent on reserve, in case it was nice enough to hold at least some of the party outside, but she called and canceled. It was miserable out there, which could cut into attendance *and* mean that the people who did show up were going to be turning her house into a mud pond.

It doesn't matter, she reminded herself. It's going to get dirty anyway, and we'll just clean it up.

Then the caterer called to say that Whole Foods had run out of both the right kind of mushrooms for the stuffed mushrooms and mint for the mojitos. Stella told her it didn't matter, they were sure to have fewer people than they'd expected, given the weather.

Then Cameron Dunn called to say that fifty members of her Jack & Jill club as well as twenty realtors in town who'd formerly declared themselves for Sladowski wanted to come to the party, and was that okay?

Stella was in the middle of assuring Cameron that that was fine when her call waiting clicked and she had to jump off that call, bracing herself against whatever disaster awaited her on the other line.

It was the school nurse, calling to tell her that Idaho had lice, and could she come pick her up?

Lice. Just the word made Stella start scratching her head. Might she have them too? She thought of all those nights she'd shared a pillow with her daughter while she read her a bedtime story. The whole drive to the Homewood CVS, she kept scratching her head.

Where did they keep the lice shampoo? Stella checked the shampoo aisle, the skin care aisle, even the section with the bug spray. God, this brought back horrible memories of coming here with Pete in high school to buy condoms, circling and circling the store until it seemed they'd be able to make it to the counter without anyone they knew seeing what they were buying.

Finally, desperate, she asked a clerk for help finding the lice shampoo. The clerk said they didn't carry lice shampoo.

"Why not?" Stella said. "Don't Homewood children get lice?"

The clerk didn't crack a smile.

"Try Bloomfield," the clerk said.

By the time she went to the Bloomfield CVS and bought the lice shampoo—two bottles, one for Idaho and one for herself, just in case—and picked up Idaho from school and got her back home, it was after noon. There were seventeen messages on her machine. It was raining harder than ever. But first things first.

It wasn't just a shampoo, she saw from reading the lengthy directions on the package. It was an experience—an extended one. And it couldn't be done in the bathtub or the shower, but had to happen over the kitchen sink, the way her mother washed her hair when she was little.

She didn't have time for lice. There was no way she could handle this today.

Idaho reached up absently and scratched her head, then scratched it again.

There was no choice.

Stella pinned one of her mother's old threadbare towels around Idaho's shoulders and massaged the shampoo onto Idaho's dry head and then did the same to her own. Then they sat there at the kitchen table for the requisite ten minutes, eating apples and waiting for the medicine to do its work. Then Stella pulled a chair over to the sink and had Idaho kneel on it and bend under the faucet while she ran the warm water over her daughter's hair, its sound syncopated with the rain falling outside the windows, after which she shampooed her own hair in the sink.

Then came the really difficult but most important part: using the tiny-toothed comb to go through every strand of her daughter's hair, from scalp to tip, teasing out the dandruff-sized nits.

I feel like a mother baboon, thought Stella.

No one in Hollywood would believe it if they saw me now.

I've never been happier in my life.

That last one came unbidden, but clear and true as her daughter's laughter.

She finished combing Idaho's hair, and enfolded her in a hug so tight and long the little girl finally wiggled free.

"What are you doing, Mommy?"

"Just loving you."

"Well, *duh,*" said Idaho, a term she'd adopted now that she was in "big kids' school," along with the jeans and sweatshirts that had replaced the frilly dresses and patent leather shoes she'd insisted on wearing only a few months ago. Her two front teeth, Stella suddenly noticed, were starting to come in, big as the Easter Bunny's.

Then Idaho ran away, up to her room to play, another new development. Given the opportunity, she'd always chosen to be with her mother rather than alone. Stella felt a throb of loss, but then thought of something her mother had said to her after she left home, once she was old enough to feel guilty about it.

"Don't be ridiculous," her mother said. "Your children are supposed to leave you. It makes me feel like I'm a good mother."

And so did Stella feel like she was a good mother too.

Late Saturday afternoon, shortly before the party was due to start, three things happened.

It stopped raining.

The band that Stella had pulled every one of her remaining strings to get to play at the benefit said they'd be there.

And Stella got a call from her lawyer in California, saying he'd gotten a special Saturday delivery of the legal documents that pronounced her officially divorced from Eddie. Eddie had gone to Japan to make a battery commercial and met a twenty-two-year-old Australian actress he wanted to marry. He'd given up his claim on any community property and agreed that they'd both walk away with what they'd brought to their brief marriage. It was almost as if they'd never met—except that, in a strange way, he'd changed her life.

Stella had anticipated feeling excited at finally wiggling free from Eddie, but now she found that the thing that was most thrilling was the idea that she'd be able to pay off her mortgage with Sladowski. She instructed her lawyer to call Sladowski's office and alert them that the debt would be paid at the beginning of the week. She'd sell stocks, cash in bonds, she didn't even want to get a mortgage. She couldn't wait to let him know that he was finally and officially and completely out of her life.

To celebrate, she called Homewood Liquors and asked them to send up twelve cases of their best champagne. No, she said, make that every bottle of champagne they had. Instead of drinking not-minty-enough mojitos, everyone at the party would swim in champagne.

The house looked magical, like a stage set, even the still-rough paint-spattered floors and the bare white walls adding to the effect. If there were no light fixtures, it was all the better; candles glittered everywhere. And if the entire place was devoid of furniture, that only made the music sound better, even if for now it was only the CDs that Stella had stayed up late creating.

Stella would not let Mary Jean do anything to help with the

party or even arrive early, knowing that Mary Jean might, at a moment's notice, drop to her knees to begin wiping a spill from the floor or grab a plunger to unstop a toilet. Mary Jean had launched a barrage of protests, but had finally given up when Stella threatened that if she insisted on helping, Stella wouldn't throw the party at all. It was gratifying to see Mary Jean turn up with her hair in a smooth chignon, her makeup perfectly in place, just ten minutes before the party was set to start, wearing one of her all-purpose black outfits.

"It looks fantastic in here," she said, surveying the house.

"You look fantastic," said Stella. "All of you do."

Caitlin was there, and the oldest son Peter, home from college for the event. He looked so much like Pete, the teenage Pete with his shaggy hair and sleepy eyes, that Stella wanted to burst out laughing. Pete was there, too, wearing civilian clothes and looking even more handsome than his son.

"Where's Franny?" Stella asked.

"I think she's staying away in protest," said Mary Jean, with a pained smile. "She vanished today, and took my Prada shoes with her."

Mary Jean stuck her foot out to show Stella a pair of worn navy pumps.

"Oh, no," Stella said. "Well, hopefully it will be so crowded no one will see your feet. And Franny will undoubtedly show up later."

At the handful of parties Stella had thrown, she remembered standing around for the first hour worrying whether anyone would actually show up. But tonight, at the stroke of seven, people started filing into the house, and they didn't stop. There were so many people there so quickly that they ran out of champagne glasses and the caterer's helpers couldn't keep up with the pace.

Stella saw Mary Jean across the living room, passing a tray full of hors d'oeuvres. She pushed her way through the crowd to her friend's side.

"You're not supposed to be doing that," she said.

"It's fine," Mary Jean assured her, with a big smile. "This way I get to talk to everyone, and I never feel awkward about moving on."

Stella swiveled around to see one of the servers holding a bottle of champagne in each hand, awkwardly trying to pour with her right while not spilling with her left.

"Here," Stella said, grabbing the still-full bottle of champagne. "I'll do that."

Mary Jean was right; it was easier to be a good host with liquor or food in your hand. Stella moved from one person to the next, draining the champagne bottle, then going into the kitchen to get a tray of hors d'oeuvres, having more fun zooming through the room as a server than she'd ever had standing still being the center of attention.

Next, Cameron Dunn and a few of her fellow Junior Leaguers joined in the act, and then Stella saw Mary Jean's kids—even Jimmy, trailed as usual by the shiny-haired Idaho—start passing food and collecting empty glasses too.

Mary Jean passed close to Stella's side, her eyes gleaming.

"They love me!" Mary Jean shouted in Stella's ear.

"They should!" Stella said back.

Finally, she thought, Mary Jean was learning to let in as much love as she put out.

Just when the party seemed to have reached its height, the noise swelling to the point where it drowned out all other thoughts, where the faces seemed like a kaleidoscopic blur, there was a flurry of activity at the door, and one of the guards Stella had hired for the event said, "Miss Powers, your special guest is here."

The first thing Mary Jean saw was the bright red hair, and her heart leaped, thinking it was Franny finally showing up from God knows where she'd been. But then she saw no, it was in fact Patty Scialfa, Bruce Springsteen's wife, with Bruce himself following right behind her. It took only a second for them to be recognized, and then a roar went up from the crowd.

"Where's Mary Jean?" Bruce said.

Mary Jean stepped slowly forward, as if being called to the Pearly Gates.

"I hope everyone from Homewood is going to vote for you," Bruce said, as Mary Jean's kids gaped at their mother being addressed by the Boss. "That's what I'm going to do, when you run for governor and president."

The band's equipment was already set up in the main hall, and the entire party followed Bruce and Patty as they joined their fellow musicians at the microphones. Then they swung into a loud rendition of "Dancing in the Dark," a later song than the ones Stella remembered Mary Jean loving so much in high school, but no matter. Bruce reached out just as he had to the young Courteney Cox in the video and pulled Mary Jean onto the figurative stage to dance with him. Stella clapped along with everyone else, thinking that now this was like a real Hollywood benefit, but finally it was for a cause she really believed in.

As Bruce launched into his next song, Stella swung around, thinking she'd take a turn through the living room, picking up glasses and napkins before the crowd repossessed it. Indeed, it was a disaster, and she moved quickly, gathering as much as she could hold in her hands and depositing it in a trashcan near the kitchen door.

Then she noticed that the side door, the one that led to the part of the lawn that was bordered by the driveway in back and the copper beech in front, was open. She crossed the room to close it, and there, under the cover of the big tree, she could just make out the glow of a cigarette. She stepped outside, worrying at first that whoever it was might set the tree on fire, realizing as the grass squished under her feet that there was little danger of that given all the rain, then recognizing, the minute she'd made up her mind to go back inside and leave the poor smoker be, that it was Pete.

"Hey," she said, since he was already looking at her, had undoubtedly, as soon as she'd set foot outside the door, known it was her, given that his eyes were already adjusted to the dark.

"Hey."

"Still smoking, huh?"

He dropped the cigarette onto the wet ground beneath the tree and ground it out.

"Don't tell Mary Jean," he said.

"I guess I owe you for not telling about my going up to Henry's that night. Though eventually she figured it out."

"I hate keeping things from Mary Jean. I should quit." He looked down at the cigarette butt. "Smoking, I mean."

There was a noise from the end of the driveway that made them both look away. They looked back toward each other, but then they heard it again: the roar of what sounded like a truck's engine, a man's shout, and then the sound of tires on the drive.

Stella stepped away from Pete, out from the cover of the tree, to see what was happening. At the same time, she noticed that Bruce and Patty and the band had stopped playing inside and that a few of the party guests were stepping outside, to get some air or, like Pete, to have a cigarette.

She could see it now, the enormous vehicle that looked like an RV coming up the driveway, one of her guards running alongside it, toting a flashlight, yelling for it to stop. Behind the RV was another car, a beat-up old red BMW.

The RV jerked to a stop, and the back door opened, a cameraman with a camera already hoisted onto his shoulder hopping out. He was followed by another man carrying spotlights who deftly set them up on the lawn, switching them on and flushing Pete out from his leafy hiding place. And then finally, out came a man with stiff hair wearing a trench coat and carrying a microphone with a news station's logo on it: the television reporter.

The guard was standing beside them now, yelling that they

had to leave, though they continued their preparations, ignoring him.

"It's all right," Stella said to the guard. "They can be here."

They looked at Stella, as if stunned to find her in person on her own front lawn.

"Stella Powers?" the reporter asked.

"Yes." Stella smiled.

"We were told there was a benefit for your friend who's running for mayor here tonight."

"Yes," said Stella. "Mary Jean Wright. You're here to do a story?"

"That's right," the reporter said, motioning to his cameraman to begin rolling.

Another reporter and a photographer got out of the red BMW, and yet another car pulled up behind them.

"Just a minute," Stella said, still smiling. "I'll get Mary Jean."

Mary Jean was standing with Caitlin and Patty Scialfa in the living room, all talking excitedly. Her daughter was looking with as much admiration at her mother as she was at Scialfa, Stella noticed. Well, she was about to have even more reason to look up to her dear old mom.

When Stella explained what was happening and pulled Mary Jean outside, not only her children but most of the rest of the party guests followed. The lawn, the huge tree, were illuminated now; even the night sky shone yellow in the television lights. The television reporter was already talking to his camera.

"They're calling Mary Jean Wright the mayoral candidate

who speaks from the heart, with her message of mom, neighborhood, and old-fashioned values," the reporter was saying straight into the camera. "Wright's candidacy gets a lot of attention thanks to her childhood friend, the actress Stella Powers. But this would-be Mayor Mom may not be all she seems."

What did they mean by that? Stella felt her smile falter, but the camera and the reporter both turned toward them, the other reporters stepping forward with their notebooks.

"Mrs. Wright," the television reporter asked, a huge smile still plastered to his face, "we hear that you were six months pregnant with your first child when you got married, right after high school. How does that jibe with your values for kids in our schools?"

Mary Jean froze, a grotesque twist of a smile illuminated on her face. Stella put her hand out, to block the view of the camera, but the television reporter kept talking.

"Miss Powers, you've been divorced three times, and you've never publicly named the father of your child. Do you think the voters of Homewood are ready for these Hollywood-style morals?"

"They're not voting for me," Stella said, putting her arm around Mary Jean, trying to lead her away, catching the looks of horror on the faces of Mary Jean's children.

"Stella, what do you think about Eddie Skinner's new fiancée?" one of the print reporters said, trotting after them. "We heard your divorce was final today, is that true? When do you think they'll get married?"

"No comment," Stella said, trying to find a way to get

Mary Jean away from the cameras and away from the crowd that was pressing closer from the house, every mouth ajar.

"Stella! Stella! What's this we hear about a love triangle between you, Mary Jean, and Mary Jean's husband Pete Wright?"

That's when they got Stella, like a fingernail in the heart. It was ridiculous, but she felt Mary Jean stiffen under her arm, and she began to move even faster in an attempt to get away from the attack.

"Mary Jean, is your husband supporting the other candidate because of his relationship with Stella Powers?"

Stella kept trying to push Mary Jean forward, but finally her friend stopped, looking toward the big tree. There was Pete, stepping from its shadows, the lights and cameras immediately turning to him, catching him in their glare.

"I'm supporting the other candidate because I've been selfish," Pete said.

With the attention momentarily focused elsewhere, Stella saw her opening and propelled Mary Jean deep into the shelter of the beech—not quite as all-consuming as it had been before Sladowski's men hacked away at it, but still a place that both let them feel invisible and gave them a view of the horror that continued to unfold.

"Mr. Sladowski promised to make me police chief, but I'm withdrawing myself from consideration for that post," said Pete, "as well as from Mr. Sladowski's campaign."

He cleared his throat, taking a step back as if this settled everything, but the cameras and the crowd only stepped toward him.

"Mary Jean Wright is not only the best candidate for mayor," he said, "but she's the only decent, honest candidate in this race. Mr. Sladowski has used public resources for his own gain, has subverted town code to ease his own tax burden while making plans to unfairly raise the taxes of the other citizens of this town. According to code 6978, paragraph 2, clause C, a citizen is not considered a public official until—"

"Mr. Wright! Mr. Wright!" one of the notebook reporters called. "Is it true that you and Stella Powers had a sexual relationship?"

"Well, that was a long time ago," Pete began, which made Stella groan out loud and turn away, as if from a fatal accident.

That's when she saw, down at the end of her driveway, beyond the reach of the bright lights, someone else standing all alone. Leaving Mary Jean for a moment, she moved to the far side of the tree and stole out of its shadows to get a better look. Yes, it was, she couldn't believe it: Henry Sladowski. Suddenly he looked her way, and when he recognized her, the smile on his face only grew bigger. He pointed at her with his thumb up, like a little boy pretending to shoot a gun, and then he slipped back into the night.

CHAPTER 16

as soon as Mary Jean woke up on Sunday morning, she had a feeling that something was terribly wrong. Immediately, her mind went to the reporters who'd shown up at the party the night before, all the awful things they'd said, what Stella had told her about seeing Sladowski grinning at the end of the driveway like a vampire. She groaned aloud when she imagined the morning's newspapers. As Pete rolled halfway toward her, she remembered how wonderful he'd been and put an arm around him, expecting that would relieve her pain. It did, but not enough. Let him sleep, she thought, as she reluctantly eased away from the warmth of his body and swung her legs out of bed. It would definitely be a long day, and she needed him to stay strong.

Everyone, it seemed, was still asleep. When they'd gotten home from the party last night, so late, she'd forgotten to check on Franny, but one of the times she'd gotten up in the middle of the night, she'd peeked into the girls' room to see them both huddled in their beds. Well, it was probably better that Franny hadn't been there to witness the uproar firsthand. She would have harangued her mother mercilessly about it.

Last night as they drove home from the party, their son Peter said, "Part of what those reporters said was true, wasn't it? Dad really did go out with a movie star, didn't he?"

"Yes, I did," Pete said, swiveling around from the front passenger seat. "She tried to get me to go to Hollywood with her, but I said no, I loved your mother, and I wanted to stay right here in Homewood."

Mary Jean swatted him.

"And because, like, Mom was already knocked up with me, right?"

Mary Jean put on the brakes and stopped right in the middle of the street, right in front of Vesuvio's. She was aware of the late-Saturday-night stragglers gawking at them, but she didn't care.

"Peter, your father was kidding about Stella wanting him to go to Hollywood. They'd broken up long before he and I got together, and we never considered anything but staying together and having you. We loved you, even before you were born. We loved each other."

She stopped herself, afraid that might have sounded like a campaign speech. She'd gotten so used to making them that sometimes her ordinary conversation came out sounding as if it had been drafted in cogent paragraphs and was meant to persuade people to her viewpoint. She turned questioningly to Pete, who smiled at her in return.

"Right?" she said.

"Right," Pete said to their son.

"Jesus, I was just kidding," said Peter.

Better let them all sleep as long as possible, she thought now, putting on a pot of coffee and stepping outside to get the newspapers and begin preparing herself for whatever horror lay ahead. She was bending down to pick up the *Star-Ledger* and the *New York Post*—the *Times* was already tucked under her arm—when a young man stepped out from behind the overgrown evergreen at the end of the driveway, startling her so that she let loose a little scream and pulled her robe closed around her neck.

"Oh, I didn't mean to frighten you, Ms. Wright," the young man said. "I just wanted to say how unfair it was, what happened to you last night."

Was he a neighbor? Someone who'd been at the party whom she somehow failed to recognize?

"Thank you," she said. "Uh . . ."

"Jeremy Stewart," he said, pulling a notebook out of his pocket. "*People* magazine."

"*The People* magazine?"

He looked confused. "Is there more than one?"

"Are you looking for Stella Powers?" Mary Jean asked.

"No, we're doing a story on you," he said, already beginning to write. "A kind of profile, on you and your family, on your background, on last night's revelations—you know, your response."

Mary Jean opened her mouth, then closed it. "I don't have a response," she said, turning back toward her house.

"What about your husband? I'd like to talk to him," said the reporter, following her down the gravel driveway.

"Leave me alone," Mary Jean snapped, badly shaken. "Leave my whole family alone."

She walked faster, feeling as if she were being chased by somebody who was trying to molest her. How did Stella stand this? Mary Jean knew she wasn't cut out for fame.

The reporter stopped walking. "I'm going to write my story, whether you talk to me or not. It would be better for you if you talked to me."

Instead of answering, Mary Jean went inside and slammed the door closed before she remembered she didn't want to wake the family. Too late: Jimmy came bounding down the stairs almost immediately, leaping into her arms.

"Hi, sweetie," Mary Jean said, kissing his cheek, which tasted like sugar.

"Hi, Mommy."

"Want to snuggle with me?" Mary Jean asked, sneaking a look out the window to see the reporter still standing there, seeming to take notes about the street and the house. Mary Jean wished she could pull shut the curtains on her life and never raise them again. She wanted this whole thing to go away.

Curling up on the sofa with Jimmy, she held her breath and opened the *Times*. Nothing. That meant a lot. If it was a story of any significance, it would be in the national paper of record, wouldn't it? The fact that it had happened late on Saturday night, that it was a small-town story and an obvious put-up job by her political opponent, would keep it out of the news. By the time Monday came around, when it might have any influence on the election, everyone would have forgotten about it.

Mary Jean was able to believe this for exactly eighteen seconds, until she began thumbing through the *Star-Ledger*. There, on the fourth page of the local section, was a story about her star-studded party being interrupted by the television cameras making accusations about her "moral history," with the news of Pete dropping from Sladowski's ticket. It was a fairly dry account, and buried inside the paper, but it was there nonetheless.

"Mommy, I want Froot Loops," Jimmy said.

"Just a minute, honey."

With trembling hands, Mary Jean pulled the *Post* from its opaque plastic wrapper. There she was, right on the cover, sheltered under Stella's arm as Stella shouted at the photographer and held up her hand to try to block the picture.

SCARLET MAMA read the headline, and then, in smaller but still prominent type: STAR IN LOVE TRIANGLE WITH WOULD-BE MAYOR AND HUBBY COP.

"What's a love triangle?" Jimmy asked.

"Never mind," snapped Mary Jean.

Then she looked down at him. "When did you learn to read?"

He shrugged. "Idaho taught me."

Oh, my God, Mary Jean thought. I've been so busy campaigning, I haven't even noticed that my son has made this amazing breakthrough.

"Why don't you go find a book to read to me?" she said, crumpling up the *Post* and stuffing it under the sofa. "I'll go get your Froot Loops."

It was eleven before the rest of the family was up, everyone but Franny.

"Where's your sister?" Mary Jean asked Caitlin.

Caitlin shrugged. "Still asleep, I guess."

"What time did she get in last night?"

Another shrug, though the fact that Caitlin wouldn't meet Mary Jean's eye was a sure sign it had been really late.

"I hope at least she brought my Prada shoes back in one piece," Mary Jean said, going for a lighter note. She didn't want to admit how disappointed she felt that Franny hadn't shown up for her party, and was hoping at least this morning she'd get to tell Franny all about it.

"I'm sure your beloved shoes are fine," Caitlin said, still looking away.

More fine than me, Mary Jean imagined her daughter thinking. Who could blame her, after what happened last night? Feeling awful that she'd dragged her family into such a mess, Mary Jean got up and hugged her daughter.

"Why don't you guys go to the mall," she said, "all of you. I think everybody deserves a treat."

"What about the guys in the driveway?" Pete asked, jerking his head toward where the reporters were just visible through the crack in the curtain.

Mary Jean had kept the SCARLET MAMA paper hidden, had not talked to Pete or the kids about the things she'd read on baristanet.com, the virtual font of local political gossip. Some of it was nasty, some of it wasn't, but all of it made her feel as if she wanted to crawl under a rock somewhere and never come out. Her family would be assaulted by the press soon enough, and she needed some time to clear her mind and figure out how she was going to handle this.

"Ignore them," Mary Jean advised now. "Just get in the car and drive away."

"What about you?" Pete said. "Aren't you coming with us?" Mary Jean shook her head.

"No," she said firmly. "I just need some time alone."

She didn't tell them this, but she'd unplugged the phone early this morning, right after she saw the headline in the *Post*. She knew that the calls would be flooding in, but she couldn't imagine that anyone on the other end would say anything she wanted to hear. The only person she wanted to talk with was Stella, and there would be time enough for that later. Now, all she wanted was to be alone in her own house.

As soon as everybody was out the door, she looked around, really looked around, able to take it in at last now that there weren't people occupying every surface, filling the place with sound and noise and smells and chaos. While she'd been campaigning for mayor, leaving her family to pick up the pieces, she'd let everything go, hadn't even noticed that she'd let it go. Not that she'd ever been a meticulous housekeeper; that was impossible, in a small house with four kids. But at least she'd kept things fairly picked up and done the laundry every few days and restocked the refrigerator and washed the dishes. At least she'd felt some measure, however illusory, of control.

Now, coats and bags and newspapers and mail littered every surface. Yesterday's dishes, and Friday's too, sat in cold gray water in the sink. The sheets on the beds hadn't been changed in—oh God, she didn't want to think about it—and the clothes that had been washed were stuffed unfolded in laundry baskets.

Was she really going to spend her first free day in weeks, and maybe her last free day for months, maybe years, cleaning her house? Was she really going to ignore the phone, refuse to look out the window, forget the press and even the election, in favor of dusting the shelves and washing the floors?

She was.

She wanted to turn on the stereo, to blast Madonna and Cyndi Lauper, but she didn't want to wake Franny. She'd do the girls' room last; if Franny still wasn't up, she'd wake her then.

First she moved through the downstairs rooms, hanging up clothes or throwing them in the washing machine or folding them and putting them away. Then she bundled away the reading material, sorted the mail, chose one drawing to save from Jimmy's mountain of school papers, and hid the rest in the bottom of the trash. She opened the refrigerator and started sifting through the food, throwing out dried cheese and sour milk and gray hot dogs, finally giving up and tossing its entire contents, even the mustard and relish. She wet a rag and moved through the house, wiping clean every surface. Then she took out the ancient vacuum cleaner and sucked up every crumb, every dust ball, every stray hair, every clot of dried mud and sliver of clipped nail on all the floors.

Then she sat down. The sun was coming in warm through the window and she turned her face to its shine, closing her eyes and feeling her heart lift for the first time all day. Maybe she couldn't control Sladowski or the newspapers or the election, but she could at least control her own house, and that gave her a sense of peace.

She opened her eyes to see the reporters, including someone new with a television camera, still camped out in the driveway, and turned decisively away, mounting the stairs. First, she tackled the bathroom, feeling the satisfying sting of disinfectant in her nostrils as she scoured the entire room, even scrubbing the brown scum from inside the shower curtain and the mildew from the grout around the faucets. Moving to the bedrooms, she stripped the sheets from the beds—all except the girls' room, where the door was still firmly closed—carrying them directly downstairs to the washing machine. Then she went back up to repeat her dusting and vacuuming routine and put fresh, sweet-smelling linens on the beds.

She wanted to savor the feeling of order and completion

that filled her now that the house was clean, rare in her experience. She'd spent so many years listing her occupation as housewife, yet seldom had she enjoyed this sense of accomplishment.

But she hadn't yet tackled the girls' room. Where *was* Franny? It was mid-afternoon now; the others would be back from the mall soon. If Franny didn't want to be woken up, too bad. If Mary Jean didn't want to face Franny's scrutiny, too bad about that too. Like it or not, Mary Jean was going in.

The twins' room was dark as night and smelled like sleep. From the doorway, even without the lights on, Mary Jean could see that Caitlin's bed was neatly made, her clothes all hung up, and her collection of miniature statues of the presidents—she was missing only James K. Polk now—lined up neatly in chronological order atop her dresser. Franny's side of the room, in contrast, was a disaster, with clothes and magazines strewn everywhere. She'd spent half an hour hunting through the mess for her shoes yesterday, but it was such a jumble she wouldn't be surprised if she found them today. The messy mountain of bedclothes that was Franny didn't stir.

"Franny," Mary Jean said softly. And then, more loudly, "Come on, sweetheart, time to get up."

When Franny still didn't move, Mary Jean flipped on the light.

"Come on, Franny," she said, crossing the room and pulling open the curtains.

It was only then, turning to the bed, that she realized something was wrong. The comforter was still mounded in the shape of a sleeping girl. But she couldn't see any face, any hand, any hair, any breath—any sign at all of her daughter.

"Franny," Mary Jean said sharply, as if that would summon her.

But she knew, even as she yanked back the covers to find an artfully arranged pile of clothing but nothing more, that her daughter was not in the bed.

"Aaaaaa!" she screamed, before she knew she was screaming.

Rushing downstairs, she grabbed for the phone, fumbled to plug in the cord.

And then, before she had a chance to lift it up, to call Pete, to call Stella, to call anyone and scream that her daughter was missing, the phone started ringing. She stared at it, felt the buzzing under her hand, felt monumentally angry that before she could call about her missing daughter, she would be forced to answer the questions of some idiot journalist. No, it was good. She wanted to torture somebody.

She yanked the receiver off the cradle. "What?" she growled.

A moment's hesitation, and then a soft voice. "M-mom?"

Mary Jean collapsed onto the nearest chair.

"Oh, my God, Franny, I just found your bed empty, and I almost had a heart attack. Where the hell are you?"

"Don't be mad, Mom. I'm in California."

Mary Jean sat there, listening to the silence as if it would explain everything.

"What do you mean, you're in California?" she asked finally.

She half expected one of Franny's typical smart answers, but instead was floored to hear her daughter burst into tears.

"What's wrong, honey?" Mary Jean said. "What's going on?"

"I thought I was ready," Franny sobbed. "I just wanted to come here. But now I've been here only one day and I've spent more than half my money and this strange guy tried to pick me up at the hotel and I can't rent a car because I'm too young and I don't know how to get anywhere."

"Just come home," Mary Jean said. "Go to the airport right now and come home."

"Why should I come home?" Franny said, still hysterical. "So I can spend my whole life babysitting for you? You're so busy, you don't even notice whether I'm there anyway."

Mary Jean felt as if she'd been slapped. She was about to tell Franny she was wrong, but then she thought, she's not wrong. I haven't had any time for her, for anyone in the family. The only time I paid any attention to her was when I wanted her to watch Jimmy. I gave her that stupid jacket instead of giving her my time, myself.

"Franny," she said gently. "I love you. I want to be there for you."

"I don't need you," Franny said, suddenly tough again. "I can take care of myself. Stella set me up with all her contacts out here, so I'll probably be working in a couple of days."

Stella. Was Franny telling the truth? Mary Jean couldn't question it; she didn't want to risk setting her off.

"Where are you, sweetheart?" Mary Jean asked.

Silence, and for a second Mary Jean was afraid she'd lost

her. The very idea that her daughter could hang up, might vanish into the West and there would be no way to find her, no way to get her back, made her wild.

"Franny, tell me where you are," she said, hearing the panic rising in her own voice.

"Why, so you can send some of Daddy's cop friends after me? I knew I shouldn't have called you!"

Mary Jean braced herself, afraid she was going to hear her daughter slam down the phone. But Franny kept breathing. Mary Jean thought back to all she had learned during the campaign about controlling her emotions, her words, about steering the encounter the way she wanted it to go. As Carlos the spa yogi had taught her, she drew in a deep, cleansing breath.

"No, Franny, calm down," she said. "I'm just asking so I can send you some money."

She was on her feet, finding a pen and a piece of paper, turning on the computer so she could track the address and get started buying herself a ticket.

"I don't believe you, Mom," Franny said.

"Really, Franny. You're right, I haven't been here for you. But I want to help you now."

Slowly, she coaxed the name and address of the hotel out of Franny, along with her promise not to go anywhere else. Mary Jean said she would call the hotel office and pay the bill for a week and wire the money and then they'd talk again. By which time, Mary Jean silently prayed, she would have her daughter safely back home.

*　　*　　*

Stella insisted on paying for Mary Jean's plane ticket, hugely expensive because she was leaving right away and had no idea when she'd be back.

"I feel responsible," Stella said.

"Franny says you set her up with all your Hollywood contacts," Mary Jean said. "Is that true?"

They were sitting at Stella's mother's dining room table, ignoring the reporters congregated on the sidewalk as well as the thumps on the ceiling from Jimmy and Idaho upstairs jumping on the beds.

"Of course not," Stella said. "I gave her the stay-in-school speech I told you I would, though I guess she outsmarted us on that one."

It turned out that Franny had gotten her high school equivalency diploma. That had been the big test she'd been studying for so diligently, not the SATs. Mary Jean had been stunned to discover that Caitlin knew about it all along, about the GED, about Franny's plan to leave, had even advised Franny to take off the day of the big party, on the theory that it would take Mary Jean and Pete longer to figure out she was gone. Not only had Caitlin lied for Franny, she'd been the one to stuff the clothes in her bed.

"I didn't think you two were that close," Mary Jean had said, dumbfounded.

"Of course we're that close," said Caitlin. "We're *twins*."

"But the thing I didn't tell you," said Stella now, "is that I caught her one night, going through my address book. Writing down numbers."

"Numbers?"

"Phone numbers. Of my agent, my manager, casting directors, everybody."

Mary Jean caught her breath. "I wish you'd told me."

"I wish I had, too," said Stella. "But it never occurred to me that she wanted those names so she could run away from home. I don't think it would have occurred to you either."

Mary Jean had to admit that, even if Stella had told her about Franny's number pilfering, it wouldn't have made her any more alarmed about Franny's intentions than she already was. She knew Franny was serious about becoming an actress, she knew Franny looked up to Stella, and from this vantage point she wasn't even that surprised that Franny had followed Stella's example and taken off. She'd wanted to believe that buying Franny a nice jacket and having Stella talk to her would keep Franny from following her impulses, but she'd also wanted to believe that running for mayor would break the waves of change that were flooding Homewood. The truth was that, whether she became mayor or Sladowski did, whether she succeeded in bringing Franny home or went to L.A. only to find her daughter had disappeared, the changes would keep on happening.

"Stella," Mary Jean said. "I'm withdrawing from the mayoral race."

"What?" Stella gasped.

"It's been on my mind today, before today—remember at the spa when I told you I thought sometimes I didn't really want to be mayor? But after what happened last night and now with Franny, I've decided for sure."

"You can't quit, Mary Jean. That's playing right into Slad-owski's hands."

"I'm not quitting because of him, Stella. I'm quitting because I just don't have it in me to step out there in the spotlight and fight back. And I've been thinking that just because my kids—well, most of my kids—are big now, they don't need me anymore. I've been treating them like deputy parents. But they still need me to be their mom. All I want to do is go find my daughter and bring her back home."

"But what about the arts programs in the schools? What about maintaining diversity, retaining the character of Home-wood?"

"I can be just as effective, maybe more effective, behind the scenes, on the school board or the town council, in one of those roles, and still have time for my family."

"But what about *you*, Mary Jean?" Stella asked plaintively. "What about how hard you've worked and how far you've come in finally thinking about yourself?"

Mary Jean took a deep breath. Homewood wasn't the only thing she'd gotten to know more intimately through running for mayor; she'd learned a lot about herself too. And while Stella had done an amazing job of teaching her how to imper-sonate a confident political animal, nobody and nothing could really change the person she was at heart. She did have to think about herself along with Pete and the kids. But not quite so much, and not quite in the way she'd been doing.

"You know how, at Nokomis, they're always talking about how all the kids have their own special gifts and talents?" Mary

Jean asked Stella. "Well, my special gift and talent isn't standing up there and being the leader. You and Franny can handle that, with your star quality, but not me. I should have realized it would take a much bigger personality than me to beat Sladowski."

"But if you quit now, Sladowski's definitely going to win," Stella pointed out.

"He's going to win even if I stay in," said Mary Jean. "People rallied around me because of you, Stella. Oh sure, maybe they wanted to believe in those values I was talking about. Or maybe they would have voted for me because they were so dazzled by you. But what happened last night gives a lot of them—the majority of them—the excuse to vote with their pocketbooks."

The doorbell rang. It was her son Peter, come to take her to the airport. Pete had been so frantic about Franny's disappearance, he'd tried to insist on going to California himself, but Mary Jean convinced him that if Franny saw him, she'd only get scared and run the other way. Mary Jean was the one Franny had the problem with, and Mary Jean was the only one who could bring Franny home.

"I need you to do a couple of things for me," Mary Jean said to Stella, casting a glance out the window. Yes, the reporters were still there.

"Anything," said Stella.

"Okay. Please keep an eye on Jimmy while I'm gone. Of course Pete and the big kids can take care of him, but he's happiest with Idaho, so I'll feel better knowing he's spending some time with you."

"Of course."

"Thank you. I'd also really appreciate it if you could get in touch with some of those people in Hollywood whose numbers Franny took, let them know what's up, that she's a minor but that I'd appreciate it if they took down her contact information in case I need to track her down."

"All right," said Stella.

"Okay, that's great. And the last thing I need you to do is to announce that I'm withdrawing from the mayoral race."

"Me?" Stella squealed. "I can't stand the idea of being the one to deliver that news."

"Please," Mary Jean said. "I've got to catch my flight now, and I think I'll break down if I have to face that gang. Please, Stella. I know you can handle it."

"I hate giving Sladowski this kind of satisfaction."

Mary Jean hated it too, but the regret it stirred up was so much less disturbing than it might have been in the face of her much larger anxieties and fears about Franny. The doorbell rang again, and she moved to hug her friend.

"Call Pete," she told Stella. "Tell him to send over all the reporters who are still hanging out in my driveway. Better make sure the *Homewood Herald* is here."

"But what will I tell them about why you're dropping out?"

Mary Jean was already moving to the door.

"Please don't mention Franny, but otherwise I don't care. Make something up. You've been in enough movies—you know how these things go."

"All right," Stella said.

"All right," said Mary Jean.

She stopped in the doorway and looked back at Stella, who seemed exhausted and harried but was still lovely.

"You know, there's only one thing I regret about doing this," Mary Jean said.

"What's that?"

"Now you're probably going to want to take me up on that deal we made and go back to California."

Stella raised her eyebrows. "What makes you think that?"

"Just a hunch. With Sladowski in office, it's not going to be so pleasant here. And who knows. We probably won't be able to afford to stay in Homewood. I couldn't very well expect you to stay here if we move away."

"One thing at a time," Stella said. "Just think about getting Franny back now. We'll deal with me later."

"All right," said Mary Jean. "Then I won't say good-bye quite yet."

CHAPTER 17

Stella sat at her mother's dining room table, trying to scribble something she could say about Mary Jean bowing out of the race that wasn't going to make her barf when she said it. Every time she looked out the window, there were more reporters and even what looked like regular people gathered in the driveway and on the sidewalk, now even spilling onto the street. This was a bigger crowd than had gathered even in the height of the frenzy after her mother's death and Eddie's dalliance.

She saw a few people carrying "Sladowski for Mayor" signs. What were they doing here? Just the sight of the signs made her not want to go out there. Jimmy and Idaho bounced on the floor above her, oblivious, while Pete and a handful of fellow officers stood guard outside. She couldn't bear the idea of the Sladowski backers cheering when they heard Mary Jean was dropping out.

If this *were* a movie, Stella would ignore Mary Jean's decision, would know that despite her friend's selfless flight to rescue her daughter, she really deep-down wanted to stay in the race. So Stella would just go out there and reiterate all of Mary Jean's genuinely wonderful beliefs and expose Sladowski's smear campaign, and he would slink away in disgrace while Mary Jean returned from California, compliant Franny in tow, to find that she'd been elected by the only unanimous vote in the history of America.

But even if all that happened with cinematic perfection, Stella feared, Mary Jean would refuse to take the mayoral post. And would be mightily pissed off at Stella to boot.

She had to do right by Mary Jean. She didn't want to risk her connection with the only person in the world besides her daughter who truly felt like family to her, the one person who'd known her for as long as she could remember. Even if she did end up moving back to California, she intended to stay close to Mary Jean forever.

But even if she would carry through on her promise to get Mary Jean out of the race, she didn't have to surrender all of Mary Jean's best principles. It might be true that the people of Homewood would ultimately vote with their pocketbooks, but it was also true, Stella knew it was, that a lot of people supported the values that Mary Jean stood for. What really killed her wasn't so much that Mary Jean wouldn't be mayor, but that Sladowski was the only alternative.

"So when you go to the polls on Tuesday," she wrote, "even if your only choice is to vote for Henry Sladowski, please remember what makes Homewood so rich—and it's not the price of our houses."

Stella paused, remembering her mother sitting at this very table, drafting the plan to set up the soup kitchen, or talking to one of her like-minded friends about how they could make birth control available to teenagers. What would her mother say now? What would her mother want *her* to say?

"We're a place that encourages our children to grow up to be their best selves, that embraces its citizens as individuals, that offers everyone who lives here a home in the fullest sense of that word."

Outside, a chant went up: Stel-LA! Stel-LA! Oh, God. It was showtime. Stella shuffled her notes, and then crumpled them into a ball. She always did better at an audition without a script. All she needed to do was open herself up to the feeling of the moment and trust that the right thing would come out of her mouth. She'd been back in New Jersey long enough to know that sounded like California bullshit, but it was bullshit that had always worked for her.

"Kids?" she called upstairs. "I'm going to go outside to talk to the people now. Want to come with me?"

The jumping stopped, and a moment later Jimmy and Idaho filed downstairs, both wearing Hermès scarves tied superhero-style around their necks, solemnly holding hands. They looked so cute together, so unself-conscious about their costumes and their attachment to each other, that Stella wanted to laugh. But she didn't want to do anything that might break their bond.

"Come on," she said. "You guys can stand on the steps with me."

When she opened the door, there was a swell of applause and a cheer from the crowd, which she hadn't expected. A gust of cold fall wind hit her in the face, unsettling her further, and she wished that she had brought her notes. Then, as she took her position at the top of the stairs, the children settling down on the steps at her feet, the TV cameras switched on their lights. Behind the reporters, she could just make out the faces of a few people she knew: Cameron Dunn was there, with her mother, along with Mary Jean's brother Billy and his wife, and a few of the moms who'd worked on Mary Jean's campaign. They all smiled at her and waved, which made her feel braver.

"Thank you all for coming," she said. "Mary Jean Wright asked me to call this press conference."

She had been planning to launch into a long preamble about Mary Jean's beliefs and why they were so important and how wonderful it had been to have everyone's support. But then she caught sight of Pete's face, ashen beneath his uniform cap. She saw Caitlin standing near her father, and Peter Junior too, and noticed how upset they looked. They're all just thinking of Franny, she realized. Nobody wants to stand here and listen to me go on and on about all this bullshit.

"Mary Jean wanted me to announce to you that she is dropping out of the race for mayor of Homewood," Stella said.

There. It was out. Sooner than she intended, but when she began to improvise, she just had to trust where it took her.

There was a roar from the crowd, shocks of horror and some applause too, and several of the reporters raised their hands and shouted Stella's name, trying to ask questions.

"Does Mrs. Wright's decision to withdraw from the race have anything to do with last night's allegations?" one reporter shouted.

"Mrs. Wright is involved in a family matter that necessitates her withdrawal from the race," Stella said.

"So the allegations are true?" another reporter called out, as if Stella hadn't spoken at all.

Stella shielded her eyes so she could see who in the crowd had asked this question, and that's when she saw him, behind everyone else, half-hiding behind a tree. Sladowski. She wanted to call him out in front of everyone, wanted to scream that it was he who'd planted all the negative stories, that he was just trying to destroy Mary Jean, and that he was a lousy lover and besides, had the tiniest penis in the Western Hemisphere.

But then Stella had a better idea. She didn't know why she hadn't thought of it when Mary Jean had first told her she was quitting. She would have loved to have gotten Mary Jean's blessing on the plan before she went ahead and announced it before the network news cameras, all the newspapers, and half the town, but it was too late for that. Stella took a deep breath.

"The allegations are an attempt by Mrs. Wright's opponents to undermine the values she stands for, a better Homewood for all its citizens," said Stella. "But those values will still be represented in this mayoral race, because in Mary Jean's place, I'm running for mayor."

There was a blaze of flashes then, as the reporters pressed forward and the TV cameras began turning and everyone began talking at once. Stella saw, with satisfaction, Sladowski whirl around and stalk away. He knew, she guessed, that she could be at least as adept as he had been at leaking little pieces of dirt to the press—and that she'd be a lot less scrupulous than Mary Jean about doing it.

As the reporters began tossing questions at her and she began talking, Stella felt restored to her element. She was comfortable being onstage, and it felt natural that she was running for mayor—more natural than standing behind the scenes coaching Mary Jean. After all, if Schwarzenegger could be governor and Reagan president, surely she could run one little town? And she'd have Mary Jean to handle the nuts-and-bolts decisions while she made speeches and got her picture taken. Already, she could tell, the crowd seemed excited at the prospect of having a real live movie star as their mayor.

Did this mean she intended to stay in Homewood? She'd announced her candidacy without really coming to a conscious resolution on that issue. If she won the race, definitely she'd stay. She had no doubt of her commitment to lead the town.

And if she lost? She'd have to think about it then. In the meantime, she'd have the pleasure of making Sladowski sweat to win the election. That was already so much fun, it might be worth it to stick around and keep doing it even if he did become mayor.

* * *

In all the years that Marty Beiserman was her agent, Stella had called him at home only a couple of times, in real emergencies: when Idaho's father left her in the sixth month of her pregnancy, for instance, and when she read the script of the movie she had been supposed to start working on when her mother died, and was desperate for his help (which he refused to give her) in getting the part.

But now, flush with the excitement of the press conference and her spontaneous decision to run for mayor, she retrieved the orange Filofax from her bag and looked up Marty's number at his Malibu house, where he was undoubtedly holed up reading scripts—or rather, reading synopses of scripts his twenty-two-year-old assistant had read for him. At least she wouldn't have to run the gauntlet of receptionists and secretaries to get through to him. If you had his beach house number, that meant he wanted to talk to you—or at least, Stella thought as she dialed, he had wanted to talk to you at one time.

She was disconcerted, then, to get his voice mail, and fumbled over her own name in her message. When she was just about to say good-bye, he suddenly picked up.

"Stella!" he cried. "I was just talking about you!"

"Really?"

"Of *course.* I was on the phone with a producer on Broadway, of all places, who's interested in you for a lead in a show that's opening next spring."

"Broadway?" Stella said. "They're actually interested in me?"

"We're in negotiations," said Marty. "They opened with

two, but I told them we couldn't take a penny under five, so I figure they'll come back with three—"

"But Marty," she interrupted. "You're not my agent anymore."

"What?" he said, sounding shocked.

"I fired you. In August. Remember?"

"I'm hurt," he said. "I *love* you. I'd do anything for you."

"That's great," she said, "because I need your help on something. It's about this girl I know, Franny Wright."

"Oh, yeah, Franny Wright. She called here before, when I was out with the dog. Said she was a friend of yours."

So Franny had been thorough about getting *all* the numbers from the Filofax, even the home numbers, and wasn't shy about using them.

"She's the daughter of a friend, of my oldest and best friend, actually. She swiped your number from my Filofax and just took off for L.A., looking to break into movies."

"Oh, yeah? Should I call her back?"

"She's very pretty, Marty. And I hear she can even act. But she's underage."

"The parents?"

"Won't sign. So I'd appreciate it if you gently but firmly tell her that you can't even consider representing her until she's eighteen. And please let her know that every other agent in the business will have the same policy."

"Sure. And what do I get for playing guidance counselor?"

"You get my promise to think about the Broadway thing, and call you back in a few days, all right?"

18

"I hope we get back in time for you to vote," said Franny. They were on the airplane, side by side, heading toward Newark Airport. Mary Jean had spent more time in planes in the past forty-eight hours than she had in her entire life. She'd always thought she was afraid of flying, but the airplanes were starting to feel positively homey, especially now that she had Franny next to her.

"Me too," she said. "I can't believe Stella's doing this."

"She'll make a great mayor." Franny beamed. "Not that you wouldn't make a great mayor too. But I think it was really smart of you to have Stella take your place."

Mary Jean was surprised at Franny's interpretation of what had happened. In all the madness of her arrival at Franny's hotel, throughout the day of Franny alternately screaming and sobbing about whether she was going to stay in California or go back to New Jersey with Mary Jean, and then in the aftermath of the discouraging meeting with Stella's agent Marty, there had been no time to talk about the election. It was only now that it was all settled and they were on the plane that the subject had turned to that.

"I didn't tell her to take my place," Mary Jean said. "That was her idea."

"Oh," said Franny. "I figured that you asked her to step in because you knew she could beat Sladowski and you couldn't."

Mary Jean felt insulted by that for about a second and a half, and then she decided maybe her daughter was right. Maybe if she'd thought of it, she *would* have asked Stella to step in. But it was undoubtedly better that Stella had thought of it herself.

"No. All I told Stella was that I'd decided not to run. I realized I needed to pay more attention to what was going on at home, and I didn't have what it took to be in the spotlight like that."

"Well, *duh*," Franny said. "I could have told you that."

It was probably a good sign, Mary Jean thought, that things were enough back to normal for Franny to start insulting her again.

"I feel guilty, though," Franny said, "if you quit because of me."

"Don't feel guilty," Mary Jean assured her. "I could have come after you and still stayed in the race. I quit because I wanted to."

She was surprised, then, to feel her daughter's hand cover her own.

"I was proud of you, you know, when you were running," Franny said. "Embarrassed, sure, but proud too. I think it kind of made me feel brave enough to take this chance and go to California."

Mary Jean rolled her eyes, but not so that Franny could see. The wages of a mother's independence were great indeed. And so were the wages of a mother's overdependence. The bottom line was, mothers were screwed no matter what.

"I just hope Stella wins," Mary Jean said.

Rather than scaling back on his attacks when Stella took her place, Sladowski had only stepped them up, accusing Stella of everything from being morally unfit to being a bad actress to violating an obscure town code about declaring candidacy in a local political race—which Pete was happy to dispute. Stella, in only two days, had fired back just as hard, and seemed to be relishing the part. Mary Jean and Franny had watched fascinated the night before as Stella paraded in one glamorous sexy outfit after another, talking about Homewood politics on everything from *E! Entertainment Tonight* to *Letterman*. Mary Jean certainly never could have pulled off that kind of publicity, but it remained to be seen how it played with the voters of Homewood.

"So," Franny said, starting to grin. "Love triangle, huh?"

"Oh, God." Mary Jean rolled her eyes.

"You know, if I'm going to go back to living at home, I want you to treat me like more of a grown-up. And not just when you need help around the house."

Mary Jean thought about that for a minute. "All right," she said.

"Like, I want you to tell me the truth about you and Stella and Dad when you were in high school. Was he really going out with both of you at the same time? And then, like, you stole him away from Stella?"

As *if,* Mary Jean thought.

"No," she said. "I always had a big crush on your dad, but he was Stella's boyfriend. It wasn't until long after they were broken up and she gave me her *permission* that I dared to go out with him. I was too afraid of making her mad."

"And then you married Dad because you were pregnant with Peter."

"Oh, I hope I would have married your dad no matter what happened. Just maybe not quite as soon."

She hesitated, and then plunged on.

"I know you're anxious for your life to get under way, Franny," she said. "But you really have time. A little time, anyway."

Franny's mouth set. "As soon as I'm eighteen, I'm going back. You heard what Mr. Beiserman said. As soon as I'm legal, I can start working."

Franny and Caitlin would turn eighteen in April.

"But graduation isn't until June."

Franny huffed and pulled as far away as possible from Mary Jean in the cramped row of the plane.

"There's no point in waiting until June. I have my GED. I don't need to go back to actual high school."

"GED or no, if you don't graduate from high school, it's going to be harder for you to get into college."

"I have no intention of going to college," Franny snapped. "You know that."

Mary Jean was about to launch into a lecture about how Franny should keep her options open, how she might go to Hollywood and find that it didn't work out after two months or two years and want to go to college then, but then she thought, don't press your luck. She'd accomplished this, found Franny and persuaded her to come back home. Trying to tell her she might want to be a banker or a teacher instead of an actress would be as fruitless as it would have been to have told the seventeen-year-old Stella not to run away to Hollywood, or to have told her own teenage self not to love Pete so much, not to marry him and have his baby.

And look, despite what any sane adult might have predicted, following those adolescent impulses had actually worked out all right.

"Okay, I'll make a deal with you," Mary Jean told her daughter.

Franny looked at her suspiciously.

"If you go back to high school and at least take the SATs, you can keep my Prada shoes."

A guilty blush spread across Franny's cheeks, but she set her mouth in a firm line.

"That's okay," she said. "You can have them back."

"I don't really need them anymore. But that's not all. When you graduate in June, I'll give you the same amount of money we gave Peter and we're going to give Caitlin so you can go to Hollywood and try to become an actress."

Franny kept staring at her as if waiting for the catch.

"You mean you'll give me money to go to acting school?"

"To go to acting school or just to live out there while you go to auditions and try to make it. I'm saying if you graduate from high school, I'll give you your college money to tide you over while you try to become an actress, even if you never go to college."

Franny stared for another second, and then leaped up and hurled herself over the armrest and into her mother's lap, hugging her so tightly Mary Jean was actually afraid for a second that she was going to stop breathing. Better not tell her right now that if she wants to go to college after she blows through all the money, she's on her own, Mary Jean thought. Better just savor every good moment I have with her, while she's still here.

Thanks to all the exercising she'd done under Stella's tutelage (which she was very happy to now be able to quit), Mary Jean managed to sprint through the Newark Airport to Pete's waiting car and then run into the voting place at Nokomis School exactly two minutes before the polls closed. It wasn't until she pulled the curtain and was standing alone in the voting booth that she felt the disappointment of not seeing her own name on the ballot. She had, she realized, really been looking forward to the moment when she would vote for herself. She had one brief flash of giving herself a write-in vote—her son Peter confessed in the car that he'd done just that—but then decided that no, she couldn't, didn't want to do that. It was Stella she really wanted to be mayor.

Since Mary Jean had never had any formal election headquarters, Stella didn't have any either where they could wait for results. There was some talk about going up to the Tree House, but Stella said that felt too closed off. She wanted to be able to see people, talk to people, whether she won or lost. So they ended up at Vesuvio's, their old haunt, occupying a booth smack in the center of the room. Before long, the place was packed with people, all crowding around Stella, who was drinking in the attention.

Mary Jean had been hoping for a private moment to let Stella know how happy she was that Stella had decided to run, but she didn't get one. Not only was Stella constantly mobbed with people, but so was Mary Jean. She could let herself feel now how uncomfortable she was in the crowd, especially at the end of these frantic last days. Finally she slid into the end of the booth, and was delighted when Mrs. Dunn, Cameron's mother, sat down beside her.

"I was sorry when you dropped out of the race," Mrs. Dunn said in Mary Jean's ear.

"That's sweet," Mary Jean said back. "But Stella will do a great job, if she's elected."

"I'm confused," Mrs. Dunn said. "Wasn't Stella dating Mr. Sladowski?"

"Ancient history," Mary Jean assured her. "Where's Cameron? Is she here?"

The pizza parlor had gotten so crowded, it was impossible

to see. Mary Jean's own family, even Jimmy, had dispersed into the crowd.

"She's at election headquarters, helping to count votes."

"Of course."

Cameron was always at the center of the action.

"So is she still on our team?" Mary Jean asked. "Or has she switched back again?"

"Cameron does a lot of business with Mr. Sladowski, so she didn't want to go overboard for Stella or you in case he ended up winning. But she's a mother and a black woman first, so in her heart she's always been on your side."

The question was how much heart would influence people's votes.

A phone rang—they'd been ringing all night—and Vic, Vesuvio's owner, screamed out to the crowd, "Hey! Would youse all please shut up? We have a winner!"

Everyone quieted down and watched him talk into the phone.

"Yeah? Yeah? What else? All right, you got it."

He hung up and looked out at everyone, raising his arms for dramatic effect.

"It is my pleasure to announce—"

Pleasure. That was a good sign. A murmur started to rise from the crowd.

"—that the next mayor of Homewood, New Jersey, is none other than our very own hometown girl—"

Now there was whooping and clapping and cheering.

"—Miss Stella Powers!"

Suddenly Stella appeared above them, standing on a plastic table, and then someone lifted Idaho to stand shyly by her side. Stella was laughing and waving. Then she zeroed in on Mary Jean, trying to wave her to stand up too.

But this was Stella's night, not Mary Jean's. Mary Jean gave her a thumbs-up and blew her kisses, but all she wanted to do now was to find her family, escape the crowd, and go home. Stella had won yet again, and Mary Jean couldn't be happier.

"So do you wish it had been you up there?" Pete asked.

They were finally alone in their bedroom again, the lights off, their whole family—to the best of their knowledge—safe asleep in their own beds.

"Only one half of one percent of me. The rest is delighted to be here in bed with you instead of talking to reporters at Vesuvio's."

"I'm happy you're here in bed with me too," said Pete. "And you know what else is great? With Stella as mayor, I can be police chief *and* be on the side of the good guys."

"Yeah, and I guess I'll be a shoo-in for town manager now," Mary Jean said. "That even pays a salary."

"We're going to need it," said Pete. "I didn't want to tell you this before, but our official eviction notice from Sladowski showed up when you were out in California getting Franny. We have to be out of here before Christmas."

"Ho ho ho. Nice. Hey, did anybody see him tonight? Did he call Stella to concede?"

"I don't know," said Pete. "All I was thinking about when

Stella won was that now we could go home and be together."

Mary Jean sighed and embraced her husband. "I'm so relieved to have Franny back here. It feels good to have all six of us under one roof."

"Yeah," Pete said. "But sometimes I can't wait until it's just you and me again."

"Pete, it's never been just you and me."

"There were those few months."

"Right, after Stella dumped you and before I got, as our child so elegantly put it, 'knocked up.'"

"We have great kids," said Pete.

"We do have great kids," said Mary Jean. "And I have a great husband."

They kissed. Then they kissed again, but before it could go further, Pete pulled back.

"Here's the thing," he said. "I think I should get snipped. You know, fixed."

She couldn't help laughing.

"Gee, honey," she said. "I was hoping we'd have a couple more."

But Pete remained completely serious. "I have everything now," he said, "that I've ever wanted."

CHAPTER 19

Stella opened her eyes the morning after the election and thought, Holy shit. I can't believe I'm the mayor of a town in New Jersey.

But then, instead of feeling horrified, she found herself breaking into a huge grin. This was her town. This was *really* her town. She could walk down the street, and everyone would talk to her and look at her, but it would be because of who she really was, and what she really did, not because of some fiction they saw up on a screen. This was real life.

Everything about last night had been so perfect, from Mary Jean rushing in just in time to vote to the spontaneous party at Vesuvio's to her overwhelming victory at the polls—Cameron Dunn told her she'd gotten over 80 percent of the vote, the biggest landslide in Homewood history. She'd carried men as well as women, longtime residents and newcomers, African American as well as white voters, the richest residents high on the hill as well as the working-class townies who were Mary Jean's core constituency. It was a rousing mandate.

The only slight flaw in the perfection was that Sladowski hadn't called to concede as she thought he would, as custom required. In fact, though the *Homewood Herald* reporter confirmed that Sladowski had gotten the word that he lost, he hadn't issued any kind of statement at all. In fact, none of the newspeople or election officials had seen him after the results were announced.

But who cared about Sladowski anymore? Stella sat up in bed, suddenly energized for the day, fueled by a sense of certainty about who she was and what she was doing. She looked at her clock: 7:25, still plenty of time before she had to get Idaho to school. She got up and went into Idaho's room—she thought of it as Idaho's room now, not her own—and sat on the edge of the little girl's bed.

"Time to wake up, sleepyhead," she said.

Idaho's eyes popped open, as they always did, and she sat straight up in bed.

"Mommy," she said, pointing toward the window. "What's that?"

Stella turned to look. She hadn't noticed anything unusual, and she thought now that that was evidence of how thoroughly she'd slipped into her old frame of reference. She hadn't even thought twice about the icy crystals glittering around the perimeter of each pane of glass.

"That's frost," she told Idaho, lifting her daughter from the bed and carrying her over to the window. The child wrapped her legs as always around Stella's waist, but she'd grown so heavy that Stella felt her arms straining even in the moment it took to look out into the yard.

"See that?" she said, pointing, to Idaho. "The way the grass is all white, like it's got sugar all over it? That's called frost. It happens in the fall, when it starts to get really cold."

Idaho nodded gravely. "It's like snow?"

The child had seen snow, when they went skiing. Like a true Californian, she considered snow something you drove to, not something that happened spontaneously in your own backyard.

"It's what comes before snow," Stella told her. "They have snow here in the winter instead of rain."

Idaho slipped out of her grasp to stand, still gazing out the window.

"We'll have snow at Christmas," she said, her voice growing excited. "Jimmy told me."

"Sometimes," said Stella. "It doesn't always snow here at Christmas."

Idaho looked at her as if she were crazy. "Jimmy said. And I saw it in a book. That's why they call it White Christmas."

"Okay," said Stella, figuring there was no point in arguing. And maybe—who knew?—this would turn out to be one of those lucky Christmases that was indeed white.

"When Santa comes here," Idaho asked, "how does he get in? Because this house doesn't have a fireplace."

Stella remembered worrying about the same thing when she was a little girl, and told her daughter now what her mother had told her.

"He parks on the roof and comes in through the kitchen door, because he wants to stop first to eat our great cookies," she said. "But maybe we'll be living in our new house, the Tree House, by Christmas. Would you like that?"

Idaho looked at her for a long time, as if she really needed a much more extended period than usual to take the full measure of her mother. Finally she responded with a single word, clearly articulated.

"No."

That afternoon, Mary Jean was waiting for Stella at the school gate. They'd seen each other briefly in the morning, but then both rushed off to do other things—Mary Jean to get Franny settled back into school, Stella to go into the city to meet the director of the Broadway show Marty had told her about—so this was their first chance to really talk.

The day had turned sunny, melting the morning's frost on the brown and gold leaves that filled the gutters, but shadows were already long, and in an hour it would be dark. The bell rang and the school doors opened and the kids poured out into the bright, crisp afternoon. Idaho and Jimmy, as usual, were hand-in-hand.

"I have something to tell you," Mary Jean said, leaning in close.

"I have something to tell you, too," Stella said, linking her arm through her friend's. "Let's go for a walk. I bet you didn't go to the gym this morning, did you?"

Mary Jean laughed, and they headed out onto the sidewalk, up two blocks and then left on Beech, walking uphill, stepping up the pace to fight back the chill in the air.

"I got offered a part," Stella burst out, unable to contain her news a second longer.

Mary Jean stopped dead, her mouth falling open. "You're not leaving . . ."

Stella chuckled and urged her friend forward again. "Not a chance. I mean a part on Broadway. It's a limited-run kind of thing. But it would mean I would have time to bring Idaho to school and pick her up and also manage town business."

"That's terrific, Stella."

"Do you really think I could handle doing a show and being mayor at the same time?"

"All these guys who've been mayor have run big-time businesses while they were in office," Mary Jean said. "I'm sure you can show up at the theater and also be mayor of this town."

Stella's copper beech came into view, and as she looked up the hill behind her house, she saw that, with the leaves off many of the trees, she could see the roofline of Sladowski's house looming above the town.

"Do you really think I can do it?" Stella said, afraid for the first time. "Be mayor, I mean."

"With your gorgeous little finger."

"I just don't want people wishing they'd voted for Sladowski."

"Not much chance of that," Mary Jean said, breaking into a grin. "That's what I have to tell you. He's gone. Left town. Turns out he was bribing certain township officials to get variances on his properties. The story's going to break in the next few days."

"How do you know this?" Stella asked, wide-eyed.

"Pete told me, of course, but I'm not supposed to tell anybody. But you're the mayor. You have to know what's going on."

"I can't believe it," Stella said. "No, I can believe it. It makes total sense. And if he'd been elected mayor, we never would have heard a thing about it."

As they drew closer to her property, Stella could see that the leaves were falling from the copper beech, which didn't look as healthy as it had last summer. She'd had an arborist look at it, but he said they wouldn't really be able to tell if any lasting damage had been done until the next spring, with the new growth.

"I'd like to think he would have been caught no matter what," said Mary Jean as they started up the driveway. "I know I would have been there watching him, and Pete would have, and there are plenty of other people in this town who didn't like what he was doing. All the people who voted for you."

The house was quiet today; many of the workmen had gone home. There was still renovation to be done, but the work had eased off after the party, in the last few days of the campaign, with Mary Jean gone and Stella too busy to direct any construction.

The truth was, even though she'd tried to do what Mary Jean advised and reclaim the Tree House as her own, even though she'd thought that by investing her own sweat in the place she could rid it of the taint of Sladowski, it hadn't worked. Everywhere she looked in the house, there he was: in the butchered tree and on the walls stripped of their molding, in the modern bathrooms, and even in the antique details they'd added back in, the doors and windows Mary Jean had discovered in the basement. They only reminded Stella of all she'd lost, and while Mary Jean loved the contrast of minimalism and antiquity, Stella was discovering that her style was really based on a cozier, more comfortable idea of home.

"So with Sladowski gone," Stella asked, "do you get to stay in your house?"

"Not a chance," Mary Jean said. "The eviction is still proceeding. We have to be out in a month."

She took a deep breath and continued, "I was thinking, Stella. What if, when you move up to the Tree House, we could work a deal for Pete and me to buy your mother's place?"

What an obvious solution. Stella was ashamed that she hadn't thought of it herself before this. There was just one catch, not even really a catch.

Stella ran her fingers over the key to the front door that she was holding in her pocket, pressed it tight once, and then drew it out and handed it to Mary Jean.

"What's this?" asked Mary Jean.

"It's the key to this house."

"But what—"

"I want you to have this house, Mary Jean. You and Pete and your kids. You're the one who has all the vision about how to fix it up, who has the family big enough to fill it. I don't want to live here anymore."

"Oh, no," Mary Jean said, her face falling.

"No?"

"You're leaving, aren't you? You're moving back to California, like I promised you that you could. Well, I was lying, Stella. I'm not going to let you go."

Stella burst out laughing. "I'm not going anywhere. I just can't take the chance that *you're* going anywhere either. The truth is, Idaho and I are happier in my mother's house."

"I can't let you do this, Stella," Mary Jean said, thrusting her hand out with the key in it. "You can't give us a house. It's too much."

"So I'll sell it to you," said Stella. "For a dollar. You'll have to pay the taxes, and believe me, that will be plenty expensive."

Mary Jean hesitated for just one more moment, and then threw her arms around Stella's neck and burst into tears.

"This is so amazing," she said. "How can I ever thank you?"

"You've already thanked me," said Stella. "You're the one who gave me a home."

"I didn't give it to you," said Mary Jean. "It was always yours."

"If you want to do something for me, you can help me fix up my mother's place. I'm happy we're going to be staying there, but it's time to make it my own." She looked at Idaho, skipping on the lawn with Jimmy. "*Our* own."

The two old friends embraced again then. Stella was struck by how much taller and more substantial Mary Jean felt, her breasts soft and enveloping, her shoulder just about the right height on which to rest your cheek. Mary Jean felt almost like Stella remembered, in the vaguest possible way, her mother feeling when Stella hugged her as a little girl. But that had been so long ago, it might only be Stella's imagination.

Jimmy and Idaho, who'd been chasing each other in the yard, raced to where their mothers stood in the darkening late afternoon, near the steps to the front door.

"We're getting married," giggled Idaho, grabbing for Jimmy's hand. "Can you watch us?"

"No, we're not," said Jimmy, flopping his head back so that he was gazing openmouthed at the lavender sky, though he didn't let go of Idaho's hand.

"Yes, we are," said Idaho decisively. "Come on, Mommy, Mary Jean, *please*. Can you be in our wedding?"

Stella and Mary Jean looked at each other and broke into smiles. They hadn't played together in a long time. But that had been the basis for their friendship, and they certainly knew how to do it again now. They joined hands and followed the bride and groom down the lawn and under the tree, where the ceremony was about to get under way, and the children would promise to love each other forever.

UP CLOSE AND PERSONAL
WITH THE AUTHOR

THIS IS YOUR FOURTH BOOK SET IN THE FICTIONAL TOWN OF HOMEWOOD, BUT THE FIRST IN WHICH THE TOWN IS ALMOST A MAIN CHARACTER. WHAT DOES HOMEWOOD MEAN TO YOU?

I grew up in the sleepy suburb of Norwood—thus, Homewood's name—and swore I'd never move back to New Jersey. But, like many people, when I had children, I did. The fictional Homewood has been kind of a shape-shifting town through the four novels, to suit my stories, but in *Suburbanistas* I wanted to deal more directly with the ways my own suburban town has changed over the years I've lived here. It's gotten richer, and more fashionable, and more expensive, and while in many ways it's a more beautiful and interesting place to live, it's lost texture and comfort and diversity. That tradeoff is what Mary Jean is trying to point out.

WHERE DID YOU GET THE IDEA FOR THIS BOOK?

One of the questions writers are asked most often is, "Where do you get your ideas?" and the answer is that each book seems to spring from a different place. My first novel, *The Man I Should Have Married*, started with the title, and my second, *Babes in Captivity*, started with the characters of the four moms. *Younger* sprang from a what-if kind of idea, and now *Suburbanistas* got its start in yet another way, from a place. The PTA of a school in my town sponsors a house tour once a year, and on that tour I saw a house that looked as if everything in it had been purchased by the same person on the same day. Who would live in such a place? I wondered. And that's how the character of Stella and the idea of a movie star moving back to her hometown and trying to buy herself a real life was born.

YOU DEDICATE THIS BOOK TO YOUR BEST FRIEND. DO YOU HAVE A FRIENDSHIP THAT'S LIKE STELLA'S AND MARY JEAN'S?

Not exactly. I've never been an actress or a local politician—or even a stay-at-home mom like Mary Jean, for that matter—and I haven't reconnected with a friend after a long estrangement. But the emotional fabric of the friendship felt close to my own experience, that quality of switching roles over time, so that you take turns being the strong one, the together one, giving each other advice. I have had the experience of being friends with a woman whose life is very different from mine, and yet in more important ways we feel exactly alike.

WHAT IS YOUR INTEREST IN LOCAL POLITICS?

I can't think of anything I'd be *less* likely to do than run for mayor, yet I do believe that people's lives are greatly affected by small decisions made at the local level. And every town has its power brokers who maneuver behind-the-scenes to influence such important factors as property values and school philosophy. What got me more excited, though, was Mary Jean's determination to step forward and not just let her town keep changing in a way that she felt was bad for her family and bad for many of its citizens. And Stella's growing realization that she can use her star power to make some important changes.

WHAT WAS YOUR PROCESS IN WRITING THIS NOVEL?

Process—how exactly you do it—is one of those things that's not talked about nearly enough by novelists, I think, at least in public. My writer friends and I discuss it all the time, but I don't often see it written about. I learned my basic process of novel writing from Elizabeth George, who writes best-selling mystery novels. I spend a long time developing my characters and settings and story—about three or four months—and work out all my scenes. Then I write a first draft extremely quickly: this book took two and a half weeks of very long, intense, uninterrupted days at a writers' colony. Then my editor and agent read the manuscript, along with a few trusted readers. Next, I spend three or four months on a very thorough revision, rewriting maybe three-quarters of the book from the ground up. And I did a third pass through the material, revising a handful of scenes and cleaning up language.

WHAT'S IT LIKE AT THE WRITERS' COLONY?

I wrote the first draft of this novel and of *Younger*, my last book, at the Virginia Center for the Creative Arts, which is in the country south of Charlottesville. It's very peaceful there and such a luxury, especially for a working mom, to have someone else cooking your meals and cleaning your room so all you have to do is write. I can write twenty or more new pages a day there, which is unthinkable in my normal life, where some days I can't even make it through twenty sentences.

YOU ALSO WRITE NONFICTION BOOKS AND MAGAZINE ARTICLES. HOW DO YOU BALANCE IT ALL?

I write fiction in the morning and nonfiction in the afternoon. Sometimes I even set my alarm for noon, to make myself switch. Once I start something, I like to keep doing it, so sometimes I have to be dragged from one genre to the next. But it's also a good balance. Fiction writing is very quiet and concentrated and can get lonely. Writing nonfiction books with my long-time partner is a nice relief from that solitary work, and sometimes I like to dive into a magazine article that lets me talk to dozens of strangers.

WHAT'S NEXT?

Because each book takes close to a year to write, I always emerge wanting to tackle something different from what I did last time. I've been looking into a lot of new things these days: memoir, which my friend Louise DeSalvo writes brilliantly and has been illuminating for me, and historical fiction. I'm also intrigued by the idea of writing a novel with at least one lead character who's a man.

Never buy off the rack again—buy off the shelf...
the book shelf!

Don't miss any of these fashionable reads from Downtown Press!

Imaginary Men
Anjali Banerjee
If you can't find Mr. Right,
you can always make him up.

2cool2btrue
Simon Brooke
If something's too cool to
be true, it usually is...

Vamped
David Sosnowski
SINGLE MALE VAMPIRE ISO
more than just another
one night stand...

Loaded
Shari Shattuck
She's got it all: Beauty.
Brains. Money.
And a really big gun...

Turning Thirty
Mike Gayle
27...28...29...29...29...
Let the countdown begin.

Just Between Us
Cathy Kelly
The fabulous Miller
girls have it all.
Or do they?

Lust for Life
Adele Parks
Love for sale.
Strings sold separately.

Fashionably Late
Beth Kendrick
Being on time is so
five minutes ago.

Great storytelling just got a new address.

DOWNTOWN PRESS
A Division of Simon & Schuster
A VIACOM COMPANY

Available wherever books are sold or at www.downtownpress.com

13459